George B. Thayer

Pedal and Path

Across the Continent awheel and afoot

George B. Thayer

Pedal and Path
Across the Continent awheel and afoot

ISBN/EAN: 9783337255619

Printed in Europe, USA, Canada, Australia, Japan

Cover: Foto ©Andreas Hilbeck / pixelio.de

More available books at **www.hansebooks.com**

ACCOUTRED FOR THE START. — (*Frontispiece.*)

Across the Continent

AWHEEL AND AFOOT.

------------ * ------------

GEORGE B. THAYER.

[Member of the Connecticut Bicycle Club.]

HARTFORD:
Evening Post Association.
1887.

PREFACE.

Close confinement to mercantile business for a dozen or more years brought on a feeling of discontent with the monotonous routine, that I at length tried to drive away by taking a little recreation on a bicycle. The machine, I found, was not only a source of great enjoyment, but it soon became a thing of practical value to me in the transaction of business. I took intense delight in riding the wheel a dozen miles to Hartford buying goods, quite content to let those who would sit inertly riding by me in the cars, and it was not long before the idea of taking a short vacation presented itself.

A vacation of more than a day was a pleasure of which I had denied myself for so many years that it was a question with me whether the sun would not stand still if I ventured out of the little orbit in which I had moved so many years. But I finally decided to run the risk. At the end of five days, after riding one hundred and seventy-five miles, I came back more than ever pleased with the mode of locomotion and its advantages in sight-seeing. So intense had become my desire to travel, to visit the places of interest here at home, that I then made business arrangements which would permit a more prolonged absence, and took a three weeks' trip of five hundred miles, and soon after a six weeks' trip of one thousand two hundred miles through the most interesting parts of New England.

Instead of quieting my rising passion for sight-seeing, these delightful journeys only added fuel to the flames.

They showed clearly to me the possibilities of a trip to California, the independence and economy possible to such a trip, and the good results to be obtained from such a mode of traveling in preference to any other. So with no desire or intention of making or breaking any records, or covering the whole distance on the wheel, the trip was started and carried out with the sole object of taking all the pleasure possible and of acquiring a knowledge of the country and the people who live in it. An account of the trip across the continent was written in occasional letters to the HARTFORD EVENING POST, as whose representative I was everywhere most courteously received. Although this little volume is to all purposes a binding of those letters, with considerable revision, in book form, I have been able when seated quietly at my own desk to give fuller details at certain interesting points, and to round out a narrative which was sometimes rather meagre from having been written out in the fields to escape too curious observation of passers-by, in a friendly barn which sheltered me from the rain, on jolting freight-trains, in the cloud-enveloped house on Pike's Peak, on one of the dizziest points overhanging the Yosemite, on a tossing steamer on the misnamed Pacific, and while waiting for the regular spouting of "Old Faithful" in the Yellowstone, as well as in many other situations not conducive to the production of comprehensive and artistic literary work.

To the wheelmen of the country, Greetings! The fraternal feeling everywhere manifested between them has, I believe, not a parallel in any social or secret order. To their spontaneous and unfailing kindness was due much of the pleasure of the trip, and if any wheelman should want a more detailed account than I have given, of any portion of the route taken, I should be only too glad to furnish him with all the information I possess.   G. B. T.

CHAPTER I.

OR this trip, which covered a distance of 11,000 miles from Hartford, Connecticut, circuitously to San Francisco, California, and return, nearly 4,300 of which was made upon the machine, a forty-six inch Expert Columbia, taking me across twenty-three States and Territories, and through hundreds of the finest cities and towns in the Union, and some of the most magnificent scenery in the world, I was equipped with a blue cap that I wore throughout the whole journey with comfort, brown blouse, thin undershirt, brown corduroy knickerbockers, brown stockings, and low canvas shoes. The baggage in the knapsack consisted of a coat, blouse, pair blue knickerbockers, three summer undershirts, night-shirt, six pairs stockings, six handkerchiefs, needles and thread, buttons, and plenty of stout string, a box of salve, a bottle of tannin and alcohol, a bottle of Jamaica ginger, razor, shaving brush, hair brush, tooth-brush, shaving soap, toilet soap, leather strap with wire hook at one end, a sponge, long rubber tube for drinking, knife and fork, shoe laces, piece of cement, box matches, a candle, coil of pliable wire, two dozen pedal-balls, pedal shaft, chain and Yale lock, pocket mirror, railroad maps, and a good supply of stationery and postal cards. On top of the knapsack was strapped a gossamer coat, gossamer leggings, rubber cap, and a pair of rubber overshoes. The whole weighed a little over fifteen pounds. It will be observed that among the articles enumerated no mention has been made of any weapon of defense. Although implored by some of my friends not to enter upon the Western wilds without a pistol, I decided to maintain my habitual faith in the honesty and good will of the average American and to depend upon diplomacy and conciliation in the circumvention of the exceptional villain. I expressed a valise along to different cities as far as Denver, but found I could carry all necessary clothing in the knapsack, and so left the valise at that place till my return from California, when I sent it directly home.

After anxiously waiting for the frost to be taken out of the ground by a warm rain that finally came, I started out on the 10th of April, 1886. The roads to Berlin were full of hard, dry ruts, and through Wallingford sandy as usual. This, in addition to the fifteen pounds of baggage in my knapsack, the soft condition of my muscles, the thirty mile ride the day before, — first one in four months,— these circumstances, taken together, had the effect to make me somewhat weary, and after reaching New Haven, and completing over fifty miles that day, I was tired. Those wheelmen who envied me the trip in the morning would have changed their feeling to pity had they seen me groping along in the dark from North Haven nearly fagged out. The next day, Sunday, was certainly a day of rest, but Monday I rode up the gentle grade of the Farnham drive to the top of East Rock in the morning, and in the afternoon about the city with a Yale student, Mr. Geo.

Kimball of Hartford, — a fine rider, who struck a gait that outwinded me and that would have used him up in a day or two, I think. For variety, I spent a couple of hours looking over the fine specimens of ancient life in Peabody museum, and afterwards made the acquaintance of Messrs. Thomas and Robbins of the New Haven Club. Tuesday, a drizzling rain prevented a start till nearly noon, and the ride around Savin Rock to Milford was anything but enjoyable, especially when wearing a rubber suit which retained the perspiration like a hot house, which it really was for me. It was the bitter with the sweet, and the bitter came first, for the roads improved to Stratford and Bridgeport, at which latter place the open-hearted J. Wilkinson, a dealer in bicycles, accompanied me through the city and on to Fairfield, showing his nationality by characterizing places in the road as "beastly." A decided fall in the temperature was now followed by a thunder storm which drove me under shelter for the night at Green Farms.

Inquiries for a wheelman at South Norwalk, the next morning, brought out in reply, " There is a man down at the carriage-shop, beyant, that could fix your fhweel, I guess "; but not looking for that kind of a wheelman, I soon found one, Mr. Chas. Warren, who piloted me along to Stamford, where I had a pleasant chat with William A. Hurlburt, the well known State representative. At Greenwich I met three riders, two of whom it was plain to be seen by the dusty condition of one side of their suits had taken recent tumbles. One was Consul E. W. Reynolds, another Dr. E. N. Judd, vice-president of the Greenwich Club, and I did not learn the name of the third. So with this unknown quantity it is safe to leave the reader to ponder over which two of the three took headers, for I could not be so base as to give a clue to the names of the unfortunate ones, all three of

whom were very fine gentlemen. Other wheelmen soon
came up, meat carts and express teams stopped on the corner, small boys gathered around, and innumerable dogs
filled in the chinks, till fearing the knapsack would soon be
arrested for obstructing the highway, I reluctantly dragged
it away and carried it along to Port Chester, where, with a
parting look at the Sound, I started across the country to
White Plains and to Tarrytown. The roads improved all
the forenoon, and from the Sound to the river were very
good. It was nearly dark at Tarrytown, but having some
acquaintance with the accommodating landlord at the American House, Sing Sing, I kept on by the monument that marks
the spot of Major Andre's capture, down into "Sleepy Hollow," made memorable by Washington Irving, and up to
the Old Dutch Church, built in 1699. With a mania which
I shall never entirely outgrow, for finding the oldest dates
in a grave-yard, I opened the creaking iron gate, and walked
in among the tipsy tombstones, and, with the scanty aid of
the twilight and the full moon, found many dates nearly as
old as the church itself. The iron latch snapped back into
place with a remarkably loud click, it seemed to me, as I
came out, for everything was wonderfully still, even for a
grave-yard, and as I went slowly on through the woods,
meeting Italian organ-grinders, passing bands of gypsies
camped out by the roadside, and coasting silently down unknown hills in the dark, I really think I must have looked
like a genuine goblin astride of a silver broomstick. But
there was a novelty about it that I rather enjoyed.

CHAPTER II.

OON after leaving Port Chester, frequent explosions attracted my attention, and when within two miles of Tarrytown I came to a cluster of cheap shanties out in the woods, and found that it was the location of Shaft No. 11 of the new aqueduct for New York city. This shaft was only sixty feet deep, and as dump cars of rocks were constantly coming up, and empty cars going down, I thought it would be a fine thing to go down into the bowels of the earth. But no amount of entreaty, no amount of newspaper influence behind me would induce the foreman to give his consent without a permit from head-quarters, so I rode over to Tarrytown, hunted the city all over, and finally got the coveted piece of paper from D. D. McBeau, the superintendent. I laid awake half the night thinking of the grand chance before me, and started off next morning from Sing Sing to Shaft One, eight miles directly out of my way, over a hilly and muddy country. Here were more cheap shanties off in the mountains and crowds of negroes and Italians loafing around in the woods, waiting for their turn to go down to work. Rum-holes were numerous and doing a thriving business. The powder and oil clerk gave me an old coat and a pair of rubber boots to put on, and when the empty car was ready I crawled over into it and boldly stood up in the mud beside an Italian, who grinned and said something I could not understand. While waiting for the bell to ring I found this hole was 360 feet deep instead of sixty. That information caused me to look over the side of the car down into the dark where the loaded car comes up — the cars go up and down like the buckets in a well — and try to imagine how far down a fellow would go. If anything should break I did not suppose it would jar me much more to drop 360 feet than it would sixty, but it was the uneasy feeling falling during the longer interval that I began to believe I would avoid. What would happen afterwards I never thought of, but it was the long time going down so far before anything could happen that troubled me. I did not want to run the risk of waiting so long. Then I began to think of what they told me before I got into the car, how the day before the cable slipped, a wheel or something dropped — I did not mind much what they said I was so intent on getting into that car — and how the brains of the man beneath were scooped up into a cigar-box and taken away, and how twelve men were sitting on that cigar-box, or all there was of the man's body below his shirt collar, at the same time I was hanging over that black hole. I did not object so much to being carried away in a cigar-box, or being sat upon afterwards, but somehow I did not think it such a big thing to go down after all. I began to imagine how it looked down there, and the more the workmen urged me the less I wanted to go. It wouldn't pay anyhow. I could just as well imagine how it looked and not go. All this time if the bell had rung I should have had no choice, but I finally crawled out, just in time, feeling very foolish, and returned the coat and boots unsoiled. A mile farther I came to Croton dam and the head of the new aqueduct. I may use that hard earned and once highly prized piece of paper some other time when I feel more like it. A brief description of this great work may not be uninteresting.

The present aqueduct runs near the Hudson River, but the rich property holders along its course would combine to effectually prevent another aqueduct from boring its way through their fine grounds, so the only thing to be done was to go back five or six miles into the mountains and tunnel the whole distance of thirty-five or forty miles. The head of the two aqueducts are close together, but whereas the old one winds along the banks of the Hudson on the surface, the new one takes a straight course from New York, the first nine miles being a bee line. Every mile or two holes are dug down into the mountain, these shafts varying from 50 to 400 feet in depth, and then tunnels are started out in opposite directions till they meet those being dug from the next shaft. This tunnel goes through solid rock, under swamps and ponds, through mountains, and finally passes under the Harlem River, eighty feet beneath its bed, into the city. Think of a hole eighteen or twenty feet in diameter being dug as far below the surface of the earth as the Genius of Connecticut on the dome of the Capitol at Hartford is above it; this hole going from Hartford down under the Meriden hills and coming out at New Haven. How do those railroad tunnels through the Alps compare with this ? There are about twenty-five of these shafts, and six or seven hundred men are constantly working, day and night, down in the bowels of the earth. The tunnels are lighted by the Schuyler Electric Light Company of Hartford. The average fall to New York is eight inches to the mile, and the water will not run much faster than a mile an hour. I have prob-

ably ridden over this tunnel half a dozen times during the
past two days, and every farmer along its course for twenty-
five miles knows about how far underneath him these men
are working Frequently an explosion that shakes buildings
five miles away reminded me of what was going on.

Asking of a good woman to-day how much the bread and
milk I had of her would be, she replied, " Five or ten cents
if thee is able to pay."

After a few minutes pleasant talk at Peekskill with Chief
Consul E. F. Hall, a slight built, dark complexioned gentleman of, perhaps, 30, wearing glasses, I hired a boatman and
crossed the river. a mile and a half wide at this place, to
Jones's Point. This was done partly to avoid the sandy
roads running far east from the river to Garrison's, but
principally to get a better view of the entrance to the Highlands. The sun was only half an hour high, but I loitered
along, never thinking of the night. The road which winds
along the side of the mountain was too stony to ride; but
who would want his attention diverted by riding when there
was such grand scenery on all sides? The West Shore
trains were rushing up and down along the river fifty feet
almost perpendicularly below me, the Hudson River trains
on the opposite side were just as busy, and the sun brought
out the features of Anthony's nose with great distinctness
as it rose nearly 1,500 feet straight up from the east bank
of the river. The sun went down some time before I began
to wonder if any farmers lived along that rugged region, for
not a house was in sight for miles, but hearing some one
chopping upon the side of the mountain somewhere, I
pushed my machine up a cow-path till my wind was all
gone, and found there was a house half a mile farther on.
Coming to the barn, in front of which a good looking woman
of 30 was milking, I told her how I hoped to reach West

Point that night, but the rough roads delayed me, and could
I stay over night? The husband was inside, she said, and
seeing some one in there in the dark I retold my story, only
to find out I was talking to the hired man. Finally the husband, who was in a box stall milking, came out and said
"yes" without more ado. The house was close to the river,
and soon after supper was over, and we were all sitting in the
dining-room talking, a knock was heard. The man of the
house said "Come in," but no one came. Soon the knock
was repeated, with the same answer, and finally the door
slowly opened and a small, dried up, middle-aged man came
shuffling in, blinking and muttering "Is John here?" But
John was not there; so Walter sat down by the stove and
immediately fell into a deep reverie, occasionally arousing
himself to inquire for John. Finally John came in, and
then it seems Walter wanted to be taken home in John's
boat, up the river about a mile. So John said, good natur-
edly, "Come out and get in then," and walked across the
gang-plank, out to where the boat was moored. Walter
started out into the bright moonlight, going very unsteadily,
and reached the gang-plank without any serious trouble, but
here he slowed up. The women-folks said "Help him
across, John," but Walter started, very cautiously, without
waiting for help, and had got half way across when he
stepped off into the air and went down out of sight with a
splash. John was so tickled he laid down in the boat and
roared, and when Walter came up, bareheaded and looking
very sleek, John couldn't stop laughing long enough to help
him, leaving him hanging there by the gang-plank in the
water up to his neck, sputtering, "Zis the river John, zis the
river?" But poor Walter was soon helped out, wrapped up
in blankets, and taken home in the boat.

The ride next morning of five or six miles to West Point

was over a road that would compare favorably with the best
city roads, and after spending an hour about the grounds,
seeing all the captured Mexican cannons, and wondering
where the captured cannons of the war of 1812 were — I
guess that was not a very good war for capturing cannons —
I crossed to Garrison's and found a road that for fifty miles,
and probably farther, is as fine as there is anywhere about
Boston. The grades are easy, the coasting so perfect I
almost forgot there was a brake on the machine. For
miles and miles fine rows of elms and maples line the sides
of the road. To say I enjoyed it seems tame. At Cold
Spring I explained the workings of the cyclometer to a gentleman, and opposite the "Cro' Nest," meeting the same one
again, he returned the favor by showing me the situation of
the Storm King Bridge, that is soon to be built. It is at
the northern entrance to the Highlands and at one of the
wildest parts of the whole river. On both sides are high
mountains with bold fronts, the one on the east jutting out
into the river. Around this projection there is just room
enough for one team to pass between the rocks and the river,
the railroad tunneling through the rocks at this point. It is
to be a cantilever bridge, and, if I understand it, is to be
built nearly a mile in length and upon four or five piers.
These iron piers are raised to the height of nearly 250 feet
above the river, but how deep the river is at this point I did
not learn. At other points it is 200 feet and over. When
these piers are at the required height an arm or span is
built out in one direction and another of equal length in
the other direction, and so on till the spans meet in the center between the piers. It is like building four or five
immense capital T's and extending the arms out till they
meet. Imagine those men up in the air 250 feet, and working out on the end of one of those immense spans 500 feet

from the center of the pier.　At Po'keepsie I found quite a nest of wheelmen at the office of the Buckeye shops, a policeman escorting me to the place to the evident delight of all the small boys, who thought I was under arrest. Representative Adriance is a tall, sandy complexioned gentleman of 35 or 40, with a full beard, and Captain Edward A. King is dark complexioned and smooth, full faced, and under 25.　Both of these gentlemen treated me very cordially, as did others there, and I would be glad to be walked off by a policeman any time to meet such fine fellows in a strange city.　Saturday morning, after crossing from Rhinecliff to Kingston and traveling twelve miles over some sandy roads that would have been impassable but for a fair sidepath, I found, upon reaching Saugerties, that I had made a mistake by not going up the east side and crossing to the same point, but forgot all about it as the terraced Catskills came in view.　At Palenville the hard work commenced, pushing the machine to the top, and, after two hours of sweating and puffing, I arrived.　Since a boy I had been told there was plenty of room at the top, and so I found it, 1,200 of them, all empty.　Notwithstanding that fact, I was obliged to take an apartment on the first floor front, that is, the piazza.　The board was very plain, too.　The one under me was not only planed but painted.　I did not stay long.

Distance traveled in six days, 251 miles.

CHAPTER III.

NOW that the trees are bare, the terraced appearance of the Catskills is plainly visible, and in climbing up by the new mountain road to the Hotel Kaaterskill, along the northern slope of the Kaaterskill Clove, one wonders at first why the numerous little houses scattered all along up this Clove are not in danger of the catastrophe that befell the Willey House in Crawford Notch, New Hampshire. The sides of the Clove are as steep as the Notch, although not as high, but the rock formation of the Catskills preserves these little hamlets. A landslide here would have to go down a gigantic pair of stairs, while in the White Mountains it would be like slipping off a gothic roof. Half an hour's rest was sufficient after the tough climb of four miles up the gentle grade, as they called it, of the new road. It was very steep all the way up, and at places very dangerous, a single wire holding up a row of posts which themselves seemed bent on going over, being the only protection against a fall of fifty feet or more. I reached the falls in the rear of the Laurel House just as the western sun was filling the Clove with rainbows, and after convincing myself with some diffi-

AN ENTERTAINING ESCORT. — (*Page 31.*)

culty that the whole mountain would not tip over if I stepped too heavy, I crawled around the amphitheatre, little by little, till the water came down directly between the stairs and myself. The ice all around the pool rose up very much like the crater of a volcano, down into the center of which the water plunged from 150 feet above. While I was creeping along backside of this ice crater there was a loud crack, loud enough to be heard above all the other noises, and my feet went down about three inches. A thin shale of ice under my feet had broken, that was all, but my heart came up as my feet went down, and it remained about six inches above its ordinary level for some time.

That night the lively conversation, accompanied by sly winks, and short little words of the gouty but genial proprietor, J. L. Schult, helped to make the evening pass pleasantly, especially when Mr. Schult, of Dutch descent himself, would slyly refer to the Yankee origin of his wife, a quiet, kind lady of Connecticut parents.

Sunday morning came off delightfully clear and cool, and after a ride of a couple of miles by the railroad station and the lake, on one side of which the ice still covered the surface while on the other side buds on the trees were bursting, I reached the Mountain House and sat down for a few minutes, but wishing to be alone crossed over to the Pine Orchard Hotel. A few steps farther brought me to the Beach House where, avoiding contact with people when Nature had so much to say to me, I sat down under the shade of the Catskill Mountain House, and for four hours was undisturbed as I lay there taking in the fine view of the Hudson, the finest, I think, to be had from any of the mountain hotels. If any one is puzzled to account for so many hotels in this section of the mountains, he is no more confused than I was when I had the same building pointed out to me at different

2

times as the Mountain House, the Pine Orchard Hotel, the Beach House, and the Catskill Mountain House, but like the various officers which centered in *Pooh-Bah* they are all one.

Celebrated as the Catskills are, Connecticut can boast of some hills that out-rank them in one respect, and that is age. The Litchfield Hills in plain sight across the river are not only the tallest in the State but they claim to be about as old as the Adirondacks. The river Saguenay has worn a wrinkle 1,500 feet deep down the face of some rocks of the same age. But the Connecticut hills don't show their age like that, old as they are. They were well along in their youth when the rocks were born over which flow the waters of Niagara, and the White Mountains, now both bald and grey, had then not even been thought of. They were in the meridian of life when the Rockies came upon the stage, and had passed that point long before the Alps, Pyrennes, Himalayas, and the rocks of which the pyramids are built, had risen above the surface of the ocean. So their real grandeur consists, certainly not in their size, but in the fact that the group of mountains to which they belong, the Laurentian range, as well as the Adirondacks, has remained above the sea level longer than any other land upon the face of the globe. Not once during this time have they ever bowed to the god of the sea. They are not so pretentious as some of their richer and more lofty followers, but in their ripe old age the Litchfield Hills have acquired a weather-beaten and a most enviable title to the first families of creation.

I understood from a wheelman that the coasting down the other side of the mountains toward Catskill was fine, and to enjoy that was my idea in working so hard to get the machine up, but the road was too steep and rough and so all the labor was lost. Crossing the river again at Catskill I rode on to Hudson by moonlight, and the next day kept on, over mostly fine roads, through Kinderhook, where some writers claim the identical "Sleepy Hollow" of Washington Irving is located, to Albany. Washing off some of the dust and dirt I put on a coat and went up to the capitol. Finding I was a stranger those in charge furnished a guide, who took me all over the magnificent structure. To give an idea of the cost of the interior decorations, it will be enough to state that one side of the senate chamber is covered with slabs of Mexican onyx, the cost of this room alone amounting to over one million dollars. On the way out of the city I stopped at the Albany Bicycle Club House, a large two story building, situated on a prominent corner, with a fine lawn in front. The house is nicely furnished, with all conveniences, but the club has of late become more of a social than an athletic club. At Schenectady the only glimpse I had of Jacob W. Clute, the active wheelman of this thriving city, was through the cracks of the court-room door as he was cross-examining a witness, but S. R. James, who has a large crockery establishment here, mounted his tricycle and piloted me along the sidewalks to the tow path. Mr. James has been at different times president and captain of their club, and is a good sized man of sixty, with side whiskers and moustache.

On the tow-path, at last. A path nearly 300 miles long and perfectly level for forty, fifty, and sixty miles on a stretch. How I looked forward to it. How I longed to get to it. How I thought the hard work was over when I reached it. What fun it would be to ride for hours without a dismount ; what time I could make. This and a great deal more I had thought about, read of, and talked over. The great tow-path, the bicyclers' paradise ! Now I was there. Well, to state facts, it is no path at all, it is a common highway, and a very common one too, for everybody uses it. The soil is a mixture of clay and coarse, very coarse, gravel. Round, loose stones

filled the ruts and every part of the road. The inside edge
of the bank is cobbled and the outside edge full of little cross
ditches. Now, where was a wheel to go ? Go in the middle
and the wheel would take a serpentine course ; try to follow
a rut and the loose stones would throw the wheel in and out.
The outside edge was terribly jolting, the inside edge dangerous, for a variation of an inch or two and the course of
the wheel would throw a rider into the mud and water ten
feet below in the empty canal. But for all that I tried the
celebrated tow-path for ten, twenty, thirty miles, and long
miles, too. After bumping along for a mile or two I would
get off and walk. Then pound along for two or three miles
farther and dismount again, more to prevent the saddle from
becoming ruined than anything else, for even a Kirkpatrick's
saddle couldn't stand everything. Water is as necessary to a
wheelman as to a locomotive, and yet there was none to be
had excepting at the lock-houses several miles apart and then
only in a well, down in some warm swamp; no gushing little
streams of sparkling, cool water, such as spring out of the
rocks and hills all along the regular highways. The only
shade was under the bridges that cross the canal at frequent
intervals, where a rider can sit down in the dirt and think
how nice it might be on the grass beneath the shade of a
pine tree. No matter what part of the road you took it required the strictest attention to business, and after following
a rut with every muscle hard and every nerve taut for an
hour or two, it became monotonous, to say the least.

The canal follows the south side of the Mohawk River and
passes through very few villages, while on the other side of the
river are many places, through each of which there must be
a mile or two of nice riding, yet I stuck to the canal on prin-
ciple for six long hours, and left it at Fonda for good. It may
be, when the boats are running, that the mules' kicking abil-

ities are employed, when they slack rope, in firing the million of round stones out of the road, and in that way make the tow-path rideable, but if every mule on the line of the canal had kicked me, personally and individually, with all four feet and all on the same spot, I should not have been any sorer than I was that night. The next day fifty-six miles were made with less labor and decidedly more pleasure over the common roads than was the forty-five miles the day before, and if the tow path was the only way to Buffalo, the next train home would have had me for a passenger. All the way to Syracuse the tow-path, from what I could see in crossing it, is very much the same rough riding, and whenever anyone advised me to take it to a certain place I writhed with pain at the very idea.

At Little Falls the West Shore double tracks, the canal, the river, the four tracks of the New York Central, and the highway are all brought into close proximity by the perpendicular ledges of rocks on both sides of the valley, and the rocks along the highway and in the river are worn and scooped out by action of the elements, very much as they are at Diana's Baths, near North Conway. It is no uncommon occurrence on the Central road to see a passenger train chasing and overtaking a freight train, while a third train will scoot in between the two, with a fourth train close on to them. There is nothing dull about a trip up the Mohawk valley, even alone on a bicycle.

It is the general opinion that the mud this spring has been the deepest of any for many years, some say twenty-five years; and often I ride over places, now dry and dusty on the surface, that bend and crack like thin ice. A wagon laid up beside the road, with a wheel wrenched off by the deep hard ruts, or a place where rails and boards have been used to extricate a mired horse, are sights of almost daily occurrence.

Once I passed a hole in the road where a fine pair of draft horses were ruined. A week sooner and the roads would have been impassable for a bicycle. Even now the ruts prevent any very fast riding. The road scraper has only been used in a very few places, and as the roads have become more dry and dusty the small wheel has become more independent. going off to one side on little excursions of its own, to the natural disconcertment of its rider. After traveling over 400 miles I have had no tumbles, but as I was following a narrow ridge between two ruts, a fly, about as large as the head of a pin, flew into my eye, immediately enlarged itself to the size of a barn, and the next instant I was in the dust. It takes the weak things of this world to confound the bicyclist. The religious crank who has painted the stones and rocks of Connecticut with warnings in regard to the future life has been using the same means of conversion all over York State, and in many places he has taken advantage of alarming situations to enforce his arguments. For instance, in the Highlands below West Point is a deep ravine, down the sides of which the road winds and crosses a bridge nearly 100 feet above the river, on which is posted a sign "dangerous." The bridge totters under my feet, and right here, painted in staring blue letters are these words : " Prepare to meet thy God," and " Repent now or you will go to hell."

The knapsack attracts considerable attention along the route, especially from the dogs. Some only give a single low grunt, while others of more sound than sense follow it for a quarter of a mile or more; but every dog has something to say in regard to the trip. Coasting down into Peekskill the knapsack was accompanied by seven (actual count) dogs of various sizes and colors, some turning hand springs, others whirling around within a very small circle, and all performing some sort of gymnastic evolutions in front, on the side of, or behind the knapsack, and each one displaying his vocal powers to the best of his ability. Sometimes a dog of light weight and wit will chew away at my canvas shoes while they are revolving on the pedal, and another will tug away at my stocking while I drink at a well, but constant exposure has so toughened my sensibilities that I can walk along with the cold nose of a savage bull dog bumping against the calves of my legs without a shudder.

Going from Ilion to Frankfort I had a lively brush with a horse car, the highway and track running side by side, of such uncertain result that the passengers became as interested in the race as the driver himself. When passengers took or left the car the stops would give me the lead, but then the driver would run his horse and leave me behind, for the road was not the best, but I finally left them behind for good.

At Utica I met a dozen or more of the members of the bicycle club at their rooms during the evening. The members are mostly young men and nearly all riders, and bicycling has certainly taken a firm hold at this place. Messrs. Arthur J. Lux and F. E. Manchaw were especially friendly to me. But at Syracuse, where I stopped the next night, the atmosphere is very different. With equally good roads, a larger population, with club rooms, rent free, in the Y. M. C. A. building, a beautiful structure in a city of fine buildings, with all things seemingly favorable, the club hardly numbers a dozen lifeless members. Will. H. Olmstead, the first bicycle rider in Syracuse, a middle aged gentleman with a full black beard, kindly assisted me with information. For six miles out of Utica the sidewalk is without a single gutter to oblige a dismount, and at Syracuse there seems to be the same regard for the personal comfort of bicyclists. That day I met the first unpleasant treatment at a farm-house. Stopping for something to eat, the farmer, who was coming in from the barn to dinner, said rather sharply, "What do you do for a living." I told him what I was doing. "Why don't you go to work and earn your dinner," said he. That "riled" me a little, but I only said I expected to pay for what I had, and had intimated nothing to the contrary. He softened perceptibly, and as the savory smell wafted from the kitchen had increased my ravenous appetite, I jingled the few coins in my pocket in retaliation, till the crabbed old man actually smiled and invited me in, as cordially as it was possible for one of his disposition to do. Then disliking to beg and buy both I said so, and went a few rods to the next house, where I could not force any money on the good woman for the bountiful meal I had there.

I stopped for a meal at a way-side hotel, when, upon leaving, the German proprietor, knowing of the intended length of my trip, said, "Hold on one minute," and he ran back into the house. Returning directly with a small business card three or four inches square, on the back of which was a railroad map of the United States, in which the State of Connecticut did not appear larger than the end of a lead pencil, he said. "There, now, you go 'long, and when you come to a road you just take out your map and there you are. You will have to ask no questions. I am glad I thought of it." Thanking him, I went on.

Passing through places with such familiar names as New Hartford and Vernon, by houses — built of small cobblestones, the size of an egg, laid in cement in rows like bricks, and arched over the doors and windows, making a very pretty appearance — by cheese factories with the accusing question painted in large black letters on a board nailed to the whey tank, "Who Steals the Whey?" (every farmer helps himself to enough whey to pay for the milk he brings, and it looks as if some helped themselves to a little more)

by acres of hop-poles already stuck, by droves of mules
all tied together, with an immense draft horse leading them
along and another bringing up the rear: genuine horse
guards, that trudged along past the bicycle without so much
as deigning to look at it, while the captive mules, the tow-
path mules, shied out at it; through Oneida Castle and
through Auburn, where a minstrel brass band marching
through the streets and a knapsack and bicycle going down
the sidewalk gave the small boys and big ones, too, for that
matter, altogether too much to attend to just at dinner-time,
I finally came to the lake at Cayuga. Here a pleasant ride
of half an hour across the lake in a row boat made a very
agreeable change from the hot, dusty riding of the last
three or four days, and then on to Geneva for the night.
Next morning a cold rain drove me into a barn and finally
into the farmer's house where I surprised the ancient granger
in the act of making up his weekly letter to an agricultural
journal. Here ends the second week of the trip.

Distance traveled during the week 288 miles; distance
from starting point 557 miles.

CHAPTER IV.

At Niagara and along Lake Erie.

T Canandaigua I had a short interview with Doctor A. G. Coleman. He is short and rather thick set, with gray hair and full beard. His conversation was very entertaining; his bicycling experience in Denver and California naturally interesting me very much.

The artificial hatching of trout at Mumford, New York, is a sight that is well worth a journey, even from a long distance. The ground occupied is small, only two or three acres, and the building in which the hatching is done is only the size of an ordinary barn, but there is an immense amount of interest concentrated in this small area. There are a dozen or fifteen small ponds, perhaps ten feet square, boarded up on the sides, in which are the various kinds of trout from a year to twelve or fifteen years of age. Brook, salmon, California brook, and German trout are the principal kinds raised here. I laid down on a plank that crosses one of the ponds, where the water comes pouring into it, and put my hand down into the water. Probably five hundred of these speckled beauties, the common brook trout, varying from one to two pounds in weight, were struggling to get through the wooden grates into the water above, and they wriggled and twisted through my fingers and bit the flesh as if they resented the interference, but otherwise paid no attention to it. Many would even allow me to take them out and hold them for a few seconds. The water was actually solid with fish, for there were over 3,000 of them in this one pond. Lying on the grass beside another pond in which were some fine specimens of salmon trout, there were within a foot of my hand trout varying from a foot to two feet and a half or three feet in length and weighing from five to eighteen pounds, all lying perfectly still on the bottom, too lazy to stir. Then I went into the building where Jim — everybody knows Jim after one visit — told me how they propagate and care for the millions of tiny things, even selecting individual cases for special care. Half a dozen men were here picking out the poor eggs and doing different kinds of work. The eggs are about half as large as a lead pencil in diameter, and the poor ones are white, the others colorless. In one of the many shallow troughs in the building through which water is constantly running were thousands of eggs spread out just ready to hatch. When they break through the shell the little fish are scarcely longer than the egg itself, which remains attached to them and is finally absorbed. Millions of these eggs, as well as millions of these little trout not an inch long, are annually shipped to all parts of the country. Seth Green came in, and a few minutes' chat with the jovial, gray bearded, two hundred and fifty pound man would make anyone wish to come again and know him better. Then I went out to see them take the spawn. During the spawning season the trout run up a long covered sluiceway at the head of each pond, and a net placed at the lower end of this covered

brook catches every fish in it after the boards are removed
and the trout driven down with a pole. The men hauled
out about a bushel and a half at the first pond and about
two bushels at the second, and emptied them into tubs
filled with water. The females were parted from the males,
— they separated them much faster than a farmer could sort
rotting apples — and then the females were taken out by
the men on their knees and squeezed dry of every egg in
them. Occasionally a few drops of milk were pressed from
a male into the pan with eggs to fecundate them, which
occurred in a few seconds, and the males were thrown back
into the pond, the female being put into a separate pond and
tenderly cared for. Thus, in about fifteen minutes 50,000
eggs, or about three quarts, were obtained, and this process
is carried out every day during the season. The female
brook trout only live to be five or six years old, such neces-
sarily rough handling naturally shortening their lives, and
the males are turned loose down the stream after about the
same age, but the salmon trout attain the age of fifteen or
eighteen years. To put an edge to the enjoyment of this
visit, that was intense to one interested in all out-of-door
sports, Jim took a pan of chopped liver and the instant the
meat struck the water in one of the ponds, three thousand
yellow bellies made the water foam and boil with their
lightning-like flashes. Then he threw some to the big ones,
those lazy fifteen and eighteen pounders. They made some
troubled waters, too, a thousand of them, four tons of trout
flesh all in motion, handsome fellows that would come sailing, mouths wide open, towards the surface and flop their
bodies, nearly a yard in length, entirely out of water. Connecticut fishermen, who tramp for miles with cold,
soaked feet and return home with a wet back and a hungry
stomach, having secured only a few ounces of trout meat,

can, perhaps, get a faint idea from this hurried description of what is to be seen here, but they ought to come and see it themselves. Of course, fishing in a hatching pond would lack the zest which men naturally feel in killing a wild thing, but "I have known it done."

Those that are turned loose down the stream make very poor eating, for their life diet of liver and lights renders their meat very tasteless. It evidently needs the piquancy of a spider or fly to give a true gamey flavor. Just before reaching Lima, I stopped at Mr. Augustus Metcalf's, to make inquiries about the roads, and his son Willard, being a wheelman, kindly invited me to stay over night. My short visit with them will always be remembered with pleasure.

All the way from Syracuse, in fact all the way from Albany to Buffalo, I took the old, original turnpike. No matter whether I finally decided to take the "lower" road between intermediate places, or the "upper" road or the "middle" road or the "river" road or the "ridge" road or the "middle ridge" road, or a plank, clay, sand, or gravel road; whatever road I happened to be on some old farmer would soon tell me I was traveling on the "old original turnpike between Albany and Buffalo." One went back so far as to say that the said turnpike followed an old Indian trail, and they all seemed to take pride in mentioning the fact that their farms are situated on what was once such a celebrated thoroughfare. But there is another fact in regard to old highways that rests on a more substantial foundation than the disputed question as to which is the "old original." The main street leading out of Utica west towards Syracuse is called Genesee street, into Syracuse it is East Genesee, out of Syracuse West Genesee, and so on through Auburn, I think, and all the principal places until Buffalo is reached by going into the city by the same Genesee street.

Going up the Mohawk valley the view one gets is not very extended, but after leaving Syracuse, clear through to Bata-via, 125 miles, the country is undulating, and from the top of the many hills a traveler gets a fine view of a most beau-tiful country.   Although the leaves were not yet out when I passed through this section, the grass was green, and the cherry trees were in bloom on Good Friday.   Fine shade trees abound along the highways, and through many of the places a double row lines the principal streets, and fine side-walks and level riding make a trip through this section, even so early in the season, very enjoyable.   Arriving at Buffalo, the instant I crossed his threshold Mr. C. W. Adams, secretary of the Buffalo Bicycle Club, made me feel perfectly at home.   He is dark complexioned, below the medium height, smooth faced, wears glasses, and is about 25 years of age.   I found in traveling farther west that his hospitable manner and winning ways have made him a favor-ite with all wheelmen who have met him.   It was not enough to take me about the finest rides in that beautiful city, after supper, and find a very entertaining escort for me about the city the next morning, but a trip to the falls and the bridge with him the next afternoon made my visit at Buffalo the pleasantest by far of any short stop I have had during a tour of many pleasant experiences.   In the city there are fifteen or twenty miles of asphalt pavements as smooth as glass, block asphalt excepted, besides miles and miles of fine park roads, and with such drives it is not strange that the club is outgrowing its old club house — old only in name — and is moving into a very large two-story building on the main street, which will soon be nicely filled up with everything that such a genuine riding, working, racing, hospitable club needs.   Judging from the dozen or more members of the club that I met, such kind, open-hearted, courteous fellows deserve all the success that the nutmeg stranger they took in could wish them, and that is unlimited. By train to the falls and out upon Goat Island on our wheels. I dared to follow where Mr. Adams led, but being ahead he didn't notice I took the inside rut of the driveway that runs around the island close to the edge, where a fall to one side would have sent my friend and machine over the bank into the rapids. I can follow as narrow a path on a wheel as anyone in some places, but around the edge of Goat Island is not one of those places. After visiting the place a dozen times or more I might, perhaps; but the first — yes, it was the first time I ever saw Niagara. When I tried to express myself about it every word sounded so flat, so meaningless, so utterly unfit. I might as well try to define the Infinite. I had nothing to say and was dumb, and am yet whenever I think of it. It seems about fifty years ago an insurrection broke out in Canada and the steamer Caroline was used by some filibustering Americans a few miles above here to help the fuss along. But the Canadian authorities finally seized the steamer, touched a match to it and set it adrift. How it came down over the rapids, all afire from stem to stern, and went over the falls, can better be imagined than described, at least by me. In conversation about the occurrence, near the stairs that lead down to where the tower used to stand, and telling how I should like to have seen it, the hackman said with a condescending air: "O yes, but that is only one of many grand scenes that you have missed by coming here late," and from his manner I inferred that strange and wonderful things had occurred on this river for the last 10,000 years at least, and that if I had come in when the doors first opened the one price of admission would have taken me through the entire show. Considering the amount of time and labor required to put this play upon the stage, or hack, rather, the wonder is, not Niagara by any means, but that these poor palæozoic hackmen can afford to exhibit for the price they do. The unfortunate delusion abroad that they charge only for the scene in the play that is being acted now is undoubtedly a great mistake, and they suffer in the estimation of the public accordingly. Their price is for what has occurred since the curtain rose in the Upper Silurian down to the present and until the curtain falls where Erie and Ontario are one. Those who come early and stay late and are not satisfied will doubtless have their money refunded at the close of the entertainment. At least such was the in-timation of the man I met. Down a couple of miles to the suspension bridge, a look at the cantilever bridge,— a struc-ture that in its construction was more wonderful than in its completed state, for the arms of the immense iron piers were built out over the river till they met in the middle — across the river and down to the whirlpool and back, and the day, a red letter one, was ended.

Thursday morning was clear and cool, and I left Buffalo with a last look at the black cloud of smoke hovering over it that stretched, thinner and thinner, far out over the lake. The roads were fine along the shore, and once or twice I laid down on the grass on the edge of the cliff that juts out over the water, perhaps forty feet below, and tried to imagine I was tired so I could have an excuse for stopping, but the cool breezes at my back urged me on and the certain pros-pect of fine road ahead kept me going, and so all day long I paddled onward, always with the wind and sometimes like it. The breeze next day blew strong from the southeast, at right angles to my course, but the road remained good. Once I stopped under a shed to avoid a slight shower, but soon found a red handkerchief hanging at my waist was not a safe thing to have around a barn-yard, for a bull over the

FROM MUD TO MEADOW.—(*Page 40.*)

.

fence near me almost immediately began to paw the ground and bellow, and so I moved on without much delay. At times the wind would blow me out of the road on to the side, and when I got fairly braced to tack against it at an angle of forty-five degrees, more or less, it would suddenly let up and back into the road I would go with a rush, the wheel leaving a sort of self-registering mark behind that indicated the velocity of the wind at the different points in the road. Notwithstanding the wind and ten miles of sand and clay, too soft and rutty to ride, the 200 miles from Buffalo to Cleveland was made in three days, with two or three hours to spare, so any wheelman can judge of the general average of the roads. I never saw as long a stretch of fine wheeling.

Just here a word about guide-boards. In Connecticut, as we all know, guide-boards are a feature of every main and almost all cross-roads throughout the State, and are usually a great help to travelers by road. But along the Sound they grew scarcer, until coming into York State they were wanting entirely. In riding over 500 miles through different parts of that State, I remember seeing but four public guide-boards, and two of those were placed there by Poughkeepsie wheelmen. The roads are no straighter than in other States, and so the only thing to do in case of doubt is to take the side of safety and ask questions. These delays many times a day amount to a great deal, but there is no other way. But the instant I crossed the State line into the northwest corner of Pennsylvania every road and cross-road had a guide board. The change is like magic. And here in Ohio they go so far in the guide-board business as to tell you which way you can go to a certain place without crossing a railroad. For instance, to-day I passed a board which read: "Painesville without R. R. crossing 2 miles," another way being shorter. For miles around Buffalo in every direction

3

the land is very low and wet, requiring much ditching, but it rises gradually on towards Cleveland, after passing Erie, which like Buffalo is situated nearly on a level with the lake, and the towns, such as Conneaut, Ashtabula, and Painesville, seem to increase in size as the land rises to a higher level, till Cleveland, largest of all, stands on a higher bluff than any. After leaving Buffalo the streams that flow into the lake gradually increase in size also, and they wear a channel down through the solid rock which rises almost per-pendicularly on each side. These ravines, at each one of which is a town or city, increase in depth as the general level of the land rises. So, as one travels west from Erie over an apparently level country, there are constantly seen larger streams, deeper ravines, higher levels, and larger cities. The Lake Shore and Nickle Plate railroads are of course obliged to cross all these ravines, and their bridges increase in height till some of them are over one hundred feet above the river bed. I passed close by the Ashtabula bridge where, many will remember, a terrible accident occurred a few years ago on a cold December night.

Speaking about railroads reminds me of a little incident of yesterday. All the railroads along the route have adopted the four whistles for a crossing, the Hudson River and New York Central being the only exceptions, I think, so the fa-miliar signal first used by the New York and New England Railroad in the Eastern States is constantly heard. Yesterday I sat down under a tree to rest a few minutes when I heard in the distance the whistle of a train, and being near the tracks, waited to see the train pass. It came no nearer for some time, but I noticed the crossings seemed to be at regu-lar intervals apart. Still the train did not come. Finally, happening to turn my head on one side the sound came from above, and looking up into the tree I saw a small brown bird that at regular intervals would swell up and utter a sound that nine persons in ten would mistake for the four whistles of a locomotive in the distance.

The other day, in turning out to pass a team, I carelessly rode into some hard clay ruts that threw me instantly,— so suddenly that I turned almost a complete somersault. That is, I thought I did, for some time, for the blow I received on the back of the head that made it snap for a while could not be accounted for upon any other supposition than that I had gone clear over and struck the back of my head on the hard ground. I did not note just the position I was in when I picked myself up; the person in the wagon did that probably; but I was painfully aware that something hit me, hard too. It was the fifteen-pound knapsack that flew up and hit me a stunning blow on the back of the head. If I had been at home I would have bandaged my head, gone into an easy chair, and called the doctor. As it was, I simply re-mounted, trundled on, and was all right again in an hour.

Nine hundred and eighteen miles in three weeks.

IDING slowly through Mentor, Ohio, a small place with two stores and a meeting-house, I overtook a man driving a raw-boned bay horse that jogged along in a lifeless sort of a way. The driver too seemed to be tired, as he leaned forward holding his body up by resting his elbows on his knees, but this shiftless acting man drove into the yard at Garfield's old home and was Mrs. Garfield's farmer. Views of the homestead and its surroundings are familiar to every one, but a large two-story stone addition is being built that alters the appearance of the house somewhat. This handsome addition is doubtless fire-proof, and the lower windows are protected with heavy iron bars, giving the whole addition the appearance of an elegant prison, but it is designed, I am told, to preserve all of Garfield's books, papers, and other valuables.

Six miles east of Cleveland, a city named after a Connecticut surveyor, is the Lake View Cemetery, at which place I stopped a few minutes at the tomb that holds the remains of Garfield, guarded by a squad of United States infantry. The use of the tomb was given to Mrs. Garfield by a private family until such time as the remains could be deposited in their final resting place on the top of a hill a short distance away. The Garfield monument, the massive foundation of which is barely finished, and of which George Keller of Hartford, is the architect, is on a site that commands a fine view of the lake, the city, and the surrounding country for miles; the most beautiful location in that part of the State.

Euclid is a small village full of rum-holes, and surrounded by mud and water, the most forsaken place I have yet seen, and in every respect, excepting distance, Euclid avenue in Cleveland is as far removed from Euclid as Paradise from Purgatory. Buffalo has streets as beautiful, with better pavements, but none as long. The poplar seems to be the popular tree, long stately rows lining the sides of the street. I was using the sidewalk on what is called the "bob" side of this street when a rider, using the pavement on the opposite, the "Nabob" side, warned me I had better get off the sidewalk, and so I rode into the city over poor pavements with the gentleman that proved to be the president of the Cleveland club, Mr. H. B. Payne. Plank roads are a necessity in the clay soil of the outer suburbs of Cleveland, but covered with two or three inches of mud, and sunken about eight or ten inches below the level of the ground, these plank roads are neither pleasant to look at nor easy to ride over. Much of the low, wet land between Buffalo and Cleveland that will not produce a profitable crop of any of the cereals, is lately being used in raising grapes, currants, and other small fruits. This industry, new for this section of the country, is assuming enormous proportions, and I passed acres and acres of land entirely devoted to grapes. In fact the country seemed to be one vast vineyard, and I could easily imagine what a delicious sight it must present in the fall of the year, and my parched mouth seemed to get drier as I rode past the immense cellars that I knew were full of the cool wine. The route I was to take to Columbus was given me very explicitly at Cleveland as far as Wellington, and from that place I was told to "go right on to Columbus," from which I understood that the latter place was only a short distance ahead. But at Wellington, wheelmen could tell me nothing, livery stable keepers could only guess at the best route, which I was equally able to do, and so I struck out blindly. I went right on, not always right, however, often wrong, but still I went. The Ohio wheelmen are to issue a road book soon, but if the information in it is no more extended than the knowledge of roads possessed by all the northern Ohio wheelmen I have met, from the consuls up to the riders of baby bicycles, the value of the book will not be very great.

And this is the kind of country I went into. Land, low, level, and wet. Very little land under cultivation and that little producing a very thin crop of wheat. Houses small and out of repair. Barns tumbling down and propped up. No pebbly brooks or clean wells, but plenty of stagnant pools and plenty of warm rain-water to drink. If a farm-house has happened to burn down the farm is deserted. Nobody seemed to be doing anything and everybody was waiting for the land to dry up or something to turn up. The farmers were all fat, good natured, and wanted to talk. The roads were in awful condition, full of hard, dry ruts, and chunks of clay, that would beat a man's brains out if his head came in contact with them. No one was going from place to place, and over a portion of one main road only two teams had passed in three days — since the last rain. Everybody seemed to have settled down into the wet clay and to become contented; as happy as a great fat hog wallowing in the mud and grunting with satisfaction. To be

sure there are a few places of three or four thousand inhabitants scattered along through this otherwise thinly populated
section, but this is the general impression a traveler gets. I
had to walk over a good portion of the road and so had
plenty of chance to observe the condition of things for
seventy-five miles south of Cleveland.

Besides, the farmers are as ignorant as they are indolent,
knowing little about their own State and less about other
States. Not one in ten of them could tell me within a hundred and fifty miles the distance to Columbus, their own
capital. One man persisted in thinking Connecticut was a
small village with a cotton mill, in the State of Rhode Island,
and I could not hammer — we were in a blacksmith's shop
out of the rain at the time — I could not hammer anything
else into the fat old simpleton's head. Then, in the large
towns along the way, as if to add insult to injury, the people, in talking to me about this section of poor roads and
poor farmers, referred to them as "Yankee roads" and
"Yankee farmers." But the people out here, although rather
despising the close, saving habits of the average New Eng-
lander, yet do respect the perseverance, the tenacity, the
sort of bull-dog grip that they think the inhabitants of the
Eastern States are noted for. They pity the farmers of
New England who contend against a stony, barren soil, but
they regard with admiration their constant endeavors to ob-
tain a competency. Here they get their living, such as it is,
so easy. At the risk of making a too egotistical illustration
of how they regard a little perseverance I will give a little
incident that occured at Wellington, a place of three or
four thousand inhabitants. A large portly gentleman, fifty
or sixty years old. sitting in a carriage in front of a fine residence, stopped me to ask the inevitable questions, where
from, where to, and all about it. Then he "hollered" loud

enough for all Wellington to hear, " Wife, wife, come out
here and see this boy; this boy from Connecticut.   Come all
the way on a bicycle, goes sixty and seventy miles a day
some days; going clear out to Denver on it.   There's an
Eastern boy for you, that's Eastern grit, that is.   That's
Eastern," and he smiled all over his round face and wished
me all the good luck in the world.

Tuesday I experienced some of the difficulties of the
Western mud.   A light drizzling rain in the morning made
the roads too slippery to ride, and walking was hardly possible.   The sticky mud accumulated under the brake and between the forks till, obliged to turn the machine around and
push it backwards with the little wheel in the air, the big
wheel finally stuck fast and slid along in the road.   Then in
pushing up hill with all the strength I had my feet would
slip back and in going down hill I slipped up, paradoxical as
it may seem.   But a heavy rain the next morning made the
highways impassable for a pedestrian even, and so I took to
the lots, avoiding the plowed fields whenever possible.
Through ordinary soil the sides of the roads would be passa-
ble, but all the holes made by cattle during the spring mud
for the last twenty-five years remain to-day just as they were
made along the sides, and when these holes are filled with
water it is not pleasant to have your foot slip into one of
them and then have the water squirt all over you, therefore
I took the lots, climbing post and rail fences, crawling
through and lifting the machine over barbed wire fences,
any way to get along, but all day I made only twelve miles
and worked hard too.

Along in the afternoon a gentleman in a buggy, the first
team I had seen during the day, offered to help me along a
mile or so.   Seated in the backside of his buggy with my
legs hanging off and dragging the machine after me, I

thought that was not just the advertised way of going "right on to Columbus," but it was to Columbus I was going, someway. If the machine was muddy the day before, it was plastered all over now. The sticky clay would accumulate under the forks and saddle, and drop off in such big chunks that at times I did not know but I had kept hold of the wrong chunk, and had left the machine back somewhere in the road. Then from the shape of the mass of mud near the locality where the cyclometer was last seen, I observed that the ingenious little appliance was gliding gracefully along bottom-side up. But all this did not last. The roads dried up before night so I could walk in them. A mound of clay beside the road marks the spot where I cleaned up the machine, and after passing through Ashland, Mansfield, and some other smaller places, the next day, thirty-five miles above Columbus I came to a "double-track" road and the hard work was over. These double-track or "summer" roads, as they are called, are made of coarse gravel on one side, and the natural soil, the clay, on the other, the clay track being preferred in the summer, and the gravel in the winter and spring. But I forgot to mention one little incident of the day before. In jumping into a team-wagon for a short ride, the corduroy breeches, with a loud report, split open across the seat, really to such an extent that a change of apparel was absolutely necessary, but before I could get to a barn, in which to disrobe, I met several teams, in which were young ladies, and I know they thought me very bold to turn about and face them after they had passed. Stopping at Cardington, I found a wheelman, Mr. Samuel Brown, who was also a tailor, and he put my breeches in riding order again

The State capitol at Columbus is a heavy, square, granite building, with piles of immense grindstones laid one on top of the other that answers for pillars in front. It has very much the appearance of an Egyptian temple, and is dark inside and dingy out. The buildings in these Western cities, whether built of marble, granite, sand-stone, or brick, all soon have the same dingy look, the smoke from the immense amount of soft coal used being the probable cause. The members of the legislature there convened all had an easy-going happy way about them, and the clerk and messengers were slow and innocent in their manners, in sharp contrast to the business-like, clean-cut appearance of many Eastern legislators, and the rapid actions of Eastern clerks and messengers. On the way out of the city I passed the insane asylum, an institution that to outward appearances will accommodate more patients and that certainly did produce more noise by yelling lunatics than the one at Middletown, Conn. Both north and west of Columbus for many miles log huts are seen on all sides, some deserted, but most of them still occupied, that confounded clay pasted into the cracks between the logs, making the best kind of protection against the weather. Great black sows with chunked little black pigs are as plenty by the roadside as hens and chickens are in the East, and they are often seen roaming around the streets in good sized towns.

Three miles west of Dayton is the Soldiers' Home, and as I rode through the entrance to the grounds, a big Dutchman stopped me, but finding my object was simply to ride about the grounds and out again, he said : " Vell, when you get up into the crowd be very careful, for some are blind and some deaf, and if you run into one h—l will be to pay." There was quite a crowd, four or five thousand of them, some fishing, some watching the alligator, all seemingly enjoying themselves about the grounds — grounds that are laid out in beautiful shape, and that contain everything almost that would make life happy. All enjoying themselves? No, not all, for over on the farther side of the grounds several hundred were laying away, with military honors, one who had gone over to the silent majority, and as they filled his grave another grave was being dug.

Mr. T. J. Kirkpatrick of Springfield, is of medium size, middle aged, light complexioned, with light-colored side-whiskers and mustache, and from my ten minutes' talk with him I am satisfied that if there had been no other route from Cleveland to Columbus than the one the local consul at Cleveland gave me, Kirkpatrick would have started out and made one for the occasion. He is one of those men who can't do enough to help you along, and is an honor to the L. A. W.

The "pike" from Columbus to Indianapolis is a road that originally must have been built at great expense, for it is raised fifteen feet or more along some of the low lands, and now is kept in excellent repair,— a broad, level, and very straight highway, so straight that in forty-four miles there are only two slight bends in it, and so level in places that for twelve miles there is not the slightest rise or depression. In the western part of Ohio the land is just rolling enough to make some very fine coasting, and at times you can look straight ahead eight or ten miles, to the top of an apparently very high hill where the telegraph poles seem to come together, they are so far off, and the task of climbing that hill makes you faint in anticipation, but long before you get there the hill has faded away (another illustration of the maxim never to climb a hill until you get to it), the grade up it has been so gradual, and then, at last, you can look back and see another hill just as high that you have come down without knowing it. The very numerous toll-gate keepers along this pike charge two cents a mile for a horse, so if I had had one of flesh and blood, the expense one day would have been $1.52, but it being of steel and rubber, and only part of a rubber tire on the little wheel at that, the cost for toll was nothing. The road from Buffalo to Cleveland I thought was high water-mark, but this pike is so uniformly good for 180 miles that it must have first place.

The appetite such a journey as this gives one is no small part of the pleasure of the trip, everything tastes so good. The truth was never more plainly stated than by a Spartan waiter. Dionysius was taking a "hasty plate of soup," at one of those free lunches they gave there in Greece so often, when, pushing back from the table, he complained that the black broth was not highly seasoned enough for him. The waiter roared it through the hall "Seasoned! We season it by running, sweating, and getting tired, hungry, and thirsty." It is truly wonderful how such exercise does increase a person's digestive ability. I can imagine to a certain degree just how Milo, a Grecian athlete, must have enjoyed himself. Twenty pounds was the amount of his daily bread, and the same quantity of meat, besides fifteen quarts of wine, taken afterwards, no doubt, for his stomach's ache. One day, feeling somewhat faint from lack of nourishment, he knocked a four-year-old in the head with his fist, and devoured the whole "beef critter" during the day. To some this may at first appear incredible, but there is one explanation, at least, that is plausible : Milo must undoubtedly have been a wheelman.

The first night out from Columbus I stopped at a farmhouse. I walked around to the side door and was just going into the dining-room, when a man, with black hair, wild eyes, and thin pale face came out. He took one sharp look at me, and turning suddenly, slammed the glass door in my face, rushed through the dining-room, and pulling a spread from the table in his flight, and covering himself up with it, disappeared. But not for a great while. As I was eating supper he came back through the room, slamming the doors in his wild rush, and ran out into the yard, as if the very devil was after him. Then I could see him out in the dark, his eyes glaring in at me through the window, and after a while, when everything was still, bang ! would go some door, and away he would run through the room into the bed-room again. Still he said nothing, had not spoken for years, they told me. Once or twice during the evening he came slowly into the room, sidling along with his face averted, and his hands apparently warding off some blow coming from where I sat, and during the night I heard an occasional crash as if the side of the house had fallen in. It was that lunatic trying to get out of the cage in which they confined him, while the inmates of the house were asleep.

Distance traveled in four weeks, 1,257 miles.

CHAPTER VI.

At Chicago.

 HAD hardly crossed the Indi-ana State line when the tire on the rear wheel broke in two pieces and came off. Luckily, I was not far from Richmond where a wheelman gave me a second-hand eighteen inch tire, which he cut down to fit the sixteen inch wheel, and by wiring it on occasionally I reached Chicago with no further trouble on my part from the wheel. Just before reaching Indianapolis, however, the machine was the cause of a broken buggy wheel. I had just dismounted to avoid a drove of cattle, when a horse, coming towards me, suddenly decided to go the other way. I stood still in my tracks but that made no difference, the horse cramped the buggy so short that the front wheel went to pieces, and had not the men jumped out and grabbed the horse by the bit, just as they did, there would have been more trouble. As it was, they left the buggy by the road-side and walked a short distance to their destination, without expressing an opinion that I was in any way to blame for the accident.

The State capitol at Indianapolis is a building of the Gre-cian style of architecture, 300 feet wide, 500 feet long, and three stories high. It has been seven years in building and two years more will be required to complete it, but the stones have become so stained and dingy from the smoke that smuts everything out of doors in all these Western cities that the structure from the outside already looks like an old building. Several of those in authority about the building were very anxious to have me know that the dirty appearance of the outside would all disappear when the building was completed, but no amount of scrubbing will make it clean until the use of soft coal is done away with. The smoke from that coal discolors everything, and the finest stone buildings are bereft of much of the beauty from this cause. The Palmer House, a stone building here in Chicago, for instance, was painted white less than two years ago to get rid of the smutty appearance that it had acquired, but even now it looks as dirty and dingy as though it had never been painted. Scrub and paint all they may there is not a building in all the West, I believe, that looks as clean and white on the outside as our own State capitol on Bushnell Park. But to return to the capitol at Indianapolis. Black and dirty as it will always look on the outside, on the inside it is to be almost entirely pure white, giving it, in comparison with the capitol at Albany and our own, a much cheaper look. But it is superior to either of those other buildings in one respect and that is, as far as I could see, there has been no settling or chipping. One of the finest corridors in the Albany capitol is so sadly marred in appearance by the settling of the foundation that the breaks and cracks in the panels on the side are noticeable to every one. But the dome to the Indiana capitol, which is to be 300 feet high, is not yet finished, and the proof of the stability of building has thus hardly been furnished. A very interesting part of my two hours' clambering over the building and about the works was the sawing and planing of

the stones used in the construction. The stone mouldings
and cornices and all the straight work on the whole building
is done by machinery just as the wood used in the construction of a wooden building is prepared in advance. The carv-
ing was the only work done by hand in preparing the stones
for the masons to place in position.

The county court house at Indianapolis is typical of one
very noticable phase of the Western desire for display. It is
a fine substantial building no doubt, but inside it is one con-
glomeration of different kinds of marble; panels, walls, bal-
ustrades, everything inside almost is marble; all the kinds
and colors that are in existence are represented here, and
many kinds are to be found nowhere else in the world but
here: all these are mixed up in the most gaudy manner possible. But look a little closer and there is not a bit of marble
there, it is all paint, imitation. And where the paint is
wearing off the fraud is badly exposed, giving the whole
building the appearance of a decided sham. Another instance of this desire for display that is not shown by counter-
feiting at least, is seen in the elegant barber's shop at the
Palmer House. Set into the tiling on the floor are nearly
four hundred silver dollars that add nothing at all to the
beauty of the floor. But many of the buildings that have
been erected here in Chicago within the last three or four
years are very substantial and whatever there is about them
is real and not flashy in appearance. Clustering around
the Board of Trade Building, which probably is the finest
building of the kind outside of New York, are many handsome structures occupying a quarter of a square, that go up
into the sky ten, twelve, and thirteen stories high.

· I have spoken of the hogs and pigs that are seen all along
the roadside through Ohio and Indiana. The numerous
sheep that are feeding along the highways show some sense

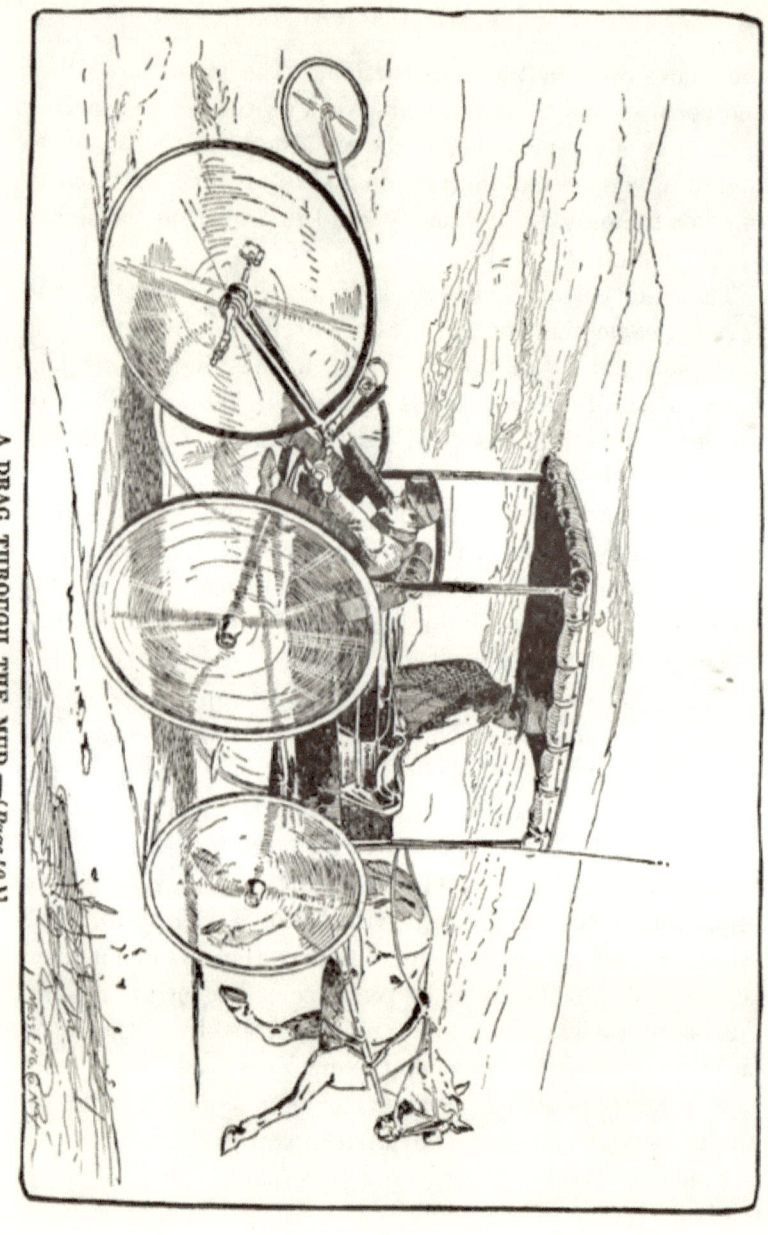

A DRAG THROUGH THE MUD.—(Page 40.)

by simply turning to one side to let me pass, and often
bleating after me as I leave them behind as if they were
sorry to have me go; but the pigs will start up and run along
ahead, scaring all the others with their short, quick grunts,
until a drove of a dozen or fifteen are bobbing along and
running into each other in their foolish attempt to get out of
the way. Then they will all suddenly stop, stand perfectly
still, and let me pass without flinching. If Eastern people
who have a prejudice against Western pork could see what
the hogs are fed upon they would have good reason to change
their opinions. The hogs eat a great deal of grass and are
not confined to any muddy, filthy pen as they are in the East,
but roam around the woods and fields as do the cows and
sheep. In the fall corn on the ear is thrown out into the
lots to them, and I can't see how pork could be fatted in any
cleaner way.

While the hog is being discussed I must tell what I saw
of the manner of his death at the Union Stock Yards just
outside of the city limits. Prominent among the many
buildings at the yards that cover 365 acres is an office of the
Illinois Humane Society, which gives a visitor the impression
that he will see nothing but kind treatment and humane ways
of killing the beef and hogs, and as far as the cattle are concerned there is nothing objectional about the process, for a
bullet in the brain renders them insensible at the outset.
But the hogs — well, this is what I saw. A dozen or more at
a time are driven into a pen in one of those immense packing
houses. A man slips a chain quickly around one of their
hind legs and they are jerked up into the air by machinery,
so that their heads are about four or five feet from the floor.
They are suspended on little pulleys which roll them along
into another pen where a man cuts their throats. This man
was standing in clotted blood ankle deep, and the squealing,

4

kicking row of hogs threw blood all over him, which he frequently washed off at a barrel of water near. A hog was
jerked up about every ten seconds, and there would be six or
eight at a time hanging with their throats cut. Before they
had time to die or grow very weak from the loss of blood
they were dropped on to an inclined board, and from there
they slipped off into the scalding tub. Sometimes two or
three would collect on this board and then they would all
slide off into the hot water together. Very few of them
were dead when they went in, and they would go plunging
and struggling around in there, throwing the water in every
direction, till gradually becoming weaker they would lie
still, a dozen of them, in the long narrow tub at a time, and
be turned over and over by men with poles very much as
cooks turn nut-cakes over with a fork in the hot fat. Why
such haste should be used in getting them into the hot water
I cannot see, and I understand the Humane Society have
tried unsuccessfully to stop such inhuman work, but this is
the sight I came unawares upon, a spectacle that I have not
enlarged upon or exaggerated in the least. The hogs were
simply drowned in hot water. The rest of the work I rather
enjoyed. The scalded hogs were taken out and placed upon
a revolving wheel, covered with scrapers, which took all the
hair off excepting around the head and legs. This wheel
was wide enough to hold three hogs at a time, and they were
turned over several times in order to scrape all sides of them.
Then men finished up the scraping with knives, the heads
were taken off with two or three strokes of the knife, and
from the time the hog was first seized by the leg till he was
cut up two or three men were at work on him all the time,
one set of men passing him along to the next, each doing certain parts of the work. Thus 2,500 hogs a day are put to
death by this one set of men, and there was machinery in this

same packing house for two other sets of men, so that seven or eight thousand hogs are scalded to death, scalded from the inside as well as from the outside, every day. This packing house is in full operation, and this is only one of many such houses in the stock-yards. I remember now there was an invitation prominent over the door of the Humane Society to make "complaints at this office," and every time I think of the horrible work being perpetrated so near by, I wonder of what earthly good is such a society. I only regret that I did not complain at the time, useless as it would undoubtedly have been, but then I did not realize what an awful sight I had seen. The enormity of the cruelty has grown on me since. But let me change the subject. A bowl of bread and milk in the middle of the day is to be had, almost for the asking, and it not only serves to quench thirst, but what strength it gives is sooner felt than if the food was of a more solid nature. One day I asked an old lady for a bowl of bread and milk, and she brought me the milk in a bowl with two huge slices of bread thrust down into the milk whole, and then she handed me a two-tined fork to eat it with. Often when I am caught out between places at night and have to ask accommodations at farm-houses, I can usually get taken in by saying "a bowl of bread and milk will do for supper."

One night, soon after the machine had been put into the front parlor,— the farmers always think the best room in the house none too good for that "silver" horse, as some of them term it — and the knapsack had been laid away in the corner, the husband came in from the barn with two pails of milk, followed by his little boy, who was just old enough to walk if no threshold or hole in the rag carpet interfered with his progress. The milk was placed in the buttery on the floor, and the little youngster of course had to see that

it was done all right.   Then the farmer came out and everything was quiet for a minute, when suddenly there was a
splash.   As it so often happens to such toddling young ones,
the little fellow's toes suddenly flew up from some unaccount-
able reason, and he sat down into one of those foaming pails
of milk.   He never said a word, but sat there perfectly still
until his mother, happening to go into the buttery, saw the
floor covered with milk, and she jerked him out of that pail
as one would pull a close-fitting cork out of a bottle, and
with very much the same kind of a sound.   When supper
was ready, in reply to her question, I said I preferred " cold
morning's milk to the warm or warmed over night's
milk."

About forty miles above Indianapolis, in a sparsely settled
district, I passed a small church filled to overflowing with
people, and a little further on I met a funeral procession.
It had been raining during the morning, but among the
fifty or more teams that formed the procession, there was
but one top carriage, two buggies, and the rest were all
heavy team-wagons.   In these farm wagons with boards for
seats, were whole families that had come a dozen miles,
probably, to attend the funeral.   From this it seems that
buggies and business wagons are luxuries that the average
Western farmer does not yet feel able to afford.

At Lafayette, I called at the home of Mr. Frank A.
Lewis, to inquire as to the condition of the roads farther on,
and his mother kindly asked me in to supper.   Before that
was finished, Frank returned with several wheelmen,
among them Mr. Wal. Wolever, a young photographer.
Here the pikes or gravel roads which made the riding
excellent so far came to an end, and there was nothing
before me for 120 miles to Chicago but black clay roads.
It had rained heavily for three successive nights, and after

riding over 1,300 miles to reach a city that is not 1,000 miles by direct routes from Hartford, I may, perhaps, be forgiven for wishing to avoid three hard days' work, without any practical return for it in knowledge or experience by taking the train to Chicago. After reaching that city, and being kindly received by friends and old schoolmates, it was with a strong feeling of thankfulness for my own safety, that I read the accounts of the terrible cyclones and floods that had passed through sections of Ohio and Indiana, carrying away bridges that I had so lately ridden over in safety, and perhaps killing men and women from whom I had so recently received kind treatment.

The system of beautiful parks that environ Chicago, and the boulevards that connect them are the pride of the city, and the citizens have good reason for being so proud of them. Only a few years ago the whole country around about the city was a low level wet prairie, but now there are six as beautiful parks as are to be found in almost any city in the country; parks filled with lakes, cascades, brooks, hills, groves, grottoes, wild animals and tame ones, and everything almost that is to be found in places where nature furnishes things to order. In Lincoln Park, for instance, is a mound of earth, a hill I suppose they call it, that is probably the highest point of land for many miles near the city, but this, like everything else in these parks, is artificial. All through Ohio and Indiana there is much land that has not yet been cleared, and these clumps and strips of timber give a variety to the country that would otherwise have been very monotonous to me, riding for hours and hours as I did over nearly level roads. These woods have little if any underbrush, and the grass through them is kept closely cropped by cows, sheep, and hogs, so that these two States are filled with hundreds of beautiful groves that invite a lazy wheelman to stop and stay awhile in the cool shade.

One day, wishing to get rid of the several days' growth of bristling beard on my face, I took out my shaving apparatus, hooked the leather strap to the brake handle, honed the razor, found an old can, brought some water from a brook near by, pinned the pocket mirror on a tree, and got as clean a shave as I ever had, washing my face with one corner of a handkerchief, and drying it with the other end.

But the open level prairie that surrounds Chicago on all sides must have a sort of depressing influence on the thoughts and ideas of those who are born and brought up without the variety of brooks, hills. mountains, and ocean. The first question usually asked me by farmers, who probably have never traveled far from their prairie homes, is : " How far do you live from the salt water ? " and when I tell them the distance. which until this trip always seemed to me considerable, but which to them, with their distances and so many things on such an immense scale, seems trifling, they act as if a sniff of the salt sea air from a distance of forty or fifty miles would be a blessing that they could hardly hope for. And yet Lake Michigan, to me, would seem a very good substitute for the ocean in everything but the taste of the water. Two of these parks are washed by the waters of this lake, and so badly washed too that the shore at Jackson Park is rip-lapped for nearly a mile, making a beautiful white-stone beach. The boulevards are laid out on as grand a scale and with as little regard to expense as are the parks. The grand boulevard is Commonwealth avenue in Boston over again, only it is twice as long, with a very broad avenue in the center and a street of good width on each side, one for equestrians and the other for wheelmen. I should judge, for it is very smooth. Ten rows of beautiful elms stretch away in a straight line for two miles, the larger ones having rows of smaller ones on each side. Drexel boulevard has two broad avenues, lined with trees on the outside, and the center filled with lovely flower-beds, for over a mile in length. Other boulevards laid out on a similar plan but not in so finished a condition, connect the different parks, making a continuous drive of nearly forty miles, all as smooth as the most fastidious wheelman could desire. Then there are the lake drives, Dearborn and Michigan avenues, and many other streets too numerous and common to mention, common nowhere but in Chicago though. Chicago wheelmen know so little about coasting, that it seemed quite a novelty to them to see an Eastern boy ride with his legs over the handles, and when I coasted down into one of the tunnels that run under the Chicago River, and disappeared in the darkness, their eyes stuck out with wonder. It was a novelty to me, too, for the dripping water gave me quite a shower bath before I came out on the other side.

Distance traveled on the wheel, 1,420 miles.

CHAPTER VII.

Across the Mississippi.

Y time was so taken up in visiting old friends and seeing the sights in Chicago that I found no opportunity to make the acquaintance of many wheelmen in that city, but I met Mr. B. B. Ayers, who kindly gave me directions for pursuing the journey westward, and so after a week's stay in Chicago I started for Minonk, 125 miles away to the southwest, to visit friends in that place, and the two days and a half passed on that journey were the hardest of the trip thus far. One would naturally think 1,500 miles of riding in the past five or six weeks would have so strengthened the muscles of my arms that they would not trouble me at least, but the hard, lumpy, rutty black clay roads of Illinois were too much for them. My elbows became so stiff I could hardly bend them, and the nervous strain occasioned by the constant jar was very exhausting. Once I was induced to take the railroad track and found very good riding for a few miles. At the station they told me the next train would not be along for an hour and it would come from the direction in which I was going, so I rode along unconcerned, for I could see ahead for miles. Suddenly, without the least warning, the sound of a short,

sharp whistle from behind caused me to jump off and into
the ditch as I never did before.   It was well I did so quickly,
for an extra locomotive immediately rushed by, and I came
to the sudden conclusion it would be a long while and the
roads pretty bad before I should again leave them to ride on
a railroad track.

Two turnpike companies once started to build a pike from
Indianapolis to Lafayette, Ind., seventy miles, but when
within two miles of each other there was a disagreement
between the two companies and that intervening piece of
road has never been finished.   Although there is a great deal
of travel over this splendid pike there is not public spirit
sufficient to fill up this gap of two miles, and for years the
traveling public have driven off the ends of these two turn-

pikes into two miles of the deepest mud fordable.   In Illinois there are no pikes even, all dirt roads; roads that are to-
day in the same condition they were when the country was
first settled; not a day's work has ever been expended upon
them.   I passed farm after farm on which were fine houses,
large substantial barns and hundreds of heads of stock,
and every indication of a rich soil and worldly prosperity,
and yet the road directly in front of these farm-houses
has remained in such a condition for years, that for six
months out of the twelve it is really dangerous for man or
beast to travel after dark.   I stopped one night in a fine
brick house that in the East would cost four or five thousand
dollars, and yet this house could only be reached by a lane in
which the mud for six months in the year was hub deep,
and a fine fat sow with a litter of pigs had full possession of
the front yard, if such a mud hole could be called a yard.
Another case I remember where the houses, barns, and stock
indicated the farmer's prosperous condition, and yet there
was no well, nothing but rain water to drink.   The fact is,
all these things — and I could keep on mentioning them to
the end of the chapter — serve to illustrate the intense Western desire for display to the neglect of comfort.   The stately
domes of their numerous court-houses seen on all sides make
a big show.   Their large barns with the farmer's name
painted on the side in red letters or shingled into the slate
roof advertise the owner's name and financial standing.
Whatever is above ground, whatever can be seen from a distance, whatever makes a great display receives the cordial
support of the average Westerner, but when you look for a
fine country road, free of toll gates, or a good, deep well, or
a nice cool cellar, or anything, no matter how much it might
add to the personal comfort of the possessor, but which is
below the surface or unseen from the surrounding country,

you may look in vain for these evidences of a moderately high state of civilization. The diet of Western families is simply abominable. It is pork, fried pork, every meal. Their meals are as monotonous as their scenery. A farmer, rich in money, lands, and houses, will live for weeks on pork, when beef, mutton, turkey, and chicken are in great abundance on all sides and so cheap as to be almost unsalable. And yet, probably because their stomachs are out of sight and the satisfying effect of a good square meal is quieting and not of the spread-eagle effect, the farmers live upon the freshest and plainest sort of food. If the Western stomach could be inflated and placed in some commanding position it would be supplied with the choicest viands and the farmers would pour out their money to fill it to overflowing.

The other Sunday I came along to a meeting-house just after the bell stopped tolling, and riding out under the shed, I slipped off my knapsack, buttoned on a clean collar, put on my coat, and went in as quietly as possible, but every one in church except one old lady looked around at me, and I lost most of the Scripture lesson in consequence of this counter attraction. From her actions, afterwards, I think the said old lady was deaf and did not hear me come in, which accounts for her apparent neglect. Soon after a portly old gentleman came waddling up the opposite aisle, and after putting his hat, cane, and numerous other articles of extra baggage over in the seat in front, he held on to the back of that seat to break the fall, finally letting go and sitting down like a trip hammer. He immediately began to box the congregation, and had gone from east around to northwest, when he fetched up against me and put me under close inspection for so long that I wickedly comforted myself knowing that I gave him a crick in the neck. Very soon many in the congregation with eyes reverently closed and heads on one side in imitation of Alexander the Great, were apparently absorbing their spiritual food through their mouths, when the choir of eleven noises followed the sermon with "Asleep in Jesus." The choir kept well together for a while, although one or two had to feel around in advance for the first note, but the last line was always too much for the tenor, and with their leader gone all discipline vanished and they came leisurely home in squads, three and four at a time. But slow and solemn as the singing was, the organist broke loose during the interlude, scampered up and down the scale, trilled, stumbled, snorted, and galloped off into the lots so far I thought he never would get back, and during his last escapade he stepped on a note that stuck, and that note loudly persisted in being heard through the benediction and sometime after the congregation had dispersed. When the organ breathed its last, the boys, old and young, all came out to see me off, and stayed so long it broke up the Sunday-school; so altogether, unintentionally, I caused a good deal of trouble.

Going through Aurora I met two wheelmen, Messrs. G. O. and Chas. W. Clayton, one of whom, but since my return I cannot tell which, accompanied me for 10 or 12 miles on my way.

Three-fourths of the area of the State of Illinois — a State eleven times as large as Connecticut — is underlaid with seams of soft coal, and at Minonk, where I spent several days in visiting relatives, is the most productive mine in the State. Over 700 tons a day are raised from a depth of 500 feet, and the machinery works with such rapidity that a ton of coal is raised and emptied in twenty-two seconds. After screening, great quantities of the coal, smaller than chestnut size, are sold to farmers, who feed it out to their hogs with beneficial results. The refuse rock and clay from this mine is carried

up an inclined railroad and dumped, making a mound perhaps seventy-five feet high.   The inhabitants think it quite a
treat to climb to the top, they get such a grand view.   It
really is the highest point of land for miles around, and the
view of a town ten miles away is to them quite a sight.
Horses in droves in the lots or loose by the roadside are very
common, but there is one peculiarity that distinguishes them
from all the other domestic animals I have seen.   The instant
they catch sight of the bicycle they invariably come boldly
toward it half a dozen paces and then turn and run like all
the other animals.   They seem to want to find out as soon as
possible the nature of the machine, but their courage is short
lived.

At Lacon I crossed the Illinois River, which was half a
mile wide at this point.   The river is very sluggish, falling
only one inch to the mile for 300 miles.

During several days I had felt sleepy all the time, doubtless due to overeating and lack of exercise in Chicago, and,
so, frequently I would lay down beside the road and sleep
soundly for an hour or two, the hard clay bed not disturbing
my slumbers in the least.   In fact I had, by this time, become quite a veteran in this respect, being able to rest peace-
fully anywhere I felt inclined to stop.

At Rock Island I left the State of Illinois, which has a
high-license system that works admirably, as far as I could
judge from the frequent inquiries made, and crossed the
Mississippi River into the prohibition State of Iowa.   Imagine my surprise to find beer and liquor sold as openly as soda
water in the city of Davenport.   The State law is circum-
vented and nullified in this manner :   The city council passed
a law obliging all dealers in soda water and like temperance
drinks to take out a license.   If a man sells soda water, and
nothing stronger, this law is not enforced against him ; but

if he sells liquor in connection with his soda he is prose-
cuted, not for selling liquor, mind you, but for selling soda
without a license   Thus, beer and liquor is sold openly, and
the city of Davenport has reaped a revenue of over $3,000
from this source within a few weeks.   Before I got through
the State of Iowa I could judge better of the practical workings of their prohibitory law, but the first day in the State
certainly puzzled me.   At one small village all the inhabitants seemed to be devoting the whole time that day to
dancing and drinking beer.   They were Germans, and it is
needless to add that there was no downright drunkenness
to be seen there.   Even in Grinnell, a place of 3,500
inhabitants, that has never had an open saloon, the "boys"
have their beer shipped in to them on such occasions as
Memorial Day and the Fourth of July.

Traveling alone as I have, most of the way, I could
appreciate to a limited extent the lonely task Thomas Stevens
performed in crossing this country as he did, but never have
I realized until I reached Iowa to what extent he had been
shut out from nearly all intelligent communication with
human beings in his journey through Europe and Asia.

About one hundred miles west of Davenport is a settle-
ment of Bohemians.   They number six or eight thousand,
and their little villages are scattered along the Iowa River
for a distance of ten miles or more.   Their system of families is very much like the Shakers in Enfield, Conn., and
beside keeping their farms up in excellent condition they
manufacture woolen goods, starch, and some other articles
of commerce.   But not one of them that I met could speak
a word of English, so that my experience for two or three
hours was in a slight degree like what Stevens suffered for
many weeks and months.   All I could do was to make signs.

Although I left Connecticut before the grass had hardly

begun to turn, since then I have seen nothing else but one everlasting sea of green. The country is more rolling in Iowa than in any of the States west of New York through which I have passed, but that change in the scenery was not of much relief. Thus far I had not seen the smallest kind of a wild flower to break the monotony of that color, green, dark and rich as it was. Imagine with what pleasure I came upon a sandy ridge of hills that were covered with a beautiful variety of wild flowers, whose colors seemed particularly bright to me, probably because they were the first I had seen in seven weeks of outdoor life. I spent an hour or more in picking flowers and in biting off the sweet tips of honey-suckles.

It is curious how many old veterans the sight of the knap-sack brings to the surface. Very often when I lay it aside for a rest some one will pick it up and try it on so handily that I know without his telling me what his experience has been. And the recent speech of that arch traitor, Jefferson Davis, stirs these old soldiers from the top of their heads to the very soles of their feet. Imagine the feelings of one of these, a large-framed, well-formed man of forty, who walked around Minonk with me, up the coal shaft and down, without much apparent difficulty, and yet this same man, John W. January, suffered a thousand deaths at Andersonville, where his feet rotted off, and where he was reduced to forty-five pounds in weight, his bones alone almost weighing that much. Jeff. Davis's words don't ex-actly stir him to the soles of his feet, but from the words he and so many others, with whom I have talked, have indignantly uttered, I think these old heroes are sorry they were not allowed to do up the job more thoroughly at the time of the war.

The bicycle is getting to be more of a wonder the farther

west it goes. Everywhere I stop crowds quickly gather, and
then the inevitable string of questions ! At Rutland, Ill., the
landlord, who was a native of Connecticut, gave me all I
could eat, but would not let me go till I had ridden all over
the sidewalks and gutters in the town, under his direction.
A few miles east of Grinnell I found I could not reach that
place the night I was expected, so I took a freight train.
While waiting for the train the whole town came down to
the station, and to escape being almost bored to death I
went out back of the station to wash my hot feet. But still
there was no rest. An Irishman who lived in Hartford
"thirty year ago," was the first to find me, then two or three
natives went through the same old list of questions, and
finally a colored gentleman came around to pay his respects,
just as I was wiping my refreshed feet on the grass. When
the train arrived I laid out on one of the long benches,
placed along the side of the caboose, and went fast to sleep,
apparently. But at every station there was something in
the air that told the inhabitants there was an object as
strange as a wild man from Borneo on board, and the
caboose was quickly filled with a gaping crowd of men,
women, and children. One passenger who had already got
some points of the trip, related all he knew and more, too,
to the assembly, and it required considerable composure to
keep on breathing regularly and keep my eyes shut with
some old woman looking right down into my face and sigh-
ing for my lifeless condition, but as long as my eyes were
closed no one asked me any questions, and 'that was a great
relief.

As this is a plain unembellished tale of a bicycle journey
in which facts are reported as they exist, not as we would
like to have them, I may as well acknowledge, though not
without a twinge, that during the first week out the chafing

AN IMPROMPTU SHAVE. — (*Page 54.*)

of a stocking strap brought out a boil on the side of my leg. The next week a second comforter appeared underneath that member, and painful as it is to acknowledge it (the bitterest pangs are now past), in a few days some six or eight more obtruded themselves, seriously interfering with the saddle. After some days of dogged persistence in riding and trying to rise above them (which efforts from the nature of the case were obviously futile), I succumbed and pleaded for a ride on a freight train ; and when that gentleman passenger, who knew the real cause of my desire to take the train, told a lady passenger who was very anxious to know, too, that I took the train because — and he hesitated — because I "had got hurt," his answer pleased me so I was sure the lady, who was looking straight at me from the opposite side of the car, would think I was writhing with pain even in my sleep. "Poor boy!" she responded, sympathetically, — "How dreadful! I do hope he will recover!"

Distance traveled on the wheel, 1830 miles.

5

CHAPTER VII.

Across the Missouri.

YCLONES are getting to be so common in this Western country that the people are endeavoring to guard against them as they do against fire, but with this difference: they do not try to protect their property against the cyclone; it is useless; they simply wish to save their lives, that is all. Insurance on property against loss by wind is now customary all over the country, but if these cyclones increase in frequency as they have in the past few years, it is only a question of time when life insurance companies will consider it an extra risk to live in this Western country. I experienced a feeling of nearness to the cyclone that was sufficient when I read the accounts of the terrible destruction of life and property in Ohio a few weeks ago, for I had a delightful journey only a few days before through some of the towns that were so soon afterwards swept away in a twinkling. But my stay in Grinnell, of a couple of weeks, was like living on an old battle-field. The dead, of course, have gone from sight, but the wounded are to be seen on all sides. I went out calling and met an old lady still suffering from an injury received four years ago. I saw another go limping by and heard she had a hip broken at the same time, and, while riding, I met a lady whose head was so crushed during that terrible storm that she now has frequent spells of insanity. I began to wonder if any one in Grinnell had escaped uninjured. Let the clouds even now gather, black and threatening, and the people live the awful experience of that night over again. The streets are soon filled with women and children, carrying what few valuables they can, all hurrying to some cave for safety. I crawled into one of these caves one day. It was in the cellar of a fine residence, and is a room not larger than six by eight feet, and not over four feet high, with strong brick walls on the sides and heavy timbers overhead, and amply ventilated, and into this small hole, not long ago, twenty-four women and children huddled for two or three hours one night, some praying, others crying, and all suffering from mortal fear as long as the storm lasted. Almost every house in Grinnell that has a cellar has a cave of some kind in it, a room boarded up and covered over thick with earth to protect the occupants from falling bricks and timbers. Not only here but all through the West a cave is now considered an essential part to every dwelling. But think of the mental suffering the people of these Western States endure whenever there is a severe storm or even indications of one. If those Eastern people could see the photographic views that I have seen of the destruction wrought by a Western cyclone, they would never assign, as a cause of their complete demolition, the flimsy manner in which the houses are built. If they could have seen the two college buildings, one built of stone, the other of brick, each as large and as solidly built as any Eastern edifice, if they could have seen these two buildings demolished and crushed like so many eggshells — in less than two minutes — what would they think of the superior safety of our Eastern houses? How many frame houses would stand such a blow? Everything was as calm and still as death that terrible night when, without any premonitory roar or warning, the cyclone struck the town like the report of a cannon, and in less than five minutes it had finished its work, ending it as easily with the two college buildings as it commenced it with the small frame houses. Although it was early in the evening, fifty-eight persons were instantly killed and many more wounded; but let it come again, day or night, it will never catch Grinnell people unawares. They watch the clouds to this day, as they would some fell demon hovering over them, and the more timid ones early rush to their caves. Many outlandish lies have been written about the power of the cyclone, but the cold fact, the bare truth is more wonderful than any stories man can invent. One only needs to come here and talk with the people about the cyclone to be convinced that their experience for a few minutes was as terrible as that of a great battle, and I was as fascinated with their stories as I ever was talking with old soldiers.

"I should know you were an Easterner from your talk," is a remark I hear on all sides, and so I have tried to learn what there is about the talk of a native of New England that distinguishes him from people west of there. It is not because he speaks so flat, for through New York every one spoke more so than I could. I pronounced the town of Fonda just as it is spelled, and yet every one there called it "Fundy." Utica was "Utiky," Lima was "Limy," and everything else was pronounced in the same flat manner. I supposed this to be a peculiarity of New Englanders, but New-Yorkers rather excel in that style of speech. Out here in Iowa, where friends have an unflinching frankness quite remarkable, they tell me whenever I say anything particularly flat my nose flies up into the air to emphasize it. That may be a trait peculiar to myself, but it is some comfort to know that people outside of New England have lingual peculiarities as marked as those coming from the Eastern States. In Ohio and Indiana. I met a great many persons who never pronounce the personal pronoun "I" as we do. It is always "Ah" instead of "I." "Ah thought so," "Ah heard so." I supposed that was more Southern than Western; but if so, many of Southern birth are now living in these States. The farther West I go the more I notice the way they roll their R's. That letter is brought out with a peculiar force in every word in which it occurs. Here, there, however, harvest, horses, father, mother, and all such words are spoken as if there were two or three r's in them instead of one. Whenever they accost me it is "O, George," while in the East it would be, "Say, George." Then two short grunts are very often used out here instead of yes or no. Emphasize the first grunt and it means no; emphasize the second, with a slightly rising accent, and it means yes. This is a common form of expression, with colored people everywhere, I think, but here, with white children, it is the most common way of saying yes or no, and many older persons use it.

They have no brooks or streams here, but everything is called a "crick," pronounced very short, too. That name is applied sometimes to good-sized rivers. These peculiarities of speech do not seem to be acquired by persons living here, who were born and brought up in the East, but their children acquire them readily, and everywhere on the trip, going and coming, I noticed these peculiarities more in the talk of the women and children than in the men. I could only account for this from the fact that men go out into the world more and come in contact and consequently talk more with persons using fewer provincialisms.

The students at the Iowa College in Grinnell had a field-day while I was there, and during the games and races I could but notice the striking difference between the features of these students and those of Eastern young men. These Iowa boys have heads large and well shaped enough, but their features are disproportionately large. Their eyebrows are large and overhanging, their cheek bones are prominent, their noses are heavy, mouths large, and under jaw bones strong and marked. There is nothing brutal or exactly coarse about their faces, but everything about them is large and heavy. I hardly saw a small-featured, clean-cut, really refined face among the one hundred and fifty young men.

The attendance at church in Grinnell is larger in proportion than in any place in the East, probably. With a population of 3,500 the regular attendance at the Congregational Church alone is eight or nine hundred.

When I left Grinnell, two members of their bicycle club, Messrs. Lee Taylor and Geo. Lewis, accompanied me for twenty miles or more, and although I was very glad of their company, the frequent tumbles they took coasting, made me sorry they had undertaken the ride, with the thermometer up in the nineties.

Iowa roads are decidedly better than those through Illinois. Although there is the same system of repairing the highways in both States — the ancient system of farmers working out their road tax where they choose — yet Iowa farmers not only scrape their roads, but in many places they were laying tiles along up the worst hills in order that the roads might be drained in the spring. I saw more work done on the roads the first afternoon in Iowa than I saw the whole week in Illinois. And there is another thing to be said in favor of these Western clay roads, roads that for hundreds of miles have been as rough as any cobble street in a New

England city (it is simply just to give the devil his due), a rider can go within half an inch of a clay rut and yet his wheel will not slide down into the rut. This has saved me many a tumble.

Another thing : during dry spells, such as we are having throughout the West now, the dust gets very fine but never very deep. The clay is so tough it does not get cut up as much as our Eastern roads do during a drought. But the coasting in Iowa, of which I expected so much, for the country is a rolling prairie, was simply dangerous. The hills are so full of hard hummocks, "dive holes" the wheel-men here call them, that it shakes a fellow up terribly. Once I went off, going down a steep hill at such a rate that my hands and knees struck the ground simultaneously, and the knapsack tunked me on the back of the head at about the same time, as if to remind me of man's fallen estate.

In almost every Western State the towns are just six miles square and the roads cross each other at right angles at intervals of one mile; consequently in traveling across the country diagonally, as I have most of the time, it was necessary to travel much farther than if the roads had been left as they were before the towns and counties were laid out. Through Iowa the old stage road followed the "divide" (what we call a ridge in the East) in many places, but when the towns were laid out the road was made straight across the country, up and down some very steep hills, in the western part of the State. The log barns, pig pens, and corn cribs, so common in Ohio and Indiana, disappear almost entirely in Illinois and Iowa, and instead appear thatched barns and sheds. Poles are set in the ground and a cheap frame fastened to them, the sides are perhaps covered with rough sheathing boards and the roof thatched with hay; that constitutes the most common barn to be seen in this part of the West. It is no wonder so many cattle perish here during the severe winters. Heavy timber is very scarce, which accounts for the lack of log cabins and other log buildings.

Speaking about timber reminds me that they have no woods out here. They always say "when you get through the timber" instead of when you get through the woods. They don't have any swamps here either, they are all "sloughs," pronounced "slews." When the Rock Island road was first built it was a common sight on looking out of the car window to see seams of coal near the surface in the cuts through which the railroad ran. Now there are many farmers in Iowa who can go out and dig up enough coal in a few minutes to last all day in their stoves.

Since I left Connecticut I have hardly seen a clear stream of water. The Croton and Hudson Rivers were both very roily from the heavy spring rains, and farther West the streams are muddy the year round. Many times I have longed to strip and take a bath, but the water was unfit for anything but hog wallows. I wonder if the black soil and the consequently black muddy waters of these Western States has had anything to do with the color of the hair on the hogs. A white hog here in the West is as uncommon as a black hog in the East. When this country was first settled the hogs were probably brought from the East, and were white. Would wallowing in the black mud and water for weeks and months during the hot summer season gradually change the color of their hair to correspond to that of the soil in which they spend so much of their time ? This question must be left to the evolutionists, who have explained, to their own satisfaction at least, so many questions of a like nature.

The cultivation of small fruits in the West has assumed

immense proportions. Strawberries have glutted the markets to such an extent that the price will hardly pay for the transportation. Five cents a quart at retail has been the ruling price in many of these Western cities. Blackberries, raspberries, and other small fruits will also be very abundant. The extent to which the farm-work is done by machinery is truly wonderful. The farmer rides while he plows, harrows, and plants the corn, and the wheat is mostly sown in drills. The expense of ditching the land has been very great, amounting in some cases to ten dollars an acre, but now a machine digs the ditch, throws the dirt one side, lays the tiling and covers it up again. Still later in the season I shall probably see the wonderful harvesting machines. Fields of corn containing from a hundred to one hundred and fifty acres are common, in fact that is about the average crop raised by every farmer here. But how they work! From 4 in the morning till 8 at night. They would as soon think of stopping "to do the chores" in the middle of the afternoon as at 6 o'clock. With all the help from the machinery and horses, the Western farmer works very hard, much harder than the New England farmer. And in Iowa he does not seem to be in very good circumstances. His house is small and in poor repair, and his barns are poorer still. With corn at 18 cents a bushel, wheat lower than ever, butter 10 and 12 cents, eggs 8 cents, and all other farmers' produce at like low figures, it requires immense crops to amount to much of an income.

The people out here also raise large families of children. Such is doubtless the case in all newly settled countries, but it is mentioned as a curious fact that people who have lived childless in the East for years, move out here, and immediately they are blessed with a goodly number of healthy boys and girls.

The gilded dome of the capitol at Des Moines can be seen for eight or ten miles in some directions, but the proportions of the dome are not so graceful as those of our own in Connecticut. The outside diameter is over 80 feet, with the inside 66 feet, while the height is 275 feet. The gilded part has a row of circular windows half way up, and compared with our own the whole dome has a decidedly more " squatty " appearance. The building is 240 by 360 feet, and inside is finished very nicely. The staircases, door casings, wainscoting, pillars, and panels are all or nearly all of genuine marble. In a country where there are so many public buildings that are decorated inside with imitations of every kind of marble known, it is quite refreshing to see so much here that is real. Thirty-two kinds of marble are used in the building. The house has only 100 members, the senate 50, the increase in population making no difference in the number of members, and yet the hall of the house is a very large room, 74 by 91 feet, and 47 feet high, and it is elegantly finished in marble, scagliola, and black walnut. These pillars of scagliola on the sides of the room are nearly as large as those at the entrance of our capitol at Hartford, and are very dark and rich in color. This material can only be used where there is little weight resting on the pillars for they are made of plaster of Paris with an iron rod in the middle. This rod is placed inside of a hollow cylinder, and plaster of Paris, variously colored, and mixed with glue to prevent its hardening quickly, is packed around it with occasionally a chunk of white plaster of Paris laid near the outside of the pillar, when the pillar is taken out of the case, placed in position and nicely polished, the various colors being brought out with a most beautiful effect. The senate chamber is finished in more elegant style, if anything, than the house, but it seemed a pity to see in such a nicely furnished room, in the rear of the president's chair, two large panels of a sickly green colored marble, that were imitations of the real article, and very poor imitations, too. But the structure taken as a whole is so well constructed, and so nicely furnished, that it seems almost incredible that the cost of the whole in its finished state will not be over $3,000,000.

In Western Iowa I encountered frequent steep hills, too steep for safe coasting; and after rather ungracefully spinning down one of the steepest, to the astonishment of on-looking pedestrians, I concluded to take a railroad train to Omaha, which I reached in a few hours, after completing my 1980th mile on the wheel.

CHAPTER IX.

At the Base of the Rockies.

OMAHA is booming as it never was before. Twenty years ago, when Congress granted a charter to the Union Pacific Railroad Company, the charter stated that the east bank of the Missouri River should be the eastern terminus of the road, but as there was no bridge over the river, the work of building the road naturally commenced on the west side of the river, and this gave Omaha a start that it has improved upon ever since. Council Bluffs, situated on the east side, about three miles from the river, has always keenly felt the remarkable success of its rival, and has used all its power to compel the Union Pacific road to make the east side of the river the terminus; but Omaha has thus far been, and the chances now are more strongly in favor than ever of its always being, the practical terminus of the road. When the bridge was built the Union Pacific trains were still made up on the west side, until Council Bluffs threatened to apply to Congress for the repeal of the charter, when a large transfer depot was built on the east side, but, mark it, as far away from "the Bluffs" and as near the river as possible. Now the stock-yards, which were first built near the transfer depot, are being removed to Omaha, wholesale firms are moving from the Bluffs over to the other side, and, altogether, Council Bluffs is to be pitied; for, since it was a good sized place itself, it has jealously seen its rival start from nothing until now it is four times as large as itself.

The bridge, which was built soon after the road was finished, is now found to be wholly inadequate, and a new double track bridge is soon to take the place of the old one, — one not so very old either. It seems a pity that so much labor should be rendered useless. The iron piers were driven down, section by section, into the shifting bed of the river, until men were working at the peril of their lives down seventy or eighty feet below the water, and these piers rise sixty feet above the river, and support an immense iron bridge; and yet all this labor and much of the material will soon be dead property, for part of the bridge has already been replaced by one with two tracks. The piers of the new bridge are of stone and two of them are finished, having been sunk to the same depth as the iron ones were. Probably the old bridge being in position helps to facilitate the building of the new one, but the old one will be all removed excepting the piers. The old ferry-boats are gone now, and all teams are driven into the rear end of a train of large box cars and thus taken across, leaving the train at the opposite end from which they entered it. There is soon to be a new Union depot at Omaha, built on an immense scale. The smelting works, already the largest in the country, are being extended. The stock-yards and packing houses are beginning to affect the Chicago business in that line of trade; the wholesale houses are drawing business clear from the Pacific coast; a new Board of Trade Building is being built, besides many other fine blocks, and, altogether, things were never booming more in Omaha than now. Most of their

streets are of asphalt, and a cable line of street cars is under
contract.

I heard a fire alarm one day and expected to see fire
engines go tearing by, but not one did I see. They have
no use for them in case of fire. Their reservoirs are situ·
ated on so high a hill that the force of the water is sufficient
to throw a stream over the tallest building. Only hose
carriages and hook and ladder companies are needed. The
city water, pumped from the muddy Missouri, is really the
purest in the world. It comes two thousand miles from the
Rocky Mountains, and passes no city that can possibly defile
the purity of its immense volume. The fine sand is filtered
from it, and the supply will be never failing.

But the river itself has changed even more in its appearance than the city, although that has grown from eighteen
thousand to seventy thousand in sixteen years; but these
changes are much more noticeable to me after an absence
from the city of that length of time than to residents. Then
the river ran south along the bluff on the east side of the
valley, turned sharply to the northwest, and soon again
turned south close to Omaha; but ten years ago, during a
high flood, the river, in a single night, cut across this ox
bow of four miles in length and only a mile wide, and com·
menced eating into the banks near the Union Pacific railroad
shops and smelting works. All the bags in the country, for
miles around, were brought to Omaha, filled with sand and
dumped into the river at this point, and engines, flat cars,
and hundreds of men were employed day and night, trying
to hold the river in check with immense rocks and broken
stones. It was a hard fight, but the sand bags and rocks
finally conquered, and now the river is roughly rip-rapped
to a depth of nearly fifty feet and for a mile in length. Six·
teen years ago there was danger the river would cut across

near Council Bluffs, and leave Omaha high and dry three
miles to the west of it; but now there is more probability
of its cutting across six miles above, and coming down into
the bend of the ox-bow again.   As it is now, this ox-bow is
"Cut-off Lake," a clear body of water that is much appreciated by boatmen and bathers.   Even nature seems to work
on the side of Omaha.

There is a peculiarity of the clay soil here, very remarkable.   In the lowering and grading of streets incident to such
a growing city, many houses are left twenty and even twenty-
five feet above the grade, and yet when the soil is dug perpendicularly down within a foot of the foundation of these
houses, brick ones as well as frame, they remain perfectly
firm and secure for months and even years, a few little
creases only being worn, by the rains and frosts, down the
face of these walls of clay.   The clay bluffs across the
river, one or two hundred feet high, are nearly perpendicular now in some places, and yet they have been exposed to
the weather for centuries, perhaps, long before the pale-faced
white settler knew of them at least.

After riding six hundred miles through the States of Illinois and Iowa, over the prairies, both level and rolling, I
am frank to acknowledge that the prospect of five hundred
miles more of the same kind of scenery did not make me
over enthusiastic to travel it on my wheel.   The riding, so
far, has not been monotonous, and I did not want it to
become so.   The object of the trip was not to make or break
records, and thus far, whenever I have found it desirable to
take a train, I have done so.   But the ride through Nebraska
would be so very similar to what I had already experienced
in Iowa, that I thought a day's ride on the cars would do
me no harm and the time saved could be very profitably
used in the mountains.   The object of my trip is to see the

most of the country in the best possible way, and thus far I think I have been fairly successful. The distance to Omaha traveled by rail has been about 250 miles, and by wheel 2,000 miles, and the total expense, including about eight dollars car fare, has been not quite forty dollars. This includes all repairs to wheel, clothes, and every expense whatsoever. I probably have stopped over night at farm houses half the time, which has been the chief aid in making the expense so light, but the accommodations have many times been better than at some of the hotels. I have ridden till nearly dark and then taken a hotel or farm-house, just as it happened. Much of the time, seventy days, since leaving home has been spent in visiting friends, but one can travel over the same route, in the same manner, without a friend to visit on the way for less than a dollar a day.

Thus far I have been very lucky in not getting caught out in many showers, and it really has rained very little where I have been. A heavy rain at Omaha prevented further progress on the wheel, at least for a few days, and decided me to take the train. Partly through the influence of Mr. Charles M. Woodman, a wheelman, employed in the Union Pacific office, I secured a ticket to Denver at reduced rates. A cap has been the only thing I have worn on my head; the skin on my nose has peeled off several times, and of course, my face and hands are as brown as my seal-brown trousers. Even corduroy breeches could not stand the pressure of those lumpy clay roads, and I have been obliged to have them reseated with thick buckskin, dyed to match. My weight has been reduced from fifteen to eighteen pounds, but a ravenous appetite soon makes up for that reduction whenever I stop riding The weight of the knapsack is hardly noticed now.

I have written sometimes of the ignorance of the farmers

DESCENT INTO THE CAVE OF THE WINDS. — (*Page 92.*)

in certain sections of the West, and perhaps now it will be no more than fair to refer to the utter lack of knowledge of their country of some persons in Connecticut. Many thought snow drifts and mud would prevent any wheeling outside of Connecticut for weeks after I started, but, as far as I could see, the roads settle in "York State" as early as in Connecticut. At any rate, I saw no snow or mud, unless it was up in the mountains. Another thing that troubled some folks was how I should to get across the streams and rivers out West. The idea that occasionally I might find a real bridge did not seem to enter their minds. The fact is, not yet have I come to the smallest creek or pond of water but which I crossed dry shod. Bridges are built here wherever they are needed, just as they are in the East. Some Connecticut people went so far as to doubt whether they had any roads out here at all. Many a one asked me how I could ride across the prairie, and they seemed to take it for granted I should ride upon the railroads, bumping along over the half-covered ties. But strange as it may seem to those persons, the people out here have horses and wagons, and ride over public highways and bridges, very much the same as we do in the East. They have churches and school-houses, Sunday-schools and revivals, morning prayers and a blessing before meals, just as they do in staid old New England. They are just as civilized and decidedly more open and free hearted than in any part of Connecticut, only perhaps they are not quite so refined; that is all the difference. To those who have seen the Western people this talk may seem superfluous, but there are many people in Connecticut, intelligent on every other subject, who show supreme ignorance in regard to the manners and customs of the people of their own country. And as for its being thinly settled, any one can judge as to

6

that when I say I have not been over half a mile from a house at any time, unless it was up in the Highlands of New York. There has been no more danger or difficulty in making the trip than there is in traveling through New England. Thus far the need of a revolver has never presented itself, neither has the idea of getting one.

Well, I took the train at Omaha and was soon gliding swiftly through the same rolling prairie that I had seen so much of in Iowa. But these waves of green soon began to subside as the ocean does after a storm, and the sun went down on a country as level and smooth as the ocean itself. From the car window I could see the roads were excellent — a mixture of sand and clay — but I did not regret that I was on twelve wheels instead of two. The newsboys on the trains out here are newsmen, full grown men. The one on the up train worked steadily all the afternoon with his papers, books, oranges, bananas, etc., and finally, when every one was tired of the very sight of him, he brought in a basket of toys. and, sitting down on the arms of the seats, amused the children in the car with snakes and jumping-jacks for half an hour or more. Great liberty is allowed passengers traveling such long distances, and little boys play leap-frog and perform all sorts of gymnastic exercises in the aisle.

Along toward midnight the passengers had begun to thin out, and almost every one had found a whole seat for himself. and had lain down with his head or heels sticking out into the aisle. The conductor came through occasionally, but was careful not to disturb any one, and in picking his way along down this gauntlet of bare heads and big feet, he would only hold up his lantern and peer into a face whenever that head hung over into the aisle where a pair of boots projected half an hour before. Everything had been quiet for sometime, and the train at midnight was running rapidly, when a low, plaintive moan issued forth from the seat just ahead of me. The voice was rather low, at first, and the sound was rather mournful. A head hung over into the aisle in a very reckless manner, and the mouth was wide open, and yet there was no complaint. The poor sufferer gradually raised his voice, and one after another in the car had risen up and looked around till the car once more seemed to be well filled with passengers. The somnorganist ran up the scale, pulled out all the stops, and, doubled up as he was, the knee-swell was used with powerful effect. It was soon becoming evident that either the head would drop clear off and roll down the aisle or that the bellows would burst, for the sound, loud as it was, came out under great pressure, when a long suffering but very patient passenger in a seat opposite jumped up and grabbing the poor fellow by the shoulder almost yelled in his ear, " Look here, stranger, do you know you have got the nightmare like a horse ? " The roars of laughter that followed were not diminished by the fact that the man opposite did not realize he had said anything to cause it. I soon found four seats together, and taking the cushions out and placing them lengthwise of the car, made a very good bed, for I am so short I could lie at full length.

The sun rose next morning over very much the same kind of a level country, but snow-capped mountains were easily seen in the distance, and a few hours later the train rolled into the station at Denver.

CHAPTER X.

On Pike's Peak.

E reached the top last night in a blinding snow and hail storm, with the lightning snapping and cracking around our heads and the thunder rolling around on all sides of us, below as well as above. But in order to have it clearly understood how it came to be "we," and how we came to get here, I must go back a little and give an account of the trip since leaving the train at Denver.

The streets of that city are not paved, but they are so hard and smooth most of the year that no one could find any fault with them. The fine sand packs down very hard. The train which I took in Omaha reached Denver so early in the morning that I found very few business men at their stores and so I rode around the principal streets, visited their fine county court-house, which must have cost in the neighborhood of $300,000, and looked with wonder at the snow-capped mountains to be seen at the end of every street, seemingly only a few miles away to the north or west. Streams of clear water run down the gutters of most of the streets, which gives to the city a very cool and refreshed appearance. But one need not look to the streams of water to feel revived; the very air was as crisp and cool as an October morning in Connecticut. It became so cold in the cars the night before that there was no sleep for any one not provided with blankets to cover him, and they tell me this is a sample of their weather all through the summer. In the middle of the day the sun is hot, but in the shade it is never uncomfortable. It is a very dry atmosphere, so that there is very little perspiration to be seen on a person's face when exercising. For several weeks the salt sweat has run down my forehead, in the heat of the day, and into my eyes, making them smart and look glossy, but here the perspiration dries before it can reach one's eyebrows. After being taken about the city and entertained by Chief Consul Geo. F. Higgins (a royal good fellow, light complexion, of medium height and build, and wearing a moustache), and after being escorted out of the city by another member of the club,— Mr. F. J. Chamard, also a light complexioned fellow, we started on for Colorado Springs together. J. A. Hasley, a member of the Kansas City Bicycle Club, reached Denver a few days before I did, intending to take a trip in the same direction I was going, and that is how we came to climb Pike's Peak together.

This chapter, and perhaps others to follow, will give our experiences nearly in the order in which they occurred.

The first thing that surprised me was the sort of grazing country to be seen on all sides. A farmer in Connecticut who would turn his cattle out into such a scanty pasture to get a living would be a fit subject for prosecution by the Humane Society. I had supposed that Colorado was the finest grazing country in the world, and was never more surprised than to see the dry, sandy, brown appearance of the country. Only at a distance did it look green; close to, but a few scanty bunches, or rather spears of grass could be

seen. Actually, such fields in the Eastern States would not
be considered fit for even sheep pastures. The only way the
herds of horses and cattle get a living is by traveling. They
are at liberty to roam over thousands of acres, and in that
way manage to subsist. The winters are not very severe,
but it is no wonder so many cattle perish when the supply of
grass, scanty at the best, is covered with a few inches of
snow. Irrigation is carried on to a great extent, but from
what I can see it was more for the purpose of watering the
stock than for bringing the land up to a high state of cultivation. So far I have seen very little land producing a fair
crop of fodder, and that is all they intend to raise. There
is no turf to be seen growing naturally.

The ride south, from Denver to Colorado Springs, was over
a very fair road, although there was probably ten miles of
walking in the seventy-five miles. To the east of us was a
level or slightly rolling country, while on the other side the
snow-covered mountains loomed up apparently only twenty-
five miles, but in reality seventy-five miles away. Even the
foot-hills, so called, mountains four and five thousand feet
above us, were twenty-five miles distant. Such is the clearness of the atmosphere one would think he could walk over
to them in a couple of hours. That afternoon, just after the
sun had sunk beneath the snowy tops, we struck some Colorado mosquitoes. The first intimation we had of their presence, while riding along at a lively gait, was a prickling sensation all over the calves of our legs, and my stockings were
actually black with them. An Eastern mosquito will usually
be somewhat embarrassed in his business affairs by a slight
motion of the body or a wave of the hand, but these in Colorado are not annoyed in the least by the circular motion of
a flying wheelman's legs, and will alight upon his calves and
proceed to business with a dispatch that is equaled nowhere

else in the world. And be it said to the credit of their excellent military discipline, they never stop drilling or desert their post till they are crushed or brushed away. Once I jumped from the machine in agony, and such a jar would tend to dislodge an ordinary specimen of this kind of animal, but not so with these; every one remained at work, and thirteen perished at a time from one slap of my hand. Many a dismount resulted nearly as disastrously to the enemy, but this cost too much in time, and brushing away while riding was finally resorted to as the least expensive means of warfare. They seemed to go in swarms like bees, and made a noise nearly as loud. The next morning we rode through another army of them, but the only lasting result of the whole fight has been to give us a very satisfy-ing occupation, whenever there was nothing more important on hand, in scratching the different areas of our legs below the knees and regularly returning to the same locality always with renewed relish.

Prairie dogs were quite common along the road, and they would sit on their little mounds and remonstrate with us in a squeaking voice for disturbing them, till we were close upon them. Jack rabbits were not so common, only three or four having been seen thus far.

That night we walked down a lane to a ranch to find shel-ter for the night, when a horse, taking fright at our machines, tried to jump over the gate at the foot of the lane, and in doing so, gate, horse, and all came down in a heap together with a crash. The horse jumped up and went off limping, but we thought the next ranch would be a safer place for us, and so we kept on a couple of miles and got an excellent supper, but our bed was on the floor in an old store-room. This slight hardship was soon forgotten in the crisp, cool air of the next morning, and we rode along, hugely enjoying

the mountain scenery on our right, till we met a drove of
horses and cattle in the road, where barbed-wire fences in-
closed the highway on both sides. The horses took fright
first and stampeded down the road followed by the cows and
calves, the seventy-five or a hundred head leaving a great
cloud of dust behind them. The ranchman, who was driving them to water, tried his best, with the vigorous use of his
lungs and a shovel in his hands, to stop them by running
backwards and forwards across the road, and after we had
dismounted and gone clear out to the fence he succeeded in
driving them past us. Coming up all out of breath and his
eyes flashing with excitement, the full-bearded ranchman
yelled, " By J——s, you fellows will get shot down here
before you go very far with them things ! If my horses had
gone over that wire fence, by J——s, I should have wanted
to put a hole through you," then cooling down a little at
our expressed regrets, he said, oaths omitted, " a while ago,
coming from Denver with a load of oats, I met a couple of
fellows on their velocipedes and they were yelling and holler-
ing, and did not offer to stop. My horses saw them first,
and started down the hill as if nothing was hitched to them.
They turned down the railroad track and took that forty
hundred of oats over those ties as if they were feathers. I
finally stopped them down in the cut, but I was mad, you
bet. Those dudes were strangers around here or they would
not have said what they did to me. They told me to go talk
to a dog and to do some other things. They did not know
enough to keep their mouths shut after they had got me into
that fix. So I just pulled my belt gun and held it up.
'Now,' says I, 'you just come back or I will corral you.
While I go out and stick up a couple of flags, you just lay
down those things and go and pack those bags of oats out
here into the road.' They wouldn't at first, but finally did,

and it did me good to see them New York dudes tugging away at them 300 pound sacks. I unhitched the horses and made them fellows pull the wagon back and load the oats in again, but they emptied both their bottles before they got through."

To appreciate this story, and the manner in which it was told, one needs to hear it highly spiced, as it was with the huge oaths and many of the strange expressions used out here. The conversation turned on other subjects, and before he finally bade us "good luck," I learned that droves of mares and a few stallions are turned out loose, and in a short time each stallion has selected his drove of mares to look after and guard, and no mare from any other drove will be allowed to come near his drove. One day a mule tried to get near a drove and the stallion was kept busy all day biting and driving that mule away, who scampered off only to return again to bother the stallion so much he had no chance to eat for hours. With cattle it is the same, the bulls selecting their drove of cows to guard and none from any other drove need apply for admission.

As we traveled south, the range of foot-hills turned to the east until we rode along nearly at the base of them. The top of Pike's Peak was plainly to be seen over these foot hills all day, and this snow-covered peak seemed to travel south on the other side of this range of hills just as fast as we did. It looked more like a hooded ghost peering over the green hills at us than a mountain peak 14,000 feet high. As we rode along it would go out of sight behind a hill, only to reappear again farther south, always keeping just so far ahead of us. This game of hide and seek did not end till we reached Colorado Springs, where the peak was directly west of us.

We had ridden but a few miles from Denver, when the thin air began to affect me. Hill climbing was out of the question, and the smallest patch of sand or the slightest up grade would make me puff like a winded horse. I tried to breathe entirely through my nose, but the suffocating feeling was unbearable, and so I rode along, mouth wide open. The dry atmosphere parched my tongue and mouth, and my tongue, shriveled to half its size, rattled around in my mouth like a wooden spoon in a bowl. Again I tried to keep my mouth shut, but that was impossible, so I made up my mind to get used to it, and rode miles without any water. Even water would only keep my mouth moist a short time.

We reached Palmer Lake, a pleasant resort 7,000 feet high, about noon. This place is nearly 1.000 feet higher than either Denver or Colorado Springs, and the grade descends both to the north and south. The foot-hills, three or four thousand feet higher, are close by to the west, and to the east the country is a rolling sea of green. But the most beautiful sight of all is the wild flowers. White, red. yellow, blue, purple, violet, in fact all the colors imaginable are seen in great profusion on all sides, acres and acres of nothing else, these beautiful little flowers not over three or four inches high growing so closely together as to crowd out what little green grass tried to grow there. In fact, while all the colors of the rainbow but this one lived closely and happily together, green seemed to be an outcast among them. And the colors which one would naturally think would be pale and faded growing in such a dry and sandy soil were just the opposite. I never saw such vivid colors. The varieties were mostly foreign to me, but I shall always remember the colors. Occasionally, rising above these fields of little flowers, were red and white thistles, red and white cactuses, and Spanish bayonets, or soap weed as they call it, all in full blossom, too.

I can't begin to describe the delightful ride down from

Palmer Lake. The coasting over a road, perfectly smooth, that wound around and over little knolls that gave a wavy motion to the ride; this was enjoyment enough in itself, but to go gliding along without using a muscle in this delightful manner, and see the foot hills, perfectly green to their tops, and the pure white peaks sparkling in the sun rising just above them, all only a mile or two away seemingly, on the right, and to the left these immense fields of the very brightest and most beautiful flowers ever seen, growing close up to the road and stretching out into the distance till their colors were lost in the pale-green of the rolling prairie — to thus imperfectly describe the scene is all I can do; one must see it to realize it.

Saturday morning, early, we reached Manitou, where water power furnishes the hotels with electric lights, and started up Ute Pass on our wheels, to visit the Grand Cavern. We were going to leave our wheels and walk up, but a guide told us it was good riding over the other side of this mountain, from the Cave of the Winds down through Williams Cañon, back to Manitou; so we pushed the wheels up a mile over a very good carriage road, six or eight hundred feet high, to the Grand Cavern, with the intention of going across, but here the fun commenced. The only way across was by a narrow trail, but the guide at the cavern said it was all down hill, and so we kept on. The trail went down the side of the mountains very steep, and we had not gone far when it was evident it was the wrong trail, and so back we started; but it took us both to get one wheel up at a time, and the way it made us puff — well, strong as we both were it took every ounce of strength we had to get back. After hunting around awhile we found the right trail, and started on in the direction of Williams Cañon, which was plainly to be seen just below. The trail came to an end at the edge of the cañon, which was three or four hundred feet straight down, but an immense hole, perhaps twenty-five feet across, went down into the bowels of the mountain about two hundred feet, to the entrance of the Cave of the Winds. Rickety ladders and shaky stairs wound down around the inside of this hole, and down these we must go with our wheels! Yes, the guide was right, it was down hill with a vengeance. We took my wheel first, it being the lightest, and Hasley went down a few rounds on the ladder and then took hold of the big wheel and held it firm so that the rubber tire slid down the ladder. I held on to the handle bar with one hand and the ladder with the other, and thus we reached the bottom of the first ladder, step by step, but safely. The next pair of steep stairs went under the shelving rocks so close that there was not room to get the wheel down, and so we lifted it over the edge of the railing, and I let it down as far as I could with one hand, and Hasley ran down to the next stairs underneath and caught the wheel as I let go. The rest of the stairs were not so steep, but a single misstep at any time would have sent us all to the bottom of this hole in unseemly haste. Getting Hasley's wheel down was a repetition of our first experience, only his was heavier, and the stairs creaked more, and it was more difficult to get his machine over the railing and let it down at arm's length, to be caught by the other underneath; but at the entrance of the cave, stairs led down under a boulder, suspended as that one was at the Flume in the White Mountains, and out into the daylight of the cañon, and we were soon down in the road, hardly realizing how we had got there.

The scenery down the cañon was so grand, and the whole trip was so exciting, that we did not regret at the end that we had taken our wheels where no other wheels have ever been, and where no other wheels ever ought to be taken again.

While we were taking a late breakfast at the Cliff House at Manitou — Manitou is at the very base and almost surrounded by mountains — a young gentleman asked us if we would escort two young ladies up to the top of Pike's Peak, and of course we were only too glad to have the opportunity. But at the last moment one of the ladies refused to go, because it would prevent her attending the first hop of the season; and the other lady who was so enthusiastic that her sense of propriety barely prevailed over her intense desire to climb up the peak, said, sadly disappointed, as she left us: "Now I will go up to my room and have a good cry," and her eyes were already running over.

The scenery up the ravine for two or three miles was magnificent, huge boulders filling the gorge, down which a good-sized stream went dashing over and under these boulders in every conceivable manner. In fact, the sides of the mountains up a thousand feet, were covered with huge boulders just on the point of rolling down, and once in a while between them we could catch a glimpse of the country below. Five miles up the trail, which is a very good foot path, is the Half Way House, and we felt much encouraged to find it had taken us only two hours. But from there up, for four miles, the trail went through timber mostly, and we began to get winded. Hasley kept his mouth shut most of the time, which I could not do from the first; but for two hours we had not a drop of water to drink.

Just below timber line, which is 12,000 feet above the sea, we met parties coming down, three and four at a time, and they encouraged us by saying: "Only four miles farther," "Keep your strength for the last two miles," "You will have to leave the trail the last mile and follow the telegraph poles up over the snow." Still our legs held out all right, but I began to get dizzy whenever I looked up or stooped to drink at a running stream of snow-water. Finally, snow was the only thing to moisten our mouths, but we both drank or ate very sparingly of this. About one thousand feet above timber line we had to cross snow-drifts one or two hundred feet across, and very soon our feet were cold and wet. Sometimes the snow would let us down to our hips, and then we would wallow along to some projecting rocks and climb up. This took my breath the worst of anything, and I laid down on the rocks, completely exhausted sometimes.

About this time a snow-storm commenced, and the wind blew so cold we could only stop a short time to get our wind. The flashes of lightning were getting to be altogether too frequent to be pleasant, and the snow and hail were so blinding we could scarcely see from one telegraph pole to another, for now we had left the trail, and were climbing straight up the side of the peak, with nothing in sight but rocks and boulders half covered with snow. Sometimes we slipped down through these boulders, and then after crawling out, the only thing to do was to lie down with our backs to the driving storm and get rested. When I started on again it was to stagger like a drunken man, for I was dizzy most of the last mile all the time. When we were sure the top must be just over the brow of the steep hill we were slowly climbing, we finally reached there only to see those telegraph poles leading almost straight up into the air and out of sight up the steepest and most rocky hill we had yet encountered. Once in the blinding snow-storm we lost track of the poles, but it was only because one had been blown down, and the next was hidden entirely from view. Finally, after crawling, staggering, and climbing up and over the last mile of rocks, and using up an hour and a half in doing it, I caught sight of a big stone house through the fog and snow, and yelled to Hasley with all the strength I had left, and that wasn't much: "Look at the chimneys."

Those who have done any mountain climbing can better imagine our feelings at that moment than I can describe them. Much as we regretted it at first, how thankful we were those ladies had not started up with us, for we never could have reached the top with them. But, as if to repay us for being deprived of their presence, those beautiful little wild flowers accompanied us all the way up, growing brighter in color. if that were possible, the higher up they grew, until on the very top of the peak, 14,147 feet above the sea, we picked a lovely little bouquet from beneath a few inches of snow. These tiny flowers, not more than an inch in height, grow close to a melting drift of snow and ice wherever there is the least bit of sand or soil to nourish them. The two signal service men, Messrs. Ramsay and Potter, did everything possible for us, and in a very short time we were ourselves again. These two men were so kind and considerate toward us, and made us feel so much at home, that we concluded to prolong our stay on the summit until Monday.

Distance traveled on the wheel, 2,075 miles.

CHAPTER XI

HE sun is about to rise," whispered Mr. Ramsay, as he softly opened our room door and then disappeared. Mr. John P. Ramsay is the Government signal officer in charge of the station at Pike's Peak, a young wheelman that everyone likes from the first. We were sleeping soundly in a comfortable bed on the top of the Peak this Sunday morning, entirely oblivious of the somewhat severe experience we had in climbing, the afternoon before, but at the first sound of the call we jumped out of bed, slipped on our shoes, and, wrapping some heavy blankets around us, went out the east door and stood on a mat, which was frozen stiff, and where the wind blew about our bare legs and up the folds of the blanket with decidedly too much freedom. We waited there fifteen or twenty minutes, shaking from head to foot, but the sight amply repaid for the discomfort. The sun was sending great broad streamers up into the sky, and a bank of black clouds, which in the distance looked like a range of mountains, still hid the sun from view. We looked over the brow of Pike's Peak, which, on top, is nothing but huge boulders and rocks imbedded in banks of snow, down upon

ABOVE TIMBER-LINE. — (*Page 94.*)

other peaks twelve or thirteen thousand feet high surrounding us on all sides, and looking cold and black in the dim light of the morning. At the base of the Peak on which we stood the level plains stretched out probably 150 miles to the east, where a band of gold was just beginning to gild that bank of clouds. No fog, or mist;. nothing obstructed the view in any direction, and everything, even in the darkness, seemed to stand out with peculiar clearness. Soon the broad streamers faded away, the band of gold rendered more dazzling by the blackness of the clouds, began to widen till the whole bank of clouds seemed to be one mountain of gold. Finally, after a long while, as it seemed to us shivering in the cold, the upper outlines of the sun could just be seen through the fiery clouds, and when the round ball stood out clear and distinct above the clouds we crawled back to bed and to sleep. Is seems almost useless to try to describe such a scene, for no one can get an idea of the sight from the most perfect description.

The house up there, built of stone, contains six good-sized rooms. Six or eight persons can be comfortably housed over night, and no one who has experienced the difficulties of the climb would complain of the food, for we had a variety and it was well cooked. I sat out doors nearly all day in the warm sun and the view was not hidden till nearly night. We could look down into the streets of Colorado Springs, fifteen miles away, almost as one would upon a checker board.

During the day several parties came up, some on horses, to within a mile and a half of the top, where snow covers the trail and renders further progress on horseback impossible, but everyone looked pale and exhausted. Hot coffee brought them around all right in a short time. A party of us went over to the north side of the Peak and tumbled

7

rocks down the side. Some of these went crashing down
nearly two thousand feet before they stopped.

During the afternoon clouds gathered, but just before
sunset the sun came out and the shadow of the Peak was
plainly seen against the clouds to the east.   Even the shadow
of the square stone house was discerned, and then two of us
went out to one end of the house, and surely, there we were,
standing like the spectres of the Brocken near the shadow
of the house, out over the plains twenty-five miles away and
fourteen thousand feet above the ground.   To be sure our
shadows were not as clean cut as though we were nearer the
object on which the shadows were cast, but anyone could see
the general form.

About 9 o'clock that night a terrific thunder storm raged
out over the plains to the northeast.   The highest clouds
were not much above, and most of them far below us.   We
heard none of the thunder and saw very little of the lightning as it flashed, but the whole mass of clouds was lighted
up incessantly.   It was a grand sight.   The whole sky to
the north, west, and south, was perfectly clear, and the stars
shone out with remarkable clearness, notwithstanding the
full moon was shining so brightly and placidly out over the
plains to the east.   Everywhere else the world was at peace,
but in the northeast those clouds made silver by the light of
the moon, were rolling and tumbling and were constantly
lighted by the fiery flashes of lightning.   And yet not a
sound was to be heard.   There was no wind, and everything
above and below was so quiet and still.   And from the
northeast, where we could see such a great commotion, there
was not the faintest sound.   If there had been no clouds
anywhere that night the stillness would have seemed natural
enough, but to see such a terrific storm raging (and I never
saw lightning before), and to see the wind tearing those

clouds all to pieces, and yet to have everything so silent you could almost hear yourself think, that was a most weird situation.

The weather on Pike's Peak is hardly more severe than it is below, even during the winter. For severity, it is not to be compared with that of Mt. Washington. The wind never blows harder than seventy-five or eighty miles an hour. The roof of the house is a common tin one. They keep up a wood fire the year round. The telegraph wires are not kept in repair, so the weather reports are only sent in by rail. Pike's Peak is not in reality a very important weather station.

As if to give us one more startling effect before we started down, the next morning opened cloudy. The morning before we seemed to be on the edge of some great ocean that stretched out to the east as far as the eye could reach, but now we were cast away at sea ourselves. The clouds covered the whole earth in all directions and were so solid and motionless that they looked like one great sea of light gray marble, beautifully carved and polished, but we were high above this sea of marble, and were looking down upon it. The sun had just risen above it when I opened my eyes, and I could hardly believe what they told me. The light brought out every line and feature of the glassy clouds, and the peak on which we were was, apparently, only about 2,000 feet above the level of this sea, for it surrounded us on all sides. Occasionally, here and there, other peaks pierced through the clouds like so many rocky islands, but there was not a rift anywhere to indicate that there was a beautiful earth beneath this great ocean of gray, polished marble, solid enough apparently to walk upon. Very soon the sun took the polish off the clouds, and before long they grew fleecy and soon broke up and passed away.

Leaving our friends at the top with regret, for I could have spent a month there with the utmost enjoyment, we started down and reached the base, without trouble or fatigue, in three hours and a half, a journey of twelve miles that consumed seven hours in going up, besides using the last ounce of strength we had in doing it, too. Coming down we picked a few flowers near the top to send home, but every few yards a new variety showed itself, and of course we had to get a few of that kind, too, till our hands were full of the beautiful tiny little things. Then we swore off and would not pick another one; but then another variety, prettier than any of the others, peeped up at us between the rocks, and before we came down to timber line, 12,000 feet above the sea, pockets, hands, and hats were full of the bright colored little flowers. After a hearty meal at the Cliff House we mounted, and our machines were so thoroughly rested they almost ran away with us down the grade out of Manitou.

To the Garden of the Gods next. All along the base of the mountains, from Denver south for seventy-five miles, are immense slabs of red and white sandstone projecting into the air edgewise, and running parallel with the range of mountains. Some of these slabs must have been 500 or 1,000 feet high originally, but the action of the rain and frost on their crumbling nature has reduced many of them to steep ridges of red and white soil, along the center of which runs the remnant of the original slab, looking like the backbone of some pre-historic animal. In the Garden of the Gods a few of these slabs remain with very little debris about their base. Some of them, five or six hundred feet long, stick right up into the air three or four hundred feet high, and they are so honey-combed and the edges so rounded and worn, that the action of water is plainly to be seen on them. No one can visit this part of the country without being impressed with the idea that these mountains were once the rocky shores of an immense ocean and the incessant action of the waves has wrought out all the curious-shaped rocks and ledges which make Colorado so celebrated. But when the subject is broached as to what force in nature was power-ful enough to turn these strata of rocks up edgewise in the first place, a traveling wheelman drops that subject as he would an ichthyosaurus.

Glen Eyrie is another place about a mile above, that abounds in these same slabs, not so large, and more slender and needle shaped. This place is private property and is nicely fixed up with drives, trout ponds, and fountains. The drives through these places of interest are very fine, and when we started back to Colorado Springs over a high, level road, running along a high ridge, the wind sent us along as we never rode before. On the level, a brake was necessary, and we even went coasting up good steep grades. This kind of riding lasted for nearly five miles, and was enjoyed in-tensely, but after a short stop at the "Springs" with a few very enthusiastic wheelmen, among them Messrs. Walker and Parsons, we turned about for Denver, and faced that same strong wind for fifteen miles, till we found a good rest-ing place for the night at a ranch, which is simply a good farm-house. The next morning after we got over the divide, near Palmer Lake, the wind sent us flying again down the grade. Such coasting! Sometimes side by side, at other times in single file, we passed the fields of wild flowers that seemed to have improved since we last saw them; for the pale yellow blossoms of the cactus plants, as large as the palm of our hand, were much more numerous than a few days before. Then we scattered horses and colts, cows and calves, in all directions; dreadfully scared the poor little prairie dogs that were caught away from home, and made

the others who were perched on their mounds, terribly
excited.   The little animals sometimes dig their holes in the
middle of the road, and as we went noiselessly along, we
thought we might sometimes catch them unawares, but
no.   Prairie dogs have ears.   They always heard us coming,
and would keep up a constant squeaking noise till the last
minute, and sometimes after they had dodged out of sight
they would pop their heads up once more, utter one last
squeak, and disappear for good.

I have often wondered why so many plants grow here
supplied with thorns and sharp pointed leaves.   There are
the thistles, cactus, Spanish bayonet, and two or three other
species, the names of which are unknown to me, but the extent to which their sharp points will penetrate a wheelman's
stockings can be accurately stated; even the spears of grass
are as sharp pointed as a needle.   They do say that sheep
will eat the cactus at certain times in the year.   It is not
stated at just what period in their existence the sheep do
this, but it is probably a short time before they cease to exist.   When their bill of fare is limited to a single article of
diet, men have been known to eat obnoxious things, and
probably the sheep eat the cactus for the same reason.   O
yes, Colorado is a great grazing country, noted for being
such.   It is also noted for being a country where sometimes
forty per cent. of the stock die in a single winter, simply
because there is nothing to eat.   The land will not produce
enough to keep them alive.   Let the snow come a few inches
deeper than usual, and the only thing for the stock is to
starve to death.   The ranchmen don't pretend to house their
stock or store up fodder enough to keep them alive when
the snow has covered the few spears of grass too deep to be
uncovered by pawing.   I am told that horses, raised in a warm
climate, do not know enough at first when turned out into a

field covered with snow, to paw the snow away and nibble the grass underneath, but they soon learn to do so from seeing others, but even pawing does not always save the poor creatures. I was agreeably surprised, in talking with a ranchman, to hear him express himself strongly in favor of a law to prevent anyone raising more stock than he could house and feed during the winter. The desert of Sahara, judging from what I have read, is nearly as good for farming as that part of Colorado I have seen is for stock raising. New York tenement houses and Colorado stock farms are equally good for producing young lives and for killing them off young, too. The ranchman who expressed a desire to put a hole through us for scaring his horses on our way down to the Springs, now recognized and waved his hand to us as we returned. We stopped at a farm-house to get some milk, and while waiting in the dining-room I noticed with surprise well-worn books in the book case, such as " Draper's Intellectual Development of Europe," " Geographical Distribution of Animals," by Wallace, " Elements of Geology," by Le Conte, " English Men of Letters," by Morley, other books by Geike, and many more of like nature. Think of such books as these being read out here on a Colorado ranch, 2,200 miles away from the intellectual hub of the universe ! I am sorry to say the ranchman by birth is not an American, but an Englishman.

A little farther on, and we overtook a lady on horseback. She did not hear us, but the horse did, and began to act skittish, and not knowing what to make of his actions the lady jumped off. We got by without much trouble, however, but it would never do to ride on leaving the lady dismounted. Here was a state of things. Not a house in sight for miles over the level prairie, not a wagon, box, or anything but a barbed-wire fence to assist the lady to regain the saddle, and with her long riding habit it was impossible to do it alone.   One thing, and only one thing could be done.   One of us must clasp his hands together on his knee, and in thus making a step for her, help her to mount into the saddle. Now, there were two of us, one tall, the other short.   For her to step up on the knee of the taller one would be more difficult than to step up on the knee of the shorter one.   So it fell to the lot of the embarrassed writer to do the service. The lady mounted easily to the saddle and we left her.

On reaching Denver and looking back over the trip, I felt I had accomplished all and more than I really expected to do when I left home.   Not but that I had a strong desire before I started to see the wonders in California, but I thought if I reached Pike's Peak, it would be doing a great deal, all I felt confident of doing then.   But now that I reached the goal of my spring ambition so easily, no small consideration would induce me to turn back.   I was in better physical condition than when I left home, and the farther I went the more confidence it gave me to continue the journey across to the Pacific.

Distance on the wheel, 2,158 miles.

CHAPTER XII.

Across the Plains.

NTIL now I had expressed a va-lise, with extra baggage, along to the different cities, but found I could carry everything I need-ed in the knapsack; and so, leaving the rubber suit behind with the valise, for I was enter-ing a rainless district, and putting on a thinner pair of trousers, I left Denver on the 24th of June.

We started on again, in a northerly direction, accompa-nied for several miles by Mr. J. W. Bryant, and reached Longmont, after a ride of thirty-five miles over miserable roads, rendered more miserable by the water that overflows them from the numerous ditches along the way. Here we found that a ride back to the southwest, to Boulder, and into the mining regions of Boulder County, would make a pleasant little side excursion, and so the next noon we rode over to Boulder, twenty miles, and stopped an hour or so at one of the sampling works. Here large quantities of ore are bought of the miners, and crushed and ground fine as flour, ready to be shipped to the smelting works at Denver and other points.

The process of finding the amount of gold or silver in a

sample of ore is very interesting. After the ore is reduced
to a fine powder, a small quantity of it, perhaps a teaspoon-
ful, is nicely weighed out, and put into an earthern saucer,
with perhaps ten times that amount of lead ore in the same
powdered state. The saucer is placed in a furnace, and the
lead soon absorbs the gold and silver and settles to the
bottom, leaving the worthless part of the powder to rise to
the top in the shape of dark-colored glass. This button of
lead, with the gold and silver absorbed in it, is then placed
in a little cup made of burnt bone. This cup is then placed
in the furnace and the bone absorbs all the lead, leaving a
speck of the precious metal about as large as the head of
a small pin. The gold and silver are then separated by
placing this speck in nitric acid, which absorbs the silver,
and the pure gold is left in the bottom of the glass. I
understand that this process, on a small scale, is practically
the same as that employed at the large smelting works. In
this way miners can find out at a very little expense just
what their ore is worth per ton from a comparatively small
sample.

We started up Boulder Cañon, a gorge in the mountain
that is very picturesque, but whose sides are not so perpendicular as those of Williams Cañon at Manitou. We rode
and walked up this cañon nine miles to Salina, where we
stayed at night. A large stream comes roaring down the
cañon, and the narrow gauge track of the Colorado Central
Railroad goes up at a very steep grade. The course of the
stream is so crooked and the cañon so narrow, that in the
nine miles there are over fifty railroad bridges. All along
up the cañon the sides of the mountain are fairly honey-
combed with holes, dug during the mining excitement in
1859, and since, but now the holes, shanties, and everything
about the region seems to be deserted.

Salina is a genuine mining town of perhaps a hundred inhabitants, and entirely different from anything that I expected. I supposed that even now a man took his life in his hands when he visited one of these mining towns, but during the evening, and all the time we were there, the place was as quiet and peaceable as any New England town — decidedly more so than any factory village. I saw many well-dressed young ladies and gentlemen all going in one direction, and found it was the night for the temperance lodge to meet, and that the members include all but about a dozen persons in the community. During the evening two little boys at the boarding-house seemed to want to get acquainted, and so I asked one how old he was. "My brother is eight years old, and I am ten days older than he is," he answered. How that could be the little fellow was unable to explain, and so am I.

The next morning we visited the First National Mine, which, to all outward appearances, is nothing more than a small shanty up the side of the mountain, with a heap of rocks thrown out to one side of it. Inside is a hole in the floor just large enough for a half barrel bucket to go through, and beside this hole is a trap-door just large enough to let a man's body down. The rocks are raised by a windlass run by horse power outside.

With old coats and hats on and a lighted candle in our hands, we followed the overseer down through the trap-door. The ladders down which we climbed were straight up and down, and about all I could see as I followed the others was the light of their candles. About once in fifty feet we came to a platform and then started down another ladder. The ladders went close to one side of the shaft, which was protected with heavy timbers on the sides, and on the other side was the hole down which the bucket went, two hundred and fifteen feet, to the bottom. It was rather awkward holding on to the rounds of the ladder with a candle in one hand, but I kept a firm grip till the rounds began to get slippery from the mud and water, and then the descent was anything but pleasant. Sometimes the ladders, instead of going straight down, leaned over from the top a little, and then it was hard work to keep my feet from slipping off. It was so dark in there I could only see the black bucket hole on one side and the two lighted candles beneath me, and how far down a fellow would go, should his hands or feet slip off the slimy rounds, I had no idea; only I know every nerve in my body was strung up and every muscle was hard.

At last, and it seemed an age, we got down to where the men were working. Two hundred feet down, tunnels, just large enough for men to work in, were run out in opposite directions. and at the ends of these tunnels the men were drilling and blasting. And what were these men after, down in this hole in the solid rock, over two hundred feet from the surface? Simply to get out a little narrow streak of dark-colored rock, not over two or three inches wide. This little streak went nearly straight down into the earth, and these men were following it wherever it went, excavating probably fifty tons of refuse rock in order to get one ton of the ore sufficiently valuable to work up.

Then we started up, and as I was the last to go up I was wondering all the way if I could keep my hold on the rounds if one of the others should slip and drop on me; but they did not have occasion to test my grip in that way, and we reached the top all right, only I had to stop and rest once. more because of the nervous excitement than anything else. and then you can imagine my feeling, suspended over that black hole with just strength to keep from falling, but with none to go higher. The memory of that experience will never be very pleasant to me.

Up three miles farther into the mountains and we came to Gold Hill, another mining town, full of saloons, but otherwise harmless, then down Left Hand Cañon, over a very fair road, out upon the plains again, and back to Longmont. On our way back we stripped off our clothes and took a bath in one of the ditches near the road.

A pleasant ride the next day of thirty miles brought us to Fort Collins, where I found many former residents of Connecticut.

The mosquito record of thirteen killed at one slap has been broken several times since reference was last made to the subject. The mosquitoes, which swarm everywhere, rarely trouble us about the hands or head, but the revolving motion of the legs seem to attract them, and they collect on our stockings in regular military array, every one headed toward the knee — of all the hundreds, and perhaps thousands, that have alighted on us, we never have seen one headed the other way — and many of them in straight lines, four and six in a row. Once, after enduring the pricking sensation as long as I could, I jumped off my wheel, and with a single slap on each stocking put thirty-two of the sweet singing little creatures on their way to the place where everybody sings. This was the result of the first two blows, and there were several outlying sections to be heard from that increased this number somewhat, for a Colorado mosquito that escapes death the first slap is sure to wait for the second one. In fact, one could almost tell the size of my hand by the area of crushed mosquitoes on my stockings, which was almost entirely surrounded by those still waiting and working. The reader may say the habits

of these mosquitoes are of little interest to him, but to me
the mosquitoes had points of keen interest about them.

The number of light complexioned men in Colorado is
very noticeable.   I began to observe it at Denver and at
Colorado Springs, and at Manitou it was even more marked,
till it seemed as if every man, woman, and child had light,
very light-blue eyes, and a light moustache; that is, every
one that wears a moustache of any color.   Wheelmen,
guides, cowboys, they all had the same smiling blue eyes
that seemed to win one's confidence at the outset.   Denver
is noted for having many confidence men and bunco steerers,
but there is no class of men I would sooner trust myself
with than the ranchmen, guides, and cowboys of Colorado.
They like to open one's eyes by telling what they have done
in the past, but in the mountains, mines, or on the plains a
traveler is as safe in their hands as he would be in any city
in the East.

There is a decided improvement in the general aspect of
the country north of Denver, through Longmont and Fort
Collins, upon what we saw south of that city for seventy-five
miles.   There is less stock-raising and more farming.   We
passed many fields of wheat, corn, and alfalfa.   The latter is
of the same nature as red clover and grows nearly as high as
herdsgrass.   Once sown it never needs to be restocked, and
three and sometimes four large crops are cut from it during
the season.   It is almost impossible to plow it up when once
it is thoroughly rooted, and one person told me the roots
would go down into the ground nearly fifty feet in search of
moisture.   I give this as a Colorado li— statement.   But the
only thing that will kill it out is water, too much of it, for it
can be drowned out, finally.

This brings me to the most important interest of Colorado,
and that is water.   Nearly all through the States of Ohio,

Indiana, Illinois, and Iowa, through which I have ridden, States from seven to eleven times as large as Connecticut, the great question that directly interests all the farmers, and that indirectly concerns every one dependent upon the success of farming, is how to get rid of the water. In some of those States great ditches, six, eight, or ten feet deep, and miles in length, are dug, and smaller ditches and tile drains lead into these main channels, and thus in the spring the water to a great extent is drained away, so that the land will dry off and be fit to cultivate.

But the cost of this system of drains and ditches is very great, amounting on some farms to ten dollars an acre. But in Colorado, a State over twenty times as large as Connecticut, water is the one subject uppermost in the minds of the people, as it is farther east, but here it is how to get it, not how to get rid of it. There is the same system of large ditches running for miles and miles through the country, and these are tapped at convenient points by smaller ditches, so that the water is spread out over the sandy, barren-looking country, till by reversing the means used in those other States, the land is brought up into a high state of cultivation. And it does seem as if they even reverse the laws of gravitation, and make the water run up hill, for many and many a ditch seems to go up over and around a hill that is higher than the head of the ditch. There is one advantage, too, the farmers here have over those farther east, and that is, they can have a wet or dry season, just as they choose, for the supply of ditch water is never failing. These main ditches are dug by stock companies, and the stock is in the market just as other stocks are. The water privileges are sold to the farmers, and in some cases the price is twelve to fifteen dollars an acre for perpetual lease. It is singular that in one section of the country it should cost nearly as much per acre to get rid of the water as it does in other sections to procure it.

But this ditch water is a great boon to the people in other respects than for agricultural purposes, and that is for drink. ing. At first I always preferred the well-water, but as I traveled up into the alkali districts the ditch water was much more wholesome to drink, and now I shun everything else. To be treated to ice-water at a farmer's house, appeared at - first rather extravagant on their part, but the ditch water in summer gets so warm, ice-water is almost a necessity. Still, a barrel full of this roily water bailed up in the morning and placed in the shade or down cellar and allowed to settle, will remain pure and palatable for a long while. At one ranch where we stopped, the drinking water was brought nine miles, although a well of alkali water was near the house. At another house I was pulling up the bucket over a pulley, and thought the bucket would never reach the top, when the rope broke, and down went the bucket, 140 feet to the bot- tom of the well that was not even curbed or stoned up. It is needless to say we did not stop to get the bucket out or to get a drink.

The annual rainfall is not only increasing in Iowa and Nebraska, but in Colorado also. It is a true saying, civiliza- tion brings rain. In the former States it is the natural re- sult of the breaking up of so much prairie land. That clay soil packed down hard by centuries of rain would formerly shed water like a duck's back, but once loosened and broken up, it tends to retain the water like a sponge, and the more moisture retained, the greater the rainfall. In Colorado, the extensive irrigation practiced tends to produce the same result; the dry, sandy soil is becoming moist and filled with vegetable matter, till in some instances the land needs only the usual rains to produce good crops. This increased moist-

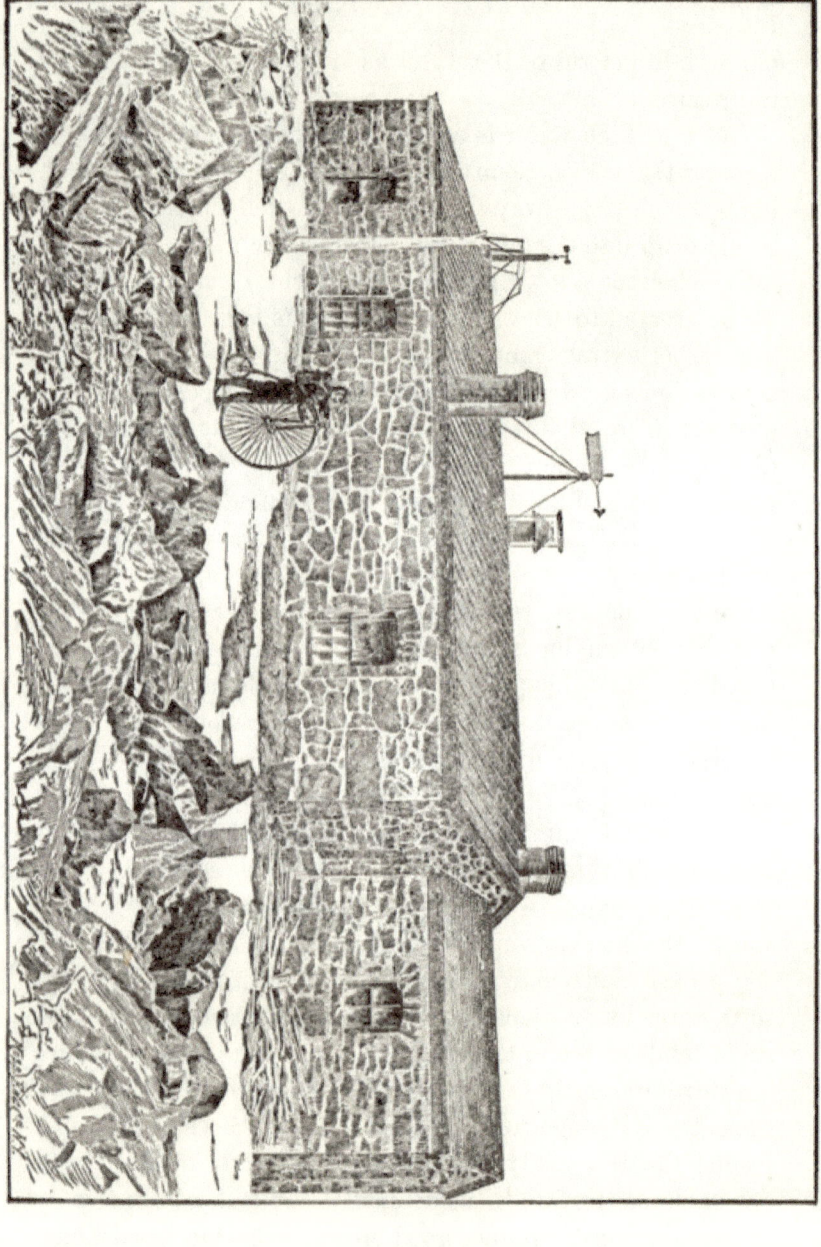

GOVERNMENT STATION, SUMMIT OF PIKE'S PEAK.—(*Page 97.*)

ure in the atmosphere has another effect, and that is upon the health of consumptives. Instances are occurring where these invalids are leaving the plains with their net work of ditches and are going up into the dryer mountain air.

Leaving Fort Collins, or "Collins" as it will shortly be called, we tarried Monday night at a large sheep ranch on the way to Laramie, where shearing commenced the next morning. The owner has nearly 10,000 sheep in his different camps, and six California shearers began shearing at the rate of about 150 sheep a day for each man. The sheep were caught by the hind leg and sat upon their haunches between the legs of the shearer, and, commencing at their necks, the white and cream-colored fleeces rolled off the sheep with surprising rapidity. Occasionally, a piece of flesh would go with the fleece, and hardly a sheep escaped without some bright red streaks or spots upon it, the blood making a sharp contrast in color against the clean white appearance of the naked sheep.

After watching the operation for an hour or more, we started up across the foot-hills to get to the Laramie road on the other side, passing a stream where the water was as red as blood from the red mud or sand being washed down. These foot-hills are immense ledges of rocks that look very much as I have seen ice packed up against the banks of the Connecticut River when the ice breaks up in the spring. Looking at these foot hills toward the west, they present the appearance of so many rounded hills of gravel and sand; but go up into and pass through them, and turn about and look at them in the opposite direction, and it seems really as if, ages ago, the crust of the earth had been broken up, as ice is in the spring, and the immense cakes of red and white sandstone had been jammed and forced up against the broad shoulders of the Rocky Mountains, till these slabs

8

of stratified rock, several hundred feet thick, overlapped each other, and some of them were even forced up into almost perpendicular positions.

Wherever I have passed through these foot-hills, whether at Manitou, Boulder, or at Fort Collins, the country has the same general appearance: that of some immense rock-jam forcing the cakes from the east up on the banks of the Rocky Mountains. Much of the red sandstone is very red, and the contrast between that and the white sandstone is strongly marked, the red and white hills being mixed up promiscuously. We followed a very good road up through the foothills for awhile, but the wagon tracks grew fewer and fewer, as they branched off in different directions, till we struck a common trail, and as we wound around the north side of a high rocky hill this trail disappeared entirely, and we found ourselves off among the barren and sandy foot-hills without the slightest road, trail, or habitation in sight for miles. We debated some time which direction to take, but finally I left my knapsack and wheel and climbed up the rocky side of that hill to get a better view, when behold, there was the Laramie road, just over the hill about a mile away. We had a hard job to get our machines over, but were soon on our way, spinning over a fine mountain road that remained good for fifty miles to Laramie, furnishing some of the finest coasting I ever had. This road for many miles was probably 8,000 feet above the sea, so that this elevation had the effect to dwarf the mountains that rose only a little higher. In fact, it is generally remarked by travelers that the Rocky Mountain scenery west of Cheyenne is very tame. Many of the hills are perfectly level on top, looking at them against the horizon, and the sides slant off, the angles being as sharp and clean cut as if the hills were built by hand.

Just before reaching Laramie we noticed, off to the east

on the plains, another Garden of the Gods, that far exceeds
in every way the one near Manitou. It was with regret that
I could only look at it from a distance of two miles or more,
but the perpendicular position, the height, and the curious
shape of the roads, standing up out of the level plains, was
certainly very interesting.

Arriving at Laramie I inquired of the first man I met,
who happened to be a good-natured Dutchman, where a certain friend of mine lived. "I don't know," he said, "but
Johnny Wilson is the one you want to see. I will go find
him for you. Any one coming so far as Conneckticut must
be taken care of. Wilson knows the whole beezness," and
he ran into his store, seized his coat and escorted us up the
main street of Laramie, calling out to every one he knew,
"These two fellows came from Conneckticut on a bicycle,"
and then he would haw-haw and laugh as if he had secured
the greatest prize in the country. In vain I told him I
wanted to find my friends before dark, but "Mr. Wilson is
the one to take care of you. He knows the whole beezness."
We stopped on the corner to find Wilson, who, it will be
surmised, is a wheelman, and men and boys, old and young,
ran to that corner as if there was a fire, and in less time than
it takes to write it, the sidewalk was blocked and the crowd
extended out into the street. Really, Laramie was more
excited at the arrival of two tired wheelmen than any place
through which I have yet passed. The next morning we
left the line of the Union Pacific and followed the old emigrant trail across the plains. The country is the dryest,
sandiest, and most barren looking of any I had yet seen.
Hour after hour we rode over a treeless and grassless country
that would have been less disappointing if it had been more
level, for as we slowly reached the crest of one long, gentle
swell, through the deep sand, another billow, higher still,

came in sight, and when we had perhaps walked to the top of that, still another, just a little higher, appeared ahead. Then over a long, level space, and we came to a shallow basin, perhaps eight miles across, on the other side of which could be seen the slender thread of our future course. Then the same rolling country with not a ranch in sight for hours.

That day we passed but one stream of water, and what made our thirst more severe was a strong head wind that dried and parched our open mouths till the flesh almost cracked open. About two o'clock we got some milk at a ranch, but that only satisfied our hunger, it did not quench our thirst. All day long we expected to come in sight of the railroad again at the top of every long hill, but every time we were disappointed, and we were doomed not to see railroad or telegraph pole for two days longer.

About 7 o'clock that night we came in sight of a ranch, (ranches out here are all slab huts), but there was no one at home, so we laid down and rested, as the next ranch was eight or ten miles farther on, and it was no use thinking of reaching it that night. Still no one came, and about dark we began to investigate. Flour, sugar, lard, coffee, salt, baking powder, and other things were found in the cupboard, but not a thing cooked. Well, now, with all these things before them, two half-starved boys would not go to bed hungry, "you bet."

Hasley started out with a tin pail to milk a cow, but the cattle ran off as wild as deers and he concluded they were "all steers, any how." Plenty of whole coffee, but no coffee-mill. I was on the point of pounding up some of the kernels with a hammer when the coffee mill was found. The smell of boiling coffee soon put a keen edge upon our already ravenous appetite. but what could we cook besides? Griddle-cakes! Somehow I remembered lard was sometimes put into griddlecakes to make them short, and in a jiffy I was trying to mix three tablespoonfuls of lard into two quarts of flour with a spoon, but the ingredients would not mix well so I used my hands, forgetting that I had just used a greasy rag with which to clean the lantern globe, and that some of the thick coat of soot might have remained on my hands. Then two tablespoonfuls of Dr. Price's baking powder was sprinkled in, and the whole wet up with water, but I must confess it was very lumpy. But if those griddlecakes, covered thick with sugar, didn't taste good! They were light and tender, and after a few trials I could turn one, the size of a dinner plate, over without a break.

Beds of hay and plenty of blankets made us comfortable for the night, and we did not lie awake listening for the folks to come home either. Some more griddlecakes and coffee for breakfast, a card, telling who we were and where we were going, and asking them to write, was left on the table, and, man like, we left the log hut that had given us such a kind shelter, without washing up the dishes.

That forenoon, we traveled over the same desolate dry country, and by one o'clock saw no signs of getting anything to eat, when suddenly we came to the edge of a high bluff, and below was a sparkling stream of cold water and several houses, a most beautiful looking spot to us. We were soon eating heartily at a ranchman's well-set table, and he not only would take no pay, but urged us to stay longer. That afternoon we overtook and passed an emigrant train of six or eight teams, but the usual head wind prevented us from leaving them very far behind, and it was not unpleasant having them so near.

Through Colorado, we saw plenty of harmless snakes by the roadside, and would occasionally stop and kill one to add variety to the trip, but for several days we had seen none of any kind.   During the afternoon I was pushing my machine along in the sand rut. leaning my arm on the saddle, and had been trudging along with my head bent down against the gale for some time, when about three feet in front of the wheel I saw a rattlesnake wriggling slowly across the road.   He stopped and so did I.   The reptile turned his head toward us, ran out his tongue and crept along into the sage brush with his tail sticking up, and disappeared.   For a long while after that, I saw a snake behind every bush, and never turned out into the sage brush to avoid the sand again as I had often done before.   Thin stockings are not the most effective armor in which to attack one of these snakes, and since I have always allowed them to go in peace.   There are plenty of dead ones along the road too, and for a few seconds, when they are curled up naturally, there is as much "business" in a dead snake as a live one.   It works upon the nerves in the same powerful way.

We met another emigrant with a very sick boy in his wagon, and the anxiety was plainly depicted on the father's face when we told him the nearest ranch was about ten miles back. and no one knew whether they had any kind of medicine there or not.   I never once thought of being ill myself off there, but fully realized the danger of a bite from a rattlesnake so far from any medical help.

That night we found good accommodations. and the next forenoon came in sight of the railroad once more. and crossed the bridge over the Platte River on the ties to Fort Fred Steele.

There was one thought that was uppermost in my mind, during this tramp of three days. and 110 miles, across the plains from Laramie to Rawlins, and that was the utter insignificance of a human being in such a place.   One crossing these plains in the cars is too closely connected, in his immediate surroundings, with the improvements of modern civilization, to fully realize the utter helplessness of a person left to his own resources on these deserts. The worldly possessions of one going afoot across these plains, no matter how rich and extensive those possessions are, dwindle into mere worthlessness. All the gold in the world would not purchase him a drop of water. His brain, no matter how active or ingenious, cannot devise anything to satisfy his cravings of hunger. There is absolutely nothing to eat. Emigrants, to be sure, start across prepared with a good supply of food and water; but let one go, as we did, without the slightest preparation in that line — for we supposed there were small places every few miles, whereas there were only two ranches together at one place, and the others averaged ten miles apart — and he will soon realize that the only thing in this world that is of any real value to him, is good muscle and a strong will to back it up. Nothing else is of the slightest account to him, and nothing he can do will give him a mouthful of food or a drop of water, if he has not the strength to go where food and water are. Of course every one has to do that as a general thing, but here it is a question of hours of hard traveling over a desert without any sort of relief till the end. Although we did not suffer for food or water to any great extent, yet I never before fully realized the helplessness of a human being when suddenly cast upon his own resources in such a place.

There is another thing that I begin to realize, but I never expect to be able to fully grasp it, and that is the size of this country. Such a trip, although it is only as yet through a very small portion of the country, helps one to faintly comprehend the Infinite. Niagara gives one an idea of the immense power of nature in motion; here one can comprehend the vastness of nature in repose. In either place the same feeling of awe and reverence comes over one, and his own insignificance stands out very prominently.

The last ten miles to Rawlins was the most discouraging of any since leaving Laramie. The road was aggravatingly level, smooth, and hard, and ran close by the railroad, but those regular trade-winds that we had faced for the last three days prevented any riding. After a while we came to a section-house, and remained there two or three hours, till the wind died down at sunset, and then we easily pushed on to Rawlins. The only bright spot in that day's experience occurred just before reaching Fort Fred Steele. I came upon a pasteboard box, about the size and shape of those used for expressing suits of clothes, lying in the road. A wagon wheel had crushed one corner, but inside, what a sight for hungry wheelmen! Nicely packed in rows were two dozen fresh, even warm doughnuts, all frosted with sugar, and four dozen cookies, looking equally tempting. Then did we not go down by the river where water was plenty and have a feast ! What we could not hold the knapsack did, and not a crumb was wasted. We felt sorry for the ranchman who probably lost his stock of pastry on his way home, but our sorrow did not seriously affect our appetites.

Distance on the wheel, 2,467 miles.

Chapter XIII.

Among the Mormons.

SEVEN cents a mile is the passenger rate upon the Union Pacific Railroad west of Cheyenne. To one accustomed to the almost uniform rate of two cents a mile on Eastern roads this at first seems high, but there are many things that the Eastern roads do not have to contend with that are sources of great expense to the Union Pacific. Water, for instance. is a large item. Trains of low box cars filled with water are almost as common on this road as gravel trains on a newly constructed one. Every eight or ten miles are section-houses for the accommodation of trackmen, and each one of these places has to be furnished with a large cistern filled with water, and this water is often brought by these trains of water cars from a distance of a hundred miles or more. Then there must be water tanks for filling the engines at certain distances, and much of this water is also brought from distant rivers. Many persons pass over the thousand miles of this road and the cost of distributing the necessary amount of water along its line never enters their thoughts, but one who wheels over hundreds of miles of this waterless country, and goes with parched tongue, mouth, and throat for hours, fully realizes the absolute necessity of having water distributed along the line of the road at whatever cost.

The wages of the employees, from the common laborer up, is considerably higher than in the East — one deserves more for living out in such a barren country — so that the more one learns of the cost of running the road the less he grumbles at the high passenger fare.

But it may be asked what has a touring bicyclist to do with the railroad, and why should he feel less or more like grumbling? It is just here. We had ridden three or four days against a wind so strong that it would not allow riding much of the time even on level ground, and to keep up this discouragingly hard work for the sake simply of riding the whole distance, was not the object of the trip. We could already realize the hardships and privations of the early settlers who crossed these same plains years ago, fighting Indians the whole time. Of that part we, of course, knew nothing, but our experience was sufficient. I do not regret it, but it is like putting one's head under water the first time to feel that queer sensation. It is unnecessary, though, to keep the head under for an hour or two to fully realize the feeling, so we thought about the plains, and took a freight at Rawlins.

There we found a wheelman, Mr. James Deitrick, chief train dispatcher on the Wyoming Division of the Union Pacific Railroad, whose kindness to us, especially in a pecuniary manner, will never be forgotten. We thought of him as the train slowly climbed the continental divide and went spinning down the other side, over the same monotonous stretch of sand and sage brush. A ride of seventy-five miles brought us to Green River at eleven o'clock at night. We knew nothing of the town, excepting that we wanted to find some other place to stay than at the $4 a day hotel, and were inquiring at a saloon (there were plenty of those open), when a little short man said: "Come over and stay with me. You are welcome to the best I have." This open-hearted fellow proved to be Frank H. Van Meer Beke, an older brother of the plucky young wheelman who started last March from New York for San Francisco via New Orleans and New Mexico. Frank was formerly a member of the Kings County Bicycle Club of Brooklyn, N. Y., and we were his welcome visitors for two days longer. If his brother Fred is anything like him he is a royal good fellow.

Green River is a place of a few hundred inhabitants, without a shade tree or a patch of green grass in the whole town. During the day we took a swim in the cold waters of the river, the first stream we had seen that empties into the Pacific Ocean, and climbed some of the high rocks in the vicinity, and from their very summits we picked out the fossil remains of many a tiny little fish that had been imbedded there ages ago, when perhaps the only dry land on the face of the earth was in the Adirondacks, Canada, and in the western part of our own State of Connecticut. In the evening (Sunday evening, July 4th) stores were open, saloons in full blast, and fireworks, cannons, and bonfires added to the turmoil. They fired Roman candles into each other's faces without the slightest warning, and the back of my shirt shows the effect of one of the bolts that scorched the skin through the flannel.

Monday our host took our machines to pieces and cleaned them thoroughly, for he was perfectly at home at that work, having had charge of a riding rink in Brooklyn, and Tuesday morning at 4 o'clock found us on our way to Evanston. We started early to avoid as much as possible the discouraging trade winds, and after crossing the river on the ties of the railroad bridge we climbed a long hill, and got a most extended view of just the same sand and sage brush. At noon, to get out of the terribly hot sun, we crawled down under a railroad bridge and ate our luncheon. We were beginning to learn to carry food along with us.

But thirty miles of sand, railroad ties, and that blazing sun drove us into another freight train, and Wednesday morning we left Evanston and before noon were riding leisurely down Echo Cañon on our bicycles. I did not regret then that I was traveling on my wheel, for the roads were good and we stopped and enjoyed the grand scenery to our heart's content. A train went whizzing by, and I saw passengers quickly calling each other's attention to a particularly interesting place in the cañon. With them it was simply a glance, and they were gone; with us, an abund-ance of time to look as long as we liked. The finest view of the best part of the cañon is to be had, I think, only from the highway. Looking up the cañon, the rocks, four or five hundred feet high projecting out into it, have very much the appearance of the bows of so many immense ocean steamers lying side by side. These rocks are a con-glomerated mixture of sand, gravel, stones, and rocks thrown together promiscuously and hardened by some pro-cess of nature into one solid mass of rock again. On the outside the whole body of rocks is colored red by some action of the atmosphere, I think, but underneath they show their natural color, that of light sandstone.

Coming down the cañon we found an overall jacket lying in the road, pretty soon we came to the tailboard of a wagon, then a ball of tobacco twine, soon after a bottle (how our mouths watered) of varnish (then they did not). Then more twine and a bunch of ropes and a bag and then more twine. For five miles we could see the trail in the road where this twine had been dragged along, and whenever it happened to catch on a bush or stone the twine would be strung along for a quarter of a mile or so. A small feed box came next and finally a good horse collar. It still remains a mystery to whom all these things belonged, and the reader must conjecture for himself. We really enjoyed wondering what we should find next.

Gophers seem to take the place of prairie dogs in the high altitudes. They are somewhat smaller, but have very much the same ways of living and are more tame. One of the little fellows stopped in front of his hole one day, within a few feet of me, sat up and ate some sage leaves, came up and sniffed at the bicycle, and, indeed, seemed very friendly. I really wanted to get hold of and squeeze him.

Traveling alone so much has made me feel very friendly toward the lower animals. I have been as much inclined to stop and talk to a horse or a little pig as to a person, and many times I longed to have the different ones wait till I could get hold of and caress them. The farther I travel the more this feeling grows on me, but there is still one animal that I have not yet learned to love or to want to squeeze, and that is a rattlesnake. But I can see I am growing in grace in that respect also. Now, when I see a snake, I don't run and jump on it, as I used to at home. The defenseless condition of my legs may have had something to do with this change of heart, but really they are the only living things that have annoyed me, thus far.

At Echo we found we were as near Salt Lake City as we should be at Ogden, forty miles further along on the line of the Union Pacific, so we started in a southerly direction over excellent roads, up the beautiful Weber Valley, and were soon eating supper at a comfortable farm-house, where everything was as homelike and pleasant as in any New England home. Desiring information, I said: "I wonder if any of those people in large canvas covered wagons we have been meeting are Mormons?" "O, yes," the farmer's wife replied quickly, "there are lots of them around here. They go out on fishing excursions this time of the year a great deal. What do you Eastern people think of the Mormons, anyway? Do you think we have horns?" You can imagine my surprise, but the farmer and his wife, too, joined in and talked so freely and pleasantly on the subject that I soon asked questions as freely as they answered them. "Yes," the farmer said, "I have been married twenty-three years and have never had more than the one wife. I may sometime take another, but I don't see my way clear to do so yet. A few Mormons around here have more than one wife, but the elections show that only one in eight throughout the whole territory are polygamists. The church does not oblige us to take more than one wife any more than it does to pay one-tenth of what we raise at tilling, and there are lots of Mormons who never do either, but if we do our whole duty we should do both. It is not enough for the Government to oblige us to give up wives we have loved and had children by, but now they are trying to pass a law to disfranchise us if we will not swear we will give up our religion. Juries are packed and we are convicted without justice. We never will give up our religion. We must submit for a while, but the time will come when we shall be delivered from our persecutors."

This and much more was said, and it all gave me the impression that if only one-eighth of the Mormons were polygamists, the extent of the blot upon the good name of the country had been greatly over-estimated, for these people were really as kind and Christ-like as any I have met in my travels. But this was one side of the question.

During the day we climbed over the Wasatch Mountains, and came down through Parley's Cañon into Salt Lake Valley. Although the sides of this cañon are not as precipitous as some, yet the rocks go boldly up into the air till their tops are covered with snow. The coasting down this cañon would have been very good, but the great number of team-wagons and Mormon camping parties made dismounts frequent and unpleasant. Just before reaching Salt Lake City, which lies to the northwest of the mouth of this cañon, we hid behind some bushes and took a most refreshing bath in one of the irrigating ditches, for the roads were very dusty all day.

Riding into the city about six o'clock, we had passed up Main street but a little way when, by chance, we met the secretary of the bicycle club. Before we had reached the hotel another member came tearing up the street after us, and in less than fifteen minutes ten or twelve wheelmen came into the hotel to welcome us, all this, too, without a minute's warning from us, or without our knowing a single person in the city by name. A few days before starting, in the spring, I clipped from the *L. A. W. Bulletin* what few names of wheelmen I could find, and thus, in almost every city, I knew some wheelman by name; but here were only four or five League members and we knew no one, but that made no difference. They heard we were from the East and they were our friends, because we were wheelmen. Mr. A. C. Brixen, proprietor of the Valley House, where we stopped, is a wheelman, and so are several of his boarders, and although at Buffalo, Denver, and many other places I have been most cordially received, the Salt Lake City wheelmen outdid all other wheelmen in their spontaneous outburst of welcome.

Shortly after supper, the sound of a brass band playing in front of the hotel, made me wonder, as I sat in my room

trying to get cool: Could it be those enthusiastic fellows had
gone so far as to give us a serenade ? Just then the music
stopped and a knock at the door convinced me.   Surely they
wanted me to come out and say something, I thought; but
what could I say? I had never made a speech in my life.
and the very idea of doing so made me blush there in the
dark in my room.   But I must go out and say something to
the crowd, and do the best I could.   So 1 did; I went out
trembling.   The music came from some theatre band out in
the street in an omnibus, and just then they drove on to the
next hotel, to advertise simply themselves, not me.   And
the expected crowd of enthusiastic admirers consisted of two
men and a boy, sitting under the trees with their feet cocked
up, reading, unconcernedly.   I did not tremble any more.
The knocker was Mr. C. E. Johnson, who wanted us to take
a ride about the city in the morning with him.   We did,
and of him I asked more questions.   " Why yes, every
member of the club is a Mormon.   There is only one who
has two wives, and since he was fined he has only lived with
one.   It amuses us to see Eastern tourists come here, as
many of them do, and appear afraid to ask us questions.
We are glad to answer all inquiries, and believe Eastern people would not be so prejudiced against us if they knew us
better,"— and much more.

The members of the club, in intelligence, personal habits,
and gentlemanly conduct, will compare very favorably with
any Eastern club, and they, from the first, showed such a
liking for us, which we could not help but reciprocate, that
I left them with more of a feeling of sadness than I have
ever experienced in parting from new friends,— and for this
reason: These young men who were so full of kindness to
us believe in a religion that the government is totally opposed
to, and which it is determined to suppress, that is, the polyg-

A HOTEL FOR TWO.—(*Page 116.*)

amous part of it. In case of trouble, and I am afraid from what little I was able to find out in regard to the situation that there will be trouble; in that case these young wheelmen will stand up for their religion, a religion they as honestly believe in as any Eastern wheelmen do in theirs.

Then I talked a few minutes with the editor of the *Tribune.* "The statement," said he, "that only one-eighth of Mormons are polygamists is misleading, certainly. The number of Mormons disqualified from voting for practicing polygamy may have been one-eighth of the whole population, but that includes every man, woman, and child, Gentiles and all. Now Gentiles and women and children are not polygamists; women and children cannot be in the very nature of the case. So that the number of Mormons, capable of being polygamists, that practice it to-day, is nearer one-half than one-eighth. As for juries being packed, the same course is being pursued here as in all courts. A man disbelieving in capital punishment cannot sit in a murder trial, for he would not convict on evidence; just so with a Mormon, he would not convict another Mormon of polygamy. The only persecution practiced is by United States deputies enforcing a United States law. The troops are quartered here in the city because there has been, and is still, need of them to preserve the peace."

I feel that what I have learned of the trouble here is only superficial, for a two days' stop, with much of my time otherwise occupied, is not a sufficient time to look up the subject; but one thing seems certain, it will be a very long and a very hard struggle, but the conclusion is foregone. Polygamy must go. Yesterday afternoon we went bathing in Salt Lake; as far as the view is concerned, it is like bathing in the ocean, you cannot see across the lake. It is only three or four years since the people of the city have

9

availed themselves of the benefits of their salt water to any great extent, but now, cheap excursions run out to the lake, twenty miles distant, and returning trains frequently bring back 2,000 passengers. Yes, it is genuine salt water bathing with a vengeance, for you can't swim in it. It is almost like trying to swim in thin mud, you can't get along any. The water is so heavy it is almost impossible to dive to any depth, and then you bob up out of the water feet first, just like a cork. It must be really dangerous to dive from any height. Sink! You can't sink if you try. You can walk clear across the lake and not go under; lie flat on your back with your hands under your head for a pillow, and one who has never been in any water, salt or fresh, could lie there all day without any trouble. Turn over and throw your arms out like a spread eagle, and it is just the same, or sit straight up, tailor fashion, and still you are high above the water; that is, high enough not to feel any nervousness about getting strangled. I never experienced such a pleasant sensation and never enjoyed bathing more, unless it was high surf bathing, and here that is impossible, for no wind, however strong, could raise very high waves on this genuinely heavy sea. The water was full of men, women, and children, all floating around, none swimming, some sitting bolt upright, others lying around in any position that was agreeable, and all unconcerned as to whether there was three or thirty feet of water under them.

I went out upon the beach to sit in the sun, to dry off, but soon looked like a miller; hair, neck, face, and hands, were covered with salt, and a bath with fresh water was of course necessary. This water in your mouth or up your nose is very disagreeable; in your eyes, painful; and to be strangled with it, simply terrible. Eyesight has been permanently injured by people opening their eyes under this water. I am told that it contains nearly three times as much salt as ordinary salt water, and the numerous streams of fresh water which empty into it, have no effect on its saline strength. Without any visible outlet, the only change noticeable is a slight rise in the water level.

Of course we had to visit the Tabernacle, which comfortably seats over ten thousand people, and when we were told the great organ was brought across the plains on ox-teams, over the same route we had just passed, a chord of sympathy seemed to vibrate between the organ and us. The Temple, which was commenced in 1853, and is to be finished in seven years, making the allotted forty years that must be consumed in its construction, is still nothing but four bare walls, nine feet thick and 100 feet high.

Distance traveled with the wheel, 2,625 miles.

WITH a full moon we had planned to travel most of the way across the alkali and sandy deserts of Nevada at night, and were on the point of leaving Salt Lake City to do so when the Grand Army of the Republic excursion tickets were issued, enabling anyone to go from there to San Francisco, up to Portland, Oregon, by water and return to Salt Lake via the Oregon Short Line. Returning by this route would take us within easy wheeling distance of Yellowstone Park, and with that inducement, in addition to being taken across Nevada and over the Sierra Nevada Mountains at half rates, we were not long in deciding to take the cars. But now the first financial difficulty stared us in the face. I had no trouble in Denver in getting identified, but, as I said, we knew no one and no one knew us in Salt Lake City. Letters, league ticket, and other papers were presented at the bank, but nothing would prevail on the officials to give us a penny. The only thing to do was to telegraph home, and that would probably delay us several days, and, with that discouraging alternative in view, we told our story to Mr. F. G. Brooks, a member of the bicycle club. "Wait till I see what father says," said he, and he carried the worthless New York drafts back to the desk. The elder F. G. Brooks hesitated a moment, and then wrote his name across the back of those drafts, and we went to the bank and received $150 in gold. And the old gentleman that did that kind act was a Mormon, through and through. Surely I had reason to like the Mormons, in every respect but their religion.

Thus far, in traveling twenty-six hundred miles or more over clay ruts and mountain roads, I had taken only two tumbles, and was beginning to think there was no such thing as headers when, in gliding serenely across the street, in front of the Utah Central Depot at Salt Lake City, I rode into a ditch, concealed with fine sand, and instantly — that word makes the time altogether too long — my nose and chin were scraping along on the hard gravel. I never took such a tumble. It was like a flash. And the knapsack, as usual, unkindly butted me on the back of the head as the ground suddenly brought the trip to a close. With the blood starting from both nose and chin, and a loosened handle bar, that at first sent a cold chill all through me with the impression that it was broken, and with a knee so badly sprained that I could only limp into the cars, these things, altogether, served to remind me that carelessness and 'cycling are incompatible.

On the way to Ogden we saw several headers at work on the wheat fields, and these served to awaken me from the dazed condition in which the only kind of a header I had ever known had put me. The field headers are mowing machines that go along in front of the horses instead of behind them, as is usual with mowing machines in the East, and as it cuts the wheat down — it simply cuts off the tops or heads of the wheat, hence the name header — the wheat falls on to a long cloth roller that revolves at right angles to the direction the machine is going. A large box wagon is

driven along at the left of the header and the wheat is carried
up on this cloth roller and loaded into this wagon. When
full another takes its place while the first wagon is being
unloaded at the stack.

The Wasatch Mountains, a range that extends from below
Salt Lake City to many miles above Ogden, are not dwarfed,
as is the case with so many other ranges of mountains, by
foot hills at their base, but they stand out bold and black, excepting where covered with snow, and are the most impressive of any mountains I have yet seen. At Ogden, through
passengers are delayed two hours between the arrival of the
Union Pacific and the departure of the Central Pacific trains.
Half of this time is a needless delay, for the mail, baggage
and express matter was all transferred long before the train
left, but this is only a sample of the manner in which both
roads are run.

The question of fast time is never considered in their
operation. A through Eastern fruit train now makes decidedly better time than the regular passenger trains; and
freight trains, as a rule, run faster between stations than
passenger trains. The time tables seem to be made with the
sole object of helping delayed trains get through on time,
no matter how slow that time is. One train we were
on was an hour and a half late at midnight, but on time
before 5 o'clock the next morning, and we did not run so
fast but that passengers could sleep as usual. There is talk
of a new fast train being put on between Omaha and San
Francisco that will shorten the time perhaps a day, but in the
East even that train would not be considered anything very
fast. Then the Central Pacific trains are not only run slow
but sure, sure that everything is all right before they start.
A brakeman comes through from the front end of the train
and calls for every one's ticket, looks at the ticket and hands

it back. Pretty soon a man in uniform, a little higher up than the brakeman, but not so high as the conductor, comes along through the train from the rear end, examines care-fully all the tickets, reads all the printed matter on them, punches them, and hands them back, after perhaps taking a passenger out of the cars to verify his statement in regard to an extra hole in his ticket made by some other official. Then after the tickets have been examined from the front to the rear, and scrutinized and punched from the rear end to the front end of the train, even before the train had started, to make the thing more binding the conductor himself comes through, punches all the tickets, and gives each passenger a plain piece of colored pasteboard without so much as a table of distances printed on it, a convenience many times to pas-sengers, and which is so rotten that it breaks and falls to pieces at the least touch. Let a passenger accidentally destroy one of these valuable pieces of plain rotten paste-board during his rolling and tumbling in his seat at night and he is looked upon by the conductor as a criminal for . wantonly destroying so much valuable property, and finan-cially crippling the railroad company in consequence, and these priceless pieces of paper are carefully gathered up at the end of each division of the road by the economical con-ductors, who, at night, shake and arouse every passenger who has so much of this valuable property of the company's concealed about his person. Most of the postal, express, and baggage cars used here are now built without doors at the ends. Perhaps the numerous train robberies have caused this innovation.

Once during that Saturday night, after leaving Ogden, I looked out of the car window and in the moonlight saw a perfectly level sea of alkali without so much as a sage bush growing upon it, and then I went to sleep again more contented than ever with the way I was crossing this part of the continent.

At one of the stations were some horned toads for sale, the first I had seen, and as I asked a passenger stand-ing near what kind of animals they were, "I think," said he, honestly enough, "they are what they call prairie dogs." All day Sunday it was sand, sage-bush, and a sun so hot that it would almost blister, and the same kind of a country we had already seen so much of east of Ogden. So I occu-pied myself most of the time writing. During the day at the different stations situated along the sandy desert the thermometer registered 102° and 104°, and yet I was not uncomfortably warm. The air would blow in at the windows as if it came direct from some furnace, and yet it was so very dry that it would not start the perspiration. Until I reached California there were only three days that were oppressively hot since the commencement of the trip, and those were in the fore part of July while crossing Iowa. In Colorado and over the plains the atmosphere was so very dry that even with the thermometer up to ninety, as it was in Iowa, one could exercise without feeling the heat nearly as much.

At Truckee we left the train at 12 o'clock at night, and as we wanted to be off early the next morning for Lake Tahoe, fifteen miles up the Truckee River, we decided not to go to bed. There were several bales of hay on the freight house platform, and one had burst open. Into that hay we crawled and slept till daylight, keeping comfortably warm till nearly morning, but I had to go behind the freight house and remove my clothes in order to shake out the innumera-ble spires of hay that pricked me from head to foot.

We got started soon after four, and the road was decid-edly better than I had reason to think it would be, and the grade was easy, but the dust rather uncomfortable. But that is to be expected in a country that has so little rain in so many months, and where the roads are used as much as this one is the fine dust gets very deep. Going up, a couple of young deer remained in the road till I was nearly upon them, and even when I dismounted they didn't run, but stayed within six or eight feet of where I stood. They appeared so tame I wanted to get my hands upon them and stroke their hair, but Hasley, coming up, drew his revolver, and I hallooed "Don't shoot; they're tame." The sound of a human voice sent them up the hillside like a streak, and I saw it was the glistening nickel that fascinated them.

The waters of Lake Tahoe are very clear, and it never freezes over, as I was told, although the weather is sufficiently cold; but really I do not see what makes the place so celebrated. It is a beautiful lake, thirty miles long, surrounded by wooded hills, but place it in New England and it would hardly be noticed among the many there fully as beautiful. The clearness of the water is remarkable, but no more so than the water of any lake situated high up in the mountains, where there is nothing but the pure white snow to furnish a water supply, and where there is no loam, mud, or vegetable matter to discolor it. There are no other attractions, unless it be the Hot Springs, and as we did not go over there, five miles away, of course I cannot form an opinion of that place.

A steamer goes around the lake once a day, carrying mail and merchandise. We rowed and fished some, that is pulled out the same fish, the minnows, that we threw in, but the rest, lying on the pebbly beach, with the sound of the swash of the waves in my ears, was enjoyed the most of any part of the day. And perhaps that is the very reason why the lake is so noted. People from the East come to it after days of travel over the sandy plains and alkali deserts of Wyoming, Utah, and Nevada, and the change from the hot, dusty ride to the clear, cold waters of the lake in the mountains, is so delightful that the lake gets its full share, and more too, of the credit for the pleasure in the change.

Both going up and coming down I must have passed hundreds of snake tracks in the road, some of them two or three inches wide. What size the snakes must have been to make such tracks I could only imagine; but the woods were surely full of snakes.

Taking the train again at midnight, I was soon asleep, but something awoke me just as we were rounding Cape Horn. The brakeman, the night before, told me it would be seven o'clock before we should pass that point of interest, so I went to sleep unconcerned about waking in time, but something startled me as a call in the morning would, and I rushed out upon the platform, rubbing my eyes open, just as we were passing around the side of the mountain. It was barely light, but the sight of two huge locomotives followed by a train of twelve cars rushing around near the edge of a precipice four or five hundred feet high will not soon be forgotten, and the manner in which the railroad twists and turns around the sides of the mountains down into Colfax is worth getting up pretty early to see. As far as the eye can see from this point down into the Sacramento valley, California is of one hue — straw-color. The ripe wheat is, of course, that color, but the common grass has dried up and changed to the same, whereas on the plains the dried grass is of nearly the same color as the soil. The morning was not clear, so the view was not very extended; but we were soon looking at objects that were of more practical value to hungry wheelmen than the prevailing color of the country. We had the best "two-bit" meal at Sacramento we had found in many a week.

The dome of the capitol, which from a distance resembles the dome at Washington, naturally draws sightseers to visit the capitol building, but the edifice looks old and out of fashion compared with many other State structures. Above the first story, which is of granite, it is built of brick plastered over and painted. The senate chamber and house of representatives are furnished simply with cushioned and cane-seated chairs, standing around promiscuously; no desks for any one excepting clerks and presiding officers. The ascent to the lantern above the dome is by winding stairs that twist about a wooden pole in the center of the upper part of the dome, and it seemed as if the whole building shook as we went up and down these stairs.

Salt Lake is a city laid out with very large blocks and built up of very small houses, and Sacramento is a city of verandas. All the sidewalks in the business portion of the city are covered and the verandas are often two stories high. These add greatly to the comfort of pedestrians, and we could fully appreciate them with the thermometer at a hundred and over. Still, notwithstanding this intense, dry heat, we started out in the middle of the afternoon and made thirty-two miles before dark over roads that were certainly excellent. The fine sand which covers the surface of the whole valley, during the rainy season packs down very hard and the wind keeps the surface of the roads in many places free of dust, so that they are as hard and smooth as concrete.

That evening we went out into the farmer's garden and ate all the fresh figs we wished. These figs are about the same shape and a little smaller than Bartlett pears and the skin is almost black. They are pink inside and have a sweetish taste that becomes fascinating. The figs we have in the East must be of another variety, for the black skin cannot be removed before drying. The next morning we passed some century plants growing by the roadside in front of a farm-house.

The roads were good for twenty miles farther, but then we began to get up into the foot hills and naturally the riding was not so good; but still after waiting three hours or more in the shade at noon we made nearly fifty miles more during the day towards the Big Trees. That evening, after asking in vain for shelter for the night at two or three places, we laid down under a tree, feeling too tired to care much where we stayed. There was no particular hardship about sleeping on the ground, for the night was warm and the ground dry, and there was no dew. I was asleep in no time, but not for long. The ants had pre-empted that section long before and were soon active in finding out who was trying to jump their claim. I did not mind their crawling up my pant legs or down the back of my shirt, or through my hair, or across my face, for I could go to sleep with a whole army walking all over me, but when an ant suddenly took it into his head to bite it served to unpleasantly disturb my dreams. After wasting a good part of the night in changing lodgings, I finally slept soundly whether the ants did or not.

The next day, after riding and walking about equal distances for thirty miles, we reached the Calaveras Big Trees, a little less than one hundred and ten miles and two days' journey from Sacramento. The heat, 102° in the shade, was so intense that the cement softened under the tire so much that it could easily be removed, and the three or four inches of hot, fine dust was very hard on the feet; but after a cold bath and half an hour's rest the verdict was that it paid. Although there are woods all over the mountains, and trees over a hundred feet high in many places, yet the grove proper comprises but about twenty-five or thirty acres.

I must say that trying to describe the trees themselves is beyond my power. I can only tell what I did. There are smooth drives through the groves, so I rode. Most of the trees are standing, but there was one that had fallen. The inside is hollow, and about fifty feet from the base is an immense hole in the side. Into this hole with my bicycle I went, and rode through the inside of the tree for nearly two hundred feet, emerging through another hole into the daylight again. There is a knothole near this point large enough to allow a man of giant frame to enter or crawl out of.

The inside of the tree was covered with charcoal, and it was quite dark in there, so I felt my way along as I rode, getting my hands black, but I washed some of it off at a pool of water that fills the inside of the tree at one point. The basin of water is two or three feet above the level of the ground, and where the water comes from and what forces it up out of the ground into the hollow of this fallen tree is a mystery. There is no rain here for months, and evaporation in this dry air must tend to exhaust the supply wherever it comes from, and yet the pool always remains at the same level.

This tree, "The Father of the Forest," is one hundred and twelve feet in circumference at the base, and, judging from what remains of it, four hundred and fifty feet was its height when standing. I have no doubt a sixty-inch wheel could be ridden through where I went. A driveway, or rather a tunnel, has been cut through another standing tree, and the stage drives through there frequently. I found plenty of room above and on either side in 'cycling through it. Imagine four wheelmen abreast riding through such a place.

A pavilion has been built over the stump of another tree

that was cut down several years ago, and I rode around and cut figure eights on the smooth floor of this stump. The diameter of this tree, at the base, is thirty-two feet, but it was cut off about five feet from the ground, and is twenty-five feet in diameter across the top. Five men worked a month, boring auger holes into it, and when it was completely cut across it would not fall, and so ropes and pulleys had to be used to pull it over. When it fell it shook the ground for miles around, like an earthquake. Thirty-two dancers are easily accommodated on the stump.

There are about ninety trees of similar dimensions in the grove, and they bear the names of generals, statesmen, noted women, and others. These trees all show the effects of fire, but younger trees growing by their side, that are certainly from one to two hundred years old, have not the slightest marks of the flames upon them. The date of this ancient fire that burnt the inside out and killed so many of the trees is beyond conjecture, but the age of these giant sequoias must be reckoned up among the thousands.

A description of these other trees might be given, but it would simply be a repetition of wonders. Seeing so many trees all the way up from Murphy's that, to me, seemed prodigious, when I first reached here the grove did not impress me, but every time I look at them now they appear larger. As in looking from the rear end of a moving train, as soon as the train stops the ties, rails, and everything begin to enlarge in size, apparently, so with these trees, a couple of days of rest has given me a much better idea of their immensity than could be had at first sight.

Distance on the wheel, 2,768 miles.

Chapter XV.

In the Yosemite Valley.

ROM the Calaveras Big Trees to the Yosemite is one hundred and eight miles, and it took me three days to make the journey. The wheelman, Mr. J. A. Hasley, whom I met the day I reached Denver, who made a good companion on the trip to Pike's Peak and across the plains to Salt Lake City, and who bore the blazing hot sun of California as far as the Trees, there decided not to continue the trip farther. For several days it was evident he was beginning to lose interest in sight-seeing, after a month's constant application to it, and when he had the misfortune to lose his purse with something over twenty dollars in it, he decided to get to San Francisco by the quickest and cheapest route, which was by the Stockton boat, an opposition line of steamers taking passengers for ten cents, a distance of one hundred miles. So now I am alone again. The first of the three days' journey was used up in coasting most of the fifteen miles down to Murphy's, over the same road we had worked so hard in getting up to the Big Trees, and then getting a few miles in a southerly direction beyond the Stanislaus River.

During the afternoon, while riding along on the side of a

high hill, I passed a sign, which read " 500 yards to the Natural Bridge, the world's greatest wonder, and don't you forget that." Believing it to be a fraud of some kind, I left the machine and walked down a steep narrow path to the bottom of a ravine, perhaps 500 feet below the level of the road. Here were two men clearing out the entrance to a cave from which ran a good-sized stream of water. The surroundings looked as if a land-slide had once choked up the ravine, but that the stream of water had finally worked its way through underneath the mass of rocks and earth, and had formed a tunnel perhaps four hundred feet long and twenty or thirty feet high. Water was constantly dripping from the roof of the tunnel, forming stalactites of various sizes and shapes. To more fully impress me with the importance of his discovery, the old bachelor who owned the place, stated that it had taken forty-two millions of years to bring the place into its present form and shape. Whether it had or not, I felt well paid for visiting a place of which I knew nothing until I saw the sign.

The Stanislaus and the Tuolumne Rivers flow down from the Sierras in a westerly direction, and in going southerly from the Big Trees to the Yosemite, one must naturally cross them. The crossing is easy enough ; there is no trouble about that. It is getting down to them that causes the trouble, and getting up away from them again. The profile of the route I took resembled an immense letter W. It is a thousand feet down to the Stanislaus River, and twelve hundred or more down to the Tuolumne, and the two rivers are but a few miles apart.

The zigzag road-down to the rivers is too steep and dangerous to coast, and once down, walking is the only way up again. When I came to the Tuolumne River, I believe I could have thrown a stone down to the suspension bridge, a

A RATTLESNAKE DISPUTES THE WAY. — (*Page 118.*)

thousand feet or more below, and yet it took four miles of walking to get down to it, and after climbing up five miles farther, I could look across the valley about a mile and see where I had been three or four hours before. I would not believe it till I looked, but the thermometer was 105° down at the bridge. Notwithstanding all this there was something about such mountain scenery, combined with the roar of the river so far below, that compensated for the heat and fatigue. Probably half the entire distance between the Trees and the Valley had to be traveled afoot on the hot road, but there is another grand view of the Tuolumne River, and a small grove of big trees to vary the monotony of the last twenty miles of hill climbing.

When we left Sacramento, it was with the vague impression that it was somewhere in the neighborhood of two hundred and fifty miles to the Yosemite, but the first day out the distance was reduced to below two hundred by some one of whom we made inquiries. We were entirely ignorant of the nearest route, but by making frequent inquiries we kept on, generally in the right direction. The second day the entire distance was further reduced to one hundred and twenty-five miles, then the distance from the Trees to the Valley was put at twenty-five miles by some one who knew it all, but such good news was not lasting, for the very next man who had "traveled over that section," said it was one hundred and seventy-five miles between the two places.

And so it was throughout the entire trip: First, we were almost there, then at night, perhaps fifty miles farther away than in the morning. Finally, after six days of hard work, with one object, the Yosemite constantly in view, the answer to an inquiry came back, "eight miles down to the hotel," and in less than a mile, while rounding a bend in the road, the grandest sight I have lived to see, suddenly burst upon

10

me. It was sudden, because I supposed it would be five miles farther before I should see anything but fine trees and bushes, and grand beyond description. I forgot my aching feet and tired legs, and walked along almost unconscious of them, down the zigzag road into the valley, which runs up in a northeasterly direction, the road entering it at the lower end.

The word valley hardly describes it, for the sides are perpendicular and almost a mile high, and this immense chasm is ten miles long and hardly a mile wide. The roar of the Merced River, so many thousand feet almost perpendicularly below, is heard even before one gets a glimpse of the river itself or even the valley, and my first thought was, is there any bottom to this chasm. On the opposite side of the valley I recognized Bridal Veil Fall from the many views I had seen of it, and a little farther down the road, which runs dangerously near the edge of precipices four and five hundred feet high, El Capitan came suddenly into sight, the most prominent object to be seen in the whole valley from that point of view.

It was quite dark when I reached the hotel, which is half way up the valley, and the next morning my feet were too tired to think of much hill climbing, so I walked up the valley about a mile where it seems to separate into two branches, and taking the right hand one, climbed up a rocky trail to the Vernal Falls. Here the Merced, a comparatively small stream, falls straight down three hundred and fifty feet, sending mist and spray up the sides of the rocks in all directions, making a roar that can be heard long before one gets in sight of the falls "You can't follow that trail up by the falls ; we got wet through trying it," said a couple of tourists whom I met just below the falls, and they started off on another trail two miles farther around. But I took the shorter route, up over slippery shelving rocks that would let one slide quickly down into the pool where the waters came thundering down from a height of perhaps thirty feet, and before I got through the shower of mist and spray, up to the ladders that lead to the top of the falls, I was wet through, too. Lying on the rocks, the warm sun soon dried my clothes, and after a good meal at Snow's, a small hotel situated midway between the Vernal and Nevada Falls, I climbed up to the top of the Nevada Falls. Here the water comes rushing down over high rocks, goes through a narrow gorge under the bridge with a roar, and plunges over the cliff. Down a short distance, the water strikes a projecting rock, and the whole river is sent out with a twist into the air, one mass of white foam that spreads out into hundreds of little white rockets that never explode, but fade away into thin spray. Down farther, another projecting rock tears the water to pieces again and sends it shooting out into the air, till, when it reaches the bottom and has fallen a distance of fully seven hundred feet, there is scarcely anything left of the water but foam.

All the afternoon I lay on the flat rock at the top of the falls, and after sleeping and writing by turns, and resting all the time, I became so accustomed to the roar that I hardly realized that the water was rushing by me and falling almost directly down seven hundred feet to the rocks below. The Cap of Liberty is a very appropriate name for a mass of granite that rises up over half a mile within a few rods of the top of the falls.

The next morning, after a good night's rest at Snow's, where the roar of the falls makes a soothing sound, I started up the trail for Clouds Rest. "O you can't miss your way. Just follow the trail," is what everybody says, landlords, guides, ranchmen, and everybody of whom the question is asked: "Is there any trouble in finding the way?" This was the case in Colorado and it is so here, and one starts off on such trips with the impression that he has simply to follow his nose and he will get there. But it is the easiest thing in the world for a tenderfoot, like myself, to miss the way.

I had gone nearly three miles up the only fresh trail there was to follow, when coming to a log hut I asked how far it was to Clouds Rest. "This is not the way. You missed the trail back there a mile and a half," and so I turned back and hunted for an hour, climbed over boulders, small rocky ridges and fallen trees, tore one knee out of my trousers, ripped open my stockings, and was on the point of going back and giving up the whole trip, when I found what was the trail; but a heavy rain had completely obliterated the foot prints three days before and the trail itself was washed out of existence in many places. But up I started and walked in the direction of the peak for an hour or two, when the trail seemed to lead away from the object of my trip, and so I started straight up the side of the mountain, crawling up over rocks on my hands and knees, sometimes slipping back, but always struggling on, till I finally reached the top. Then how thankful I was that I had not turned back. The top of the peak is, perhaps, twenty by thirty feet in area, and is ten thousand feet above the sea. That is not very high compared with some mountain peaks, but it is six thousand feet above the valley, and as I write these words I can look down, almost straight down, eight hundred feet more than a mile. Think of sitting in the front row of the gallery and looking down into the parquet six thousand feet below. I am sitting in such a place now, only there is no railing or protection in front. The sight is enough to make one almost lose his senses. I

had been on top but a few minutes when there was a rum-
bling sound like thunder not very far off, and I began to
wish myself somewhere else. Whether it was a rock falling or simply the reverberation of a gun I don't know, but
it made me feel very uncomfortable for a while. The peak
is the highest of any in sight for many miles, and one can
look down into the whole length of the Yosemite Valley
as he would into a deep trench. The river, looking white
and slender down there so far, is roaring on its downward
course, but I can't hear it. The heavy pine trees from one
to two hundred feet high down there in the valley, look
like standing evergreens in a meadow. El Capitan, the
Half Dome, the Cap of Liberty, the North Dome, and all
the other immense peaks that rise up three or four thousand
feet above the valley, I can look down on as a tall man upon
a crowd of boys.

A swallow rushed by me with the whiz of a bullet, making
my heart beat with excitement for the moment, and then I
began to think how nice it would be to fly down to some of
the peaks below; but when a person begins to think of flying in such a place it is dangerous business. He might
suddenly take it into his head to try it. The peaks to the
east are all covered with snow, and the whole country for
miles in every direction has a very light colored appearance,
the granite of which it is all composed giving it that look.
The mass of rocks that are entirely bare, free from all kinds
of vegetation, is fully one-half of the entire area of the
country within view.

Straight across the valley, and only a little lower down, is
a mass of granite, smooth as a floor, containing hundreds of
acres, with scarcely a tree or shrub on it. It is less than a
mile away, and yet what an awful chasm between us, a
chasm deeper than it is wide. The distant views from

Pike's Peak are more extended, but there are no such perpendicular heights as are here seen on all sides.

I cannot give any good reason for feeling so, but it takes all the courage I have to stay here and eat my luncheon and write what little I have written. Sitting in the middle of this small area the only objects seen over the edge are from five to six thousand feet below, and it is only by going near the edge, which I don't like to do, that I can see the immense granite mountain that supports this small, flat surface, and the sight of that reassures me. But I can't endure it any longer. It is not pleasant up here alone. I feel all the time as if I was just on the point of losing control of myself. I keep thinking what if I should jump off, how would it feel going down a mile or more through the air. People who talk contemptuously of what is called altitude sickness can never have experienced it.

After an hour's unpleasant stay on top I got back to Nevada Falls all right and then took the new trail around to Glacier Point, where, after twenty-five miles of climbing during the day, I was ready to rest for the night. The next morning I went out to the point, or, that is, within ten feet or so of the edge. Glacier Point is nearly opposite Yosemite Falls, and a magnificent view of the valley, including both its branches, is to be had from this place, although it is nearly three thousand feet lower than Clouds Rest. The rock projects out over the edge of the cliff, and an iron railing has been placed there. They say, I don't know anything about it, myself, for I did not go out to this railing, but they say you can look down under yourself thirty-two hundred feet into the valley below. The feeling was sufficiently unpleasant the first time I went up the winding stairs on the inside of the dome of the capitol at Hartford, but here the height is over twelve times as great, and I did not care to try it, but some do go out there and have their pictures taken.

Down the trail to Barnard's again, and up the opposite side of the valley to the foot of the Upper Yosemite Falls. Here a small stream plunges over the edge of the rocks and falls directly down over sixteen hundred feet, ten times as high as Niagara; before the water reaches the bottom the wind has reduced it to little less than spray, and just before I got to the foot of the cliff the wind suddenly changed and I was drenched to my skin before I could get away. These falls produce a peculiar sound down in the valley that is not heard at all near them. It is that of falling rocks or sup-pressed thunder, caused probably by the water being blown against the face of the precipice. Whether it was the small volume of water compared with the Nevada Falls, or having my ardor so suddenly dampened by the shower bath, but the Yosemite Falls did not impress me as the other falls I had seen did. On the way back, a gentleman just ahead of me suddenly came upon a rattlesnake a yard long, and the man jumped into the air, and ran back like a deer, but his courage returning he struck the snake a well-directed blow with a stone, and now has the four rattles in his pocket as a trophy.

On the way out of the valley, in the afternoon, I stopped at the Bridal Veil Falls, which are nine hundred feet high. Here I met a lady painting near the falls. Two days before that I first saw her at the Nevada Falls, where, before night, she had put upon canvas a most striking picture of the falls. Now she was doing the same here, and we sat upon the rocks at the foot of the falls and had a most delightful talk, for nearly an hour, on the advantages we had (she traveled horseback) over common tourists who depend upon cars and stages.

Like the Yosemite, these falls reach the bottom all blown to spray, and I began to perceive that after three days of this tremendous sight-seeing such common heights as one or two thousand feet were passed by unnoticed, and it took some such prominent figure as El Capitan to awaken any special interest. This solid, smooth, perpendicular piece of granite juts out boldly into the valley over three thousand feet high, and it easily holds first place in point of interest at the south end of the valley, as the Half Dome does at the north end.

The Half Dome rises above the valley four thousand eight hundred feet, and as its name indicates, one-half of the upper portion is rounded and smooth like any dome, but it is split in half; the other side being vertical from the top down for one thousand five hundred feet, and the lower portion descending nearly perpendicularly. And as I climb up out of the valley, over the Big Oak Flat route, and take a last look at the gigantic object below, I try to form some idea how this valley, different from any other in the world, could have been formed. But all attempted theorizing upon this stupendous subject proves unsatisfactory, and I am more than willing to leave the problem for some other fellow to solve.

Distance traveled on the wheel, 2,874 miles.

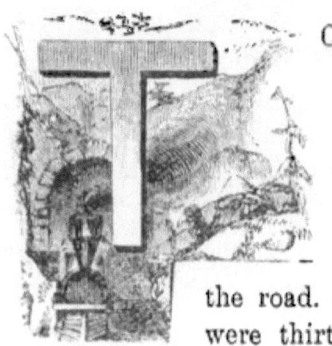

O get out of the Yosemite Valley required nearly ten miles of hill climbing, or rather walking, for there is no such thing as riding up even an ordinary hill with three or four inches of fine dust and numberless loose stones in the road. But once at the summit there were thirty miles of coasting, such as it was. Long before, in going into the valley, I had been obliged to take off the spring under the brake, for it required every ounce of strength I had to control the machine in coasting down some of those long hills without wasting any of my strength in pressing down a stiff spring. The roads were very rough, full of roots and stones, and so steep many times that it needed the full strength of the brake to keep the machine slowed down to a safe speed, but even then sometimes an unseen root or stone would throw me forward on to my feet, and the head of the machine would strike me on the lower part of the backbone till the flesh was black and blue. So in order to keep on the bicycle for any distance, I had to actually lie down on the saddle, keeping as far back on it as possible and reach the handles. In this position, with my legs sprawling out in front and the knapsack rubbing on the backbone of the machine, I rode for miles and miles, often bounding into the air, so that day-light might have been seen between myself and the saddle. It was neither a graceful nor a comfortable position, but it was the only way I could get along without walking, and to do that after walking up these same hills in a broiling sun would have been too bad. Some of the hills were too steep and crooked for coasting even, but most of them I rode down without mishap.

The next day after I left the valley, just before dark, while riding over a smooth, level strip of road, the felloe on the little wheel broke. The butt end of an eight-penny nail was sticking through the tire just at the point of fracture, but whether that was the cause of the breakage or not I cannot say. But this I did know, the machine was appa-rently useless.— forty-five miles from any railroad, and how many miles from a blacksmith's shop I had not an idea. But with the use of a piece of hoop iron and some wire that I brought all the way from Indiana, where the old rubber tire had made the only previous trouble with the machine, I bound up the felloe and it carried me thirty miles, till the next noon, when a blacksmith riveted a piece on, and made the wheel strong again.

The one hundred and sixty-two miles from the Yosemite back to Sacramento were made in three days. On the way I dropped the machine and ran a quarter of a mile across a wheat field to see a header and thresher at work. It was drawn by eighteen mules, working six abreast, and cut a swarth nearly if not quite ten feet wide. The tops of the wheat as they fell were carried up on a cloth roller into the threshing part of the machine which worked as the machine was drawn along. Four or five men rode upon the machine, doing various work, but the result of the whole was, the wheat was cut, threshed, run into bags, and the bags tied up and thrown off, as the whole establishment went along on two immense wheels. Any farmer can judge of the great number of acres of wheat such a machine will harvest in a day.

Irrigation is carried on quite extensively here, but the source of a great part of the water supply is ordinary or bored wells. Some farms have twenty-five or thirty wells, and at each well is a wind-mill. The wind blows almost invariably from the west, every afternoon, and the number of revolving wind-mills seen over the level plains of the Sacramento Valley is astonishing. They are as thick as the chimneys in a city, and when they are all in motion, hundreds of them in all directions, the sight is quite novel to an Easterner. An ordinary good supply of water is had at a depth of less than twenty feet, but let the well be carried down fifty or sixty feet and a source of water is found that is inexhaustible, the size of the bore or the quantity pumped up not having the slightest effect upon the clearness or the supply of the water.

The dust, which to Californians must almost get to be a part of their living before the season is over, is a source of great annoyance to a wheelman who has much walking to do. The roughly worn rubber tire raises a constant cloud and the taste and smell is very offensive, but there are counter odors that are really very pleasant. The dried " life-everlasting," that is very common among the foot hills, gives off a most delicious perfume, and there is constantly being wafted by the winds to our nostrils another scent so sweet as to be almost sickening. What the source of this perfume is I could not ascertain, for there was no shrub or bush in blossom to give off such fragrance, but a farmer told me it was the leaves of the laurel, a bush that is very

common in the mountains. Crush these leaves and the
smell is far from sw.eet; but diluted by the air it may, perhaps, be different. At any rate there is something in the
hills and mountains of California that constantly throws off
a perfume that is most pleasant to one breathing so much
unpleasantly scented dust.

From the plains, as soon as the feed dries up in the
summer, the cattle are driven up into the mountains, where
vegetation is much fresher, and there they remain till fall.
After making the journey once or twice the cattle start off
of their own accord for the mountains when the feed gets
scarce on the plains. This has the effect to diminish the milk
supply among the farmers, as I found out to my sorrow,
for many was the large farm-house at which I asked in vain
for a bowl of milk.

Californians delight as much as do the Mormons in camping out. It is the custom, after the harvest is over, for the
farmer to lock up his house, take his whole family up into
the mountains and stay for weeks. Many times a day I
met these parties going or coming; and taking an early
start some mornings I passed men and women lying on the
ground under their wagons wrapped up in blankets, sound
asleep, the silent running machine not disturbing them in
their slumbers In fact everywhere, at the Big Trees, in
the Yosemite, and by the roadside, along the route, everybody seems to be living out under the sky. It must be a
delightful life, for the ground is warm; there is no dew, and
by the side of a nice, clear, cool brook, where the fishing
and hunting is good, the enjoyment must be great. I really
wanted to stop with many a party I saw thus situated.

My appearance in Sacramento after a twelve days' trip of
three hundred and eighty miles in the Lower Sierras was, to
put it mildly, peculiar, and the attention I attracted from

every one was rather disconcerting to a modest man. My shoes had become so worn and torn, that the different pieces of canvas had to be tied together with strings in order to keep them on my feet. My stockings were little better than leggings — feet all gone — and what there was left of the uppers was very holey, in sharp contrast with the almost sole-less condition of my shoes. And the trousers,—well, not to mention one knee torn out and the other sewed up in a bunch, the part most intimately acquainted with the sad-dle would make a very good crazy-quilt pattern. A piece of black silk taken from an old skull cap, a portion of a pair of overalls, and a part of a pair of merino stockings were all sewed into the inside of the trousers to strengthen them, and as the different pieces wore through it left a garment of many colors, and I felt constrained to face every one. Had I brought the heavy corduroy buckskin-seated trousers, in-stead of leaving them at Denver, on account of their weight, I should not have been thus left at the last of the journey in such a deplorable condition, but a traveling wheelman who does his own tailoring whenever occasion suddenly requires, behind a stone wall or clump of bushes, or after he was dis-robed at night, cannot stop to do a very nice piece of work even if he could. It is needless to say that my first business on reaching civilization, was in a clothing and shoe store.

I had ridden from Milton that day, a distance of sixty-seven miles, and although I had eaten two hearty meals dur-ing the ride (and a hearty meal for a hungry wheelman means a good deal), yet at five o'clock, when I reached the hotel, I was half starved. At this hotel, the instant you are seated at the table a waiter on one side of you reels off: ' Beef-steak, pork-steak, mutton-chop, fried tripe, corned-beef, pork and beans, fried liver and onions, bacon, and pot-pie," with a rapidity that classes him as a gastronomic ; and another waiter on the other side, the instant you have given your order says, " tea or coffee ? " so quickly that you really believe he is about to pour from the large steaming pots which he holds in his hands, both the tea and coffee all over you if you did not respond instanter.

Before the square chunks of sugar have had a chance to dissolve in the coffee, the first waiter has returned, not only with what you have ordered, but with lots of other stuff, and as there is not room enough on the table for all the various dishes, he piles them up in a semi-circle around you, two or three layers high. I rather liked the way they had of doing business in that dining-room. Once or twice during the first meal I dug a hole through the breastwork, but at a nod the waiters quickly filled it up again, preventing my escape in that direction. I liked the place, first-rate, and so I stayed there two days — not in the dining-room, but close by. I had considerable writing to do, and thus I simply vibrated all the next day between the desk and the dining-room. It was immaterial what I ordered at the table, everything tasted so good, and so much tasted that same way. In short, I ate as never a wheelman ate before, and as this particular wheel-man will never eat again, under the same circumstances. I have forgotten just what the various dishes were that sur-rounded me at the beginning, during the progress, and at the latter part of the supper siege, but I remember distinctly that fried liver and onions were the last to enter the list and that in a few hours, they were, like the " Bloody Sixty-ninth," the last on the field and the first to leave it.

That night I had not been abed long when, in my dreams, one of those watchful waiters, seeing something troubled me, came to the bedside with an armful of liver and onions, sim-ply that and nothing more, and as he placed the dishes around on the bed in that same semi-circle, he took care to heap them up in the center of the circle so that I could hardly see out. Although such a task at first weighed heavily on me, I soon lifted the burden by devouring each dish in turn, but scarcely had I drawn a sigh of relief when another waiter appeared, more heavily loaded than the first, with the same, liver and onions, simply that; but I said I didn't want any more. Still they came, piling the dishes around and above me in an immense semi-circle pyramid, and the more I tried to do my whole duty as a wheelman by stowing away the monotonous meal before me, the more solid grew the foundation of that pyramid. But there was no escape. On all sides of the bed were those wasteful waiters filling the room, and hovering about with dishes piled along up both arms and upon their shoulders, until I seemed to be in the center of a great amphitheater of dishes of liver and onions. Even then I should not have become discouraged at that, simply that, but out in the hall there was plenty more. So, much as I dislike to acknowledge defeat, I was finally induced (but it took a deuce of a long while) to stop eating, and, in sudden awakening, throw up the whole business, liver, onions, and all.

Once more taking the train, which was ferried across the water at Benecia, the twelve heavy cars and monster locomotive not making the slightest depression of the boat, I finally reached San Francisco, the turning point on the trip. It may not be uninteresting to give the boys a few notes in regard to the cost of the journey in time, money, and muscle. The stock of muscle is of course decidedly larger than at the beginning, but the amount of flesh is about fifteen pounds less, which was all lost on the first month or six weeks. My stomach has given trouble twice, both times when after long, hard riding for many days, I ceased all work and tried to appease a ravenous appetite by eating enormously. I succeeded, both in satisfying my appetite and myself that even a

wheelman's stomach can be overloaded when he stops riding
for a few days. The water, of which I have drank very
freely everywhere, excepting across the plains, where there
was but little to be had, has caused me no trouble. Three
pairs of shoes have been worn out, and the feet of twice as
many pairs of stockings.

The distance on the wheel has been 3,036 miles, that on
the cars about 1,800, and in climbing up and about Pike's
Peak and the peaks about the Yosemite, nearly one hundred
miles more, so that the entire distance traveled has been
nearly, if not quite, 5,000 miles. The cost has been $120.
This includes repairs to machine, new clothes, and repairs of
old ones, and every expense whatsoever.

It is a curious fact, curious to me at least, that on both the
other bicycle trips I have taken, one of 500 hundred miles
down through Rhode Island and Martha's Vineyard, and the
other of 1,200 miles up through the White Mountains, the
cost per mile of distance traveled should have been so nearly
what it has been on this trip. It is within so small a fraction
of two cents a mile that I feel confident one can travel on a
wheel, in almost any part of this great country, for nearly
the same price. And it would be almost ungrateful to the
machine now not to say a word in its favor, for I have a feeling of affection towards this Columbia Expert, that is akin
to that felt by an equestrian for a strong, able horse that has
carried him safely over so much country.

Before I started on this trip the machine had carried me
3,000 miles, into mill flumes and mountain passes, and had been
put to as severe a test as it is possible for New England roads
and a Yankee rider to place upon it. It was the manner in
which it stood the test that inspired confidence to give it a
harder task, and the manner in which it has brought me here
is now known to the reader. The trip into the Yosemite

THROUGH THE SEQUOIA'S HEART.—(*Page 141.*)

was the severest strain ever put upon the machine, and, in fact, the rider; but the wheel I think would have come out in a whole condition had it not been for that butt end of an eight-penny nail. As it is, the expense of keeping the machine in good repair for three years has been less than five dollars, or one-thirteenth of a cent a mile for distance traveled.

The time taken to accomplish this portion of the trip has been one hundred and ten days, so that the living and traveling expenses combined have been but little over a dollar a day.

And now that the turning point in the journey has been reached, and as this is a " true relation," as our forefathers used to say, of the common-place adventures of a wheelman, there is only one more little incident that needs to be told, if it need be told at all, and that is in regard to a bottle. From the start I have carried one. Many cowboys and ranchmen thought the tool bag was a liquor flask, but the little bottle above mentioned was carried in the knapsack, and everywhere the knapsack went the bottle was sure to go. That bottle and the Yosemite were the two objects, great and small, that kept my spirits up during the thousands of miles, and many of them weary ones, that we traveled together. The prime motive of the journey was to see the Yosemite and carry that bottle of liquid to California. The cork was not even drawn during the entire journey, and yet that liquid had a wonderful power in keeping my spirits up. In fact, a glass of California wine has been the only alcoholic stimulant thus far drank. The object of carrying a bottle of liquid so far and not even smelling of the cork may seem to some foolish on my part, but had the liquor being used sooner the object sought could not have been accomplished, which object was to get some mixed liquor, some " 'alf and 'alf," and carry

11

it back to Connecticut.   The object was partly accomplished to-day.

Last fall, while riding along the rocky shoes of Nahant, I filled a small bottle with water from the Atlantic Ocean. To-day I emptied part of that water into the Pacific Ocean near the Cliff House, and now I have a bottle filled with water taken from the Atlantic and Pacific Oceans, and in the bottom of the bottle are some pebbles and sand, the former from the Atlantic, the latter from the Pacific.

And to-day, standing on the extreme western limit of the Great American Continent, I make obeisance to the good wheel by whose aid I have now accomplished the wonderful and laborious yet delectable journey!

CHAPTER XVII.

With the Veterans.

A BICYCLE is of little use in the city of San Francisco, that is, in the city proper. The horizontal streets are too roughly paved and the perpendicular streets are of course unridable. It may be exaggerating the case a little to speak of the streets as being perpendicular, but many of them are nearer that than they are level. The city is full of hills, such as Telegraph Hill, where there is a beer garden in the shape of an old castle, and Nob Hill where Flood, Stanford, and other California millionaires have built some of their fine residences. A cable line of street cars runs over these hills, and it is quite a treat at first to take a ride upon these cars. They go noiselessly up a grade that often rises one foot in three, as steep as the Mount Washington Railroad, and yet the speed of the car does not slacken in the least, either going up or down, the rate being somewhat faster than horse cars. Unlike the dummy or grip-car in Chicago, which has a train of three or four cars, these have only one car attached, which is often crowded to its utmost, but should the grip lose its hold on the cable the car can be instantly lifted off its wheels on to runners that would prevent the car sliding down the steep grade at a very dangerous speed.

The cable, the power which moves the cars, runs along under the center of the track entirely unseen, and the grip, a flat, iron beam, in the center of the dummy, slides along in a slot in the center of the track, and by an ingenious contrivance grasps or lets go of the running cable at the will of the gripman. The power is communicated to the cable by running it over grooved wheels at a central station in the cable car line, which is often three or four miles long. In the rapidity of transit, this system on a level is a great improvement upon horse cars, and in surmounting these long, steep hills, where horse-power would be utterly useless, it works equally well.

But to return to the bicycle. In going out to the Presidio, a government reservation, west of the city, a mile or so, and to the fort which stands just at the Golden Gate, I found excellent roads, and so on, all the way to the Cliff House, which is four miles out on the shore of the Pacific; but the drifting sand caused a few dismounts. Strange as it may seem, this sand is the cause of great expense to the people here. It drifts like snow, covering up fences, houses, and in time blocking up thoroughfares if left undisturbed.

On the way out I passed square miles of sand hills that were being blown by the westerly winds into heaps and drifts thirty or forty feet high. And one of the petty annoyances from the sand is the dust that is constantly filling every nook and corner of stores, shops, and dwelling-houses. The trouble from flies is as nothing compared to the evil which housekeepers have to endure from their greatest enemy, dust. There is something about this California dust that is more penetrating than Eastern dust, for the pedals on the machine would in other places remain in good running order for several weeks after cleaning, but here they get gummed up in a very few days.

A most novel attraction at the Cliff House is the sea lions that swarm all over a mass of rocks out in the ocean, perhaps a hundred and fifty feet from the cliff. Here hundreds of these growling, snarling animals crawl up out of the cold waves, floundering over each other in search of a warm place to sleep in, and disturbing other slumberers, thus creating a constant uproar. The grounds and flower gardens about the residence of Adolph Sutro, of Sutro Tunnel fame, are certainly very pretty — the most beautiful I have seen — and the situation, just back of the Cliff House, and higher up, is a very fine one.

After a short trip across the bay, by water and rail, to Alameda, the Saratoga of California, all interest was lost for awhile in everything else in the growing excitement attending the Grand Army Encampment. To one who had been so long in coming across the continent, the sight of those who had so recently left Connecticut was a real pleasure, and I keenly enjoyed looking at fellow Yankees, especially into the faces of those from Hartford. But it was a great disappointment to see Connecticut unheralded in the grand procession except by a small banner belonging to the New Haven Post. The colors that should have made the forty members from Connecticut who joined in the procession distinguishable in the thousands of other marching veterans, arrived an hour after the parade was dismissed.

The Avenue, which one here soons learns to know means Van Ness Avenue, is a fine broad street, just suited (as it is not a business street) for the easy formation of a parade, and the sight of the marching and counter-marching regulars, the State militia, and the ten thousand veterans, many of these carrying large silk flags, taken in connection with the scores of playing bands and drum corps, altogether, was very inspiring. Certainly the streets and buildings of San Francisco were never so gayly and handsomely decorated, and there never were so many people here.

It was interesting to see the faces of Generals Sherman and Logan as they stood up in their carriages reviewing the procession, nearly opposite the Palace Hotel. Sherman's keen eye noted everything. He frequently pointed out some veteran or banner in the procession in his quick eager manner, and seemed as anxious as a boy not to let anything escape him. He acknowledged the cheers and shouts of the passing veterans by little short, quick nods, keeping his head going and eyes winking almost continually, only occasionally waving his hat a little, which he held down at arm's length most of the time. Sometimes a veteran would leave the ranks to grasp his hand, but not very often, and if a number came at once he would waive them off with an impatient gesture as if the thing that pleased him most was to see them keep marching, marching. Every action of his was quick, active, and almost nervous, and the only time I have seen him do anything slowly was at the pavilion one evening, when he followed Commander-in-Chief Burdette around the floor with a lady on his arm during the grand march preceding the dancing. Then he was obliged to go slow. His photographs flatter him only in one respect, and that is his nose. The end of his nose is larger, fuller, redder, than it appears in his photograph, and curves at the end like a beak.

General Logan stood in his carriage almost the antipode of Sherman. Logan was slow, graceful, smiling, saw the procession pass in a calm sort of a way, and took no particular notice of anything in it but once. He replied to the hurrahs and yells of the veterans by slowly raising his black flat brimmed hat, bowing gracefully and smiling, and replacing his hat on his head.

The regulars marched by in splendid form, without so much as turning their eyes to the right, but the militia could not resist the temptation to look at Sherman and Logan, and their lines were very wavy in consequence. The veterans simply straggled by, cheering and yelling in squads or singly, just as the spirit moved them. Some Grand Army of the Republic officer, arrayed in glistening uniform and riding a fine horse, would come sailing up with his face and body as immovable as a statue, when suddenly becoming aware of the presence of these generals the officer would unbend, turn his head on a pivot, bow and smile his sweetest, but in nine cases out of ten these supreme efforts of the officers were all lost on Logan, for he was gazing with earnest look at the line of veterans.

A stout, full bearded man left the ranks and walked firmly up to Logan, grasped the hand that was always ready, and said, in a low, trembling voice, "God bless you." And I know from his looks he felt a good deal more than he said. Another rather timid man came from the ranks and shaking Logan's hand, said: "I can't help it," and walked off, hanging his head, as if he had done something foolish. Then another came rushing up with a wild glaring look in his eyes, and shaking, and yelling "Twenty-second Ohio," was off again with the moving mass. Up ran another, and, shouting the one word "Chattanooga," as Logan gave him a hearty shake, was gone.

And so it was throughout the whole review; no matter whether they came singly or whether whole companies left the ranks in a body, and made a rush for the carriages, Logan's hand was always extended, and a "Glad to see you,"

or " Yes, that's so, boys," made the old veterans feel happy;
for only when Logan was shaking, as fast as he could, a score
of uplifted hands, did his black eyes flash, and look as if he
really was, as he said he was, glad to see the crowd of com-
rades pushing eagerly toward him.   Once a great burly
six footer, crowded up, and extending his broad hand eagerly
shouted, "Touch her, God Almighty, touch her."   A veteran
who had been irrigating a little too freely, stood for quite
a while in front of the carriage, and as the old soldiers
tramped by he would call their attention, in a maudlin way,
to the personage he had in charge by saying, "don't forget
John."   But it was plain to be seen there was no danger of
that.   Then another one came up with a demijohn, and,
pouring out a glass of water and spilling twice as much all
over himself, said, "Drink with me, Gen'al, if you never
drink again," and the general did.   Then when he joined in
singing "Marching Through Georgia," all the ladies in the
windows on both sides of the street waved their handkerchiefs; but when a little raggamuffin, during a lull in the
yells and shouts of the veterans, rushed out in front of the
carriage, and called for "Three cheers for Black Jack," he
failed to get them.   It certainly required considerable
patience on Logan's part to be shaken and almost yanked
out of the carriage, as he was several times, but he bore it
with good grace, and replied to the hundreds of questions
and salutations as pleasantly as possible.

Again at the concert at the pavilion he was heartily ap-
plauded as he came in and took his seat, and while the ten
thousand persons present were clapping their hands, cheering and yelling "Logan, Logan," he sat perfectly still, looking straight in front of himself with that same far away
look in his eyes.   As nothing less would satisfy the audience
he finally climbed upon the stage, when with one accord

the thousand singers present showered him with flowers and bouquets. This time he seemed to be somewhat discon-certed and blushed as the bouquets hit him in the breast and face and knocked his long straight black hair all over his eyes. Still he bowed and bowed, and jumped down and took his seat as soon as possible. His manner certainly wins the admiration and respect of the average American.

A day's trip to Monterey on the cars is sufficient to see the beautiful grove of live oaks there and to view the old town and bay. The Hotel Del Monte is a magnificent structure, and the floral display about the hotel, in the court in the rear, where there is a garden of an acre of the most brilliant flow-ers imaginable, and many more out in the grove, this makes the whole place the most delightful resort I have seen. The beach is strewn with the bones of whales, and in places they are thrown up tons of them in heaps. I saw one curiosity hunter lugging off a vertebra that must have weighed fifty pounds. The waves would occasionally float a jelly-fish closely up on the beach, and we finally succeeded, two of us, in holding one of these quivering, slippery masses of living matter from sliding back with the waves, but wet feet was the price of the prize. Some of these masses of jelly that are about the shape of a scalloped summer squash, are nearly as large as a tub, certainly larger than a half bushel.

The water on the coast here is too cold for comfortable bathing, and hot salt water bathing is advertised everywhere, but to any one who has enjoyed the surf anywhere on the Atlantic coast the idea of swimming in a tank of heated salt water is not very attractive. For all they have no winter here the cost of fuel is greater, if anything, than where the climate is more severe. Coal costs more per ton, and is de-livered to families in fifty pound sacks. Fires are comfort-able every day in the year, and sealskin cloaks are seen in the streets all summer long. Why they don't have more big fires in San Francisco is a wonder. Acres of frame dwellings and business blocks are here, a strong wind is always with them, and after four or five months without a drop of rain it naturally seems as if the buildings must be as dry as tinder. But they tell me the red wood, which is the chief building material, does not burn very readily, as there is very little if any resin. The thing they dread most is a thunder storm. A good lively earthquake is barely noticed, and the people walk along with the ground trembling and shaking under them, and the occurrence is hardly mentioned, but let an ordinary thunder storm pass over them and it is the subject of conversation for weeks. The week before I reached here a thunder storm occurred that in New England would hardly be noticed, but here it startled the whole city, and was the occasion of many an animated discussion among the natives who still gather in little groups upon the streets to express their various opinions regarding the phenomenon.

CHAPTER XVIII.

Monterey and the Geysers.

M Y trip to Monterey, which was mentioned in the last chapter, was made in connection with an excursion arranged as a part of the Grand Army of the Republic programme. I was very glad the ride was taken on the cars, for the last fifty miles was over a section of country that strongly resembles in appearance the sage bush and sandy deserts of Wyoming and Nevada. The prospect of traveling over such roads on a wheel does not stir up in me such an enthusiastic determination to undertake their passage as it did two months ago, and the chance of meeting Eastern people on the train was quite an inducement to go by cars; but a bicycle is just the thing with which to visit the Geysers. The knapsack on this trip was left behind, not because of any inconvenience that it causes, for the longer it is used the better I like it for carrying the amount of baggage necessary on long tours, but the knapsack is the occasion of so many questions, it is such an advertisement, that whenever it is possible on these side excursions it is left behind. But although I started out wearing trousers and dressed otherwise in ordinary clothes, and entertaining the idea that I should not be so publicly bored as usual on this journey because of my ordinary appearance, this impression proved to be a false one as soon as I took the ferry for Oakland.

Every one on the boat seemed to know the machine and rider, and on a boat or train it is the same everywhere. Why they knew the machine will be explained shortly, but a few words first about being bored by so many questions. It is not because of any reserve I feel in regard to imparting information about this mode of traveling across the country, to any one interested in such touring, for four or five years ago I asked just such questions of Professor Williams of Brown University, on his return from his European bicycling tour, and whenever any one on the road or at a private house asks questions I feel only glad to answer them; but let any one on a ferry boat, at a station, hotel, or any public place commence the usual string of questions — and this string never varies from one end of the country to the other — then a crowd of listeners quickly gathers around, each one in the audience eager to ask the same or some question the others have not thought of, and it becomes disagreeable in the extreme.

The machine became known in this manner. The enterprising agent of the Columbia machine here, with a manner that he must have imbibed from Chinatown, it was so childlike and bland, and with an eye to business which I did not see him open, asked permission to " fix up the machine a little, cement the tire on good," or something, and the next morning the machine was covered with Grand Army of the Republic decorations, a big placard citing its history hung upon it, and the whole affair placed on the sidewalk in front of the agent's place of business, opposite the Palace Hotel, to be viewed by the thousands of people not only from California, but here from all parts of the country during encampment week. So that is the reason why machine and rider are so well-known in this vicinity, better known perhaps than in any other part of the country outside of New England.

The ride of three hours to Napa was a delightful one, across the bay to Oakland, then a few miles on the cars to Vallejo Junction, across the bay again, and a few miles farther by train to Napa. After stopping over night there with a new-made friend, I started out up the Napa valley in the cool of a pleasant Sunday morning. The roads were excellent and the country pretty thickly settled for California, but very few persons were stirring about, and the quiet and peaceful appearance of everything was in pleasant contrast with the noise and excitement of the past week in the city. Calistoga, ambitiously named the "Saratoga of the Pacific," on account of a few mineral springs, and a hotel that wants custom, was reached by noon, and it was twelve or fifteen miles farther before any hill climbing to speak of was neces sary. Then it all came together, about seven miles of it.

It seems strange, in passing through as much unsettled or newly settled country as I have, not once being obliged to go without food for more than six or seven hours during the day, that now, in this old inhabited part of California, I should not be able to procure a mouthful of food for eleven hours, but so it was. It was partly my fault though, for I had ridden thirty-five or forty miles, and it was two o'clock in the afternoon before I thought of being hungry, and then the hill-climbing commenced, and the farm-houses were minus.

It was nearly six o'clock before Pine Flat, five miles up the mountain, was reached, and during the last two or three miles I could not walk without staggering sometimes, and often stopping to rest, I was so faint. But a good meal of eggs and venison fixed me all right, and the next morning the summit was reached without much trouble, and only six

miles of coasting remained.   But such coasting ! The grade
is not as steep as in some parts of the Yosemite route,
Priest's Hill, for instance, on the Big Oak Flat route, but the
road is much narrower and decidedly more crooked.   It
twists around the sides of the mountain and runs so close to
the edge of precipices two or three hundred feet high, that
it must make one's head swim to ride round these turns in a
stage.

Clark Foss, the celebrated driver, who owned this route,
and was one of the twenty-five different men in different
places who drove Horace Greeley on the ride when he prom·
ised "to get him there in time " (every one who ever came
to California has heard the story ; it is the worst chestnut
ever perpetrated, but they still retail it), died about a year
ago, and his son, Charlie Foss, now drives the six-horse open
wagon.   For three or four miles I was in constant dread of
meeting the stage coming up, and had I done so on some of
those oxbow shaped curves in the road, where there is not
a foot of space on either side of the hubs, between a ledge
of rocks and a precipice, the result can well be imagined.
The stage suddenly appeared around one of these very
curves, when but a few seconds before, I had been thrown
off upon my feet by a rock in the road and was walking,
but although I was told I should hear the stage coming, I
did not till the leaders' heads appeared around the ledge of
rocks, not ten feet ahead of me.   But for striking the rock
in the road, I should surely have been coasting, and the re·
sult would have been, in all probability, I should have gone
over the edge, or the horses and stage would have done so.
Then what a volley of questions was fired at me by the
dozen passengers aboard.   The driver stopped, and for five
minutes it seemed as if everyone in the stage was talking
and asking questions, all at the same time.   Some of the

passengers had seen me before and knew of the trip, and as the stage disappeared around the curve with the gentlemen waving their hats and the ladies their handkerchiefs, and all wishing me good luck, the pleasant impression left with me will long be remembered, not only for the good feeling shown towards me, but because our meeting on that sharp curve at one of the most dangerous points of this dangerous mountain road might have terminated so differently and perhaps disastrously.

Only once did I come near having any trouble with the wheel. In crossing the numerous dry creeks that run down the steep sides of the mountain, the road makes horse-shoe curves, descending rapidly down to the creek and then rising as sharply on the other side. In coasting down into these curved gullies, one has to get his feet back upon the pedals pretty lively in order to climb up the grade on the other side without dismounting, but once the wheel slowed up quicker than I expected, and before my feet were back on the pedals, the wheel turned straight across the road and rolled slowly to the edge of the precipice. I took one look down, my heart leaped into my mouth, and I sprang out of that saddle backwards quicker than I ever did before in my life. It was undecided for a few seconds whether the machine would go over the edge with or without me, but after balancing there for a year and a half, as I remember it, I got the best of gravity and finished the ride down to the geysers in safety.

The distance from Napa, fifty-five miles, could easily have been made in a day, had I had a good meal in the middle of the day to work on ; but as it was, I saw all there was to see in an hour, and after resting another hour was ready to start on before noon.

Those who have visited the geysers lately, and also saw

them a dozen or fifteen years ago, tell me the springs are not
nearly as active now as they were then. I certainly was
disappointed. It is surely a queer place up that narrow
little cañon, with the different colored rocks — red, green,
blue, yellow, and white ones — all crumbling down in one
confused mass into the little stream of scalding hot water
that runs down through the cañon. The sides of the cañon
were sizzling and bubbling over with little hot springs, and
the steam that escapes from the holes was sickening. It
smelled like eggs that have passed their prime. Once I
poked some of the crumbling stuff down into one of these
little vent holes, and the creeping steam spitefully blew the
hot sand-stones in my face and eyes. I pushed a stone a
little larger than my fist into the most noisy hole, but the
escaping steam barely moved it. Years ago, they tell me, a
rock as large as a man could lift, would be thrown out of
this hole with considerable force. The witches' caldron, a
boiling pool of lead-colored water, not now over five or six
feet in diameter, is the most active of any of the springs,
but there is nothing that can be called a spouting geyser in
the whole cañon.

The ride down to Cloverdale, seventeen miles, was greatly
enjoyed, for the grade was just steep enough to coast, but
not to make dangerous riding, and there certainly was something very novel about gliding safely along in the wheel
track close to a ledge of rocks, with a yawning precipice
within a foot of the other wheel track, and the road winding
around projecting points of rocks, and in and out along the
side of the mountain, and yet with a grade so gentle that
the wheel kept on quietly without the use of a brake. The
mountains were so bare of trees that the fine views were un-
obstructed, and one could look down the winding valley and
see points in the road that he would eventually reach in that

OPEN-AIR TAILORING. — (Page 157.)

quiet, easy manner, always without the use of any power either to accelerate or retard the speed of the wheel. Yes, a trip to the geysers on a bicycle is well worth taking, but it is the riding and sight-seeing on the way that pays, and not the geysers. With a barrel of water, a few barrels of lime, and a little coloring matter, one could almost discount the geysers in their present activity.

The ride down the Sonoma valley, and to the point where wheelmen are obliged to take the train and ferry over to San Francisco, was through a level country and over excellent roads, and an average speed of six miles an hour was maintained throughout nearly the whole of the ninety miles of the return trip. California is over twenty-five times as large as Connecticut, and I have only seen a small portion of it, but to say, as most Californians insist, that what I have seen is a beautiful country, is certainly drawing upon the imagination to a great extent. The roads are dry and terribly dusty, the grass is dead, the streams all dried up, and the only green objects to be seen, as you look across the country, are the trees and grape-vines and occasionally a few acres of shriveled-up corn. And these are covered so thickly with dust that the color underneath is hardly discernible. To one accustomed to the refreshing showers of the Eastern States during the summer, which render the verdure so luxuriant, the dry, dead, dusty appearance of almost everything from the tops of the mountain peaks to the rocky bottoms of the dry creeks and rivers, is anything but beautiful. It looks as if the face of nature needed washing. But let one imagine the hills and mountains covered with rich, green grass and bright-colored wild flowers, as they were only a few months ago, and think of the streams and rivers brimming full, or imagine the hundreds of acres of grape-vines I have seen, loaded down with their dark, rich fruit, and he can

12

easily see that California has been and will soon be again, a most beautiful country through which to travel. We see California at its worst in August.

"Do the fleas trouble you any? We are eaten up alive with them," said an Eastern lady to me one day. My experience in Colorado with mosquitoes was sufficient, it seems, for the fleas here have troubled me very little, but they are a source of great discomfort to most travelers, and even the old residents. Persons going out for a walk will sometimes come back covered with them. The pleasure of an evening's entertainment or social call is often sadly interfered with by the presence of a flea in a lady's underclothing, and a clergyman here was once seen to suddenly leave the pulpit during service and rush for his study, and afterwards explained to some one that he had to go out and "hunt a flea," but that was not the one that "no man pursueth." It is said that some California genius has invented a flea-trap, but I hear of no well-authenticated instance in which the flea was captured.

Distance traveled on the wheel, 3,200 miles.

O pleasant was my visit in the city of the Golden Gate that it was with some regret that I left San Francisco and took the electric-lighted steamship *Columbia* for Portland. It was certainly very fortunate for me while there to make those side excursions to Monterey, to the Geysers, and to other places, and yet have the pleasure each time of returning to a good home, while so many Eastern people were cast upon the friendless hotels. This pleasant refuge was at the residence of Mr. A. B. Crosby, formerly of Rockville, Conn., into whose family I was most cordially received, and will always be remembered as a bright spot in my wanderings.

The excitement of encampment week and the excursions taken prevented my making the acquaintance of many wheelmen, but I found Mr. Cook, who took such an unfortunate fall at the Hartford races last year, Chief Consul Welch, Mr. George H. Adams, and several others, all gentlemen, as, it is almost needless to say, is the status of the great majority of wheelmen everywhere. There were a great many New England people among the five hundred or more passengers aboard the steamer, but the only Connecticut people I found

were from New Haven and Birmingham. Still we were
quite a distinguished company. The large frame, the bald
head, and smiling face of ex-Commander-in-chief Burdette,
the empty sleeve and gray head of the newly-elected Commander-in-chief Fairchild, Governor Robie of Maine, Professor Williams of Brown University, my tutor, in the sense
that his delightful account of his European trip first set me
wild to be a bicycle traveler there, and many other intelligent
ladies and gentlemen helped to form a party that cheered
and happily waved their handkerchiefs as the iron steamer
left the wharf, turned about, and passing through a fleet of
ferry-boats in the harbor, glided out through the Golden Gate,
and into a bank of fog and a gale of cold raw wind.

How different from what I anticipated. When climbing up
to the Big Trees and into the Yosemite, through the hot sand,
the suffocating dust, and under a blazing sun, how I looked
forward to this ride on the Pacific. In place of the dry and
barren country covered with dust, I pictured the broad ocean
of bright blue. Instead of hours of raging thirst I looked forward to the time when it would be "water, water everywhere,"
and plenty of ice water to drink. When I was so tired I sat
right down in the road in the dirt, with the sun pouring its
rays down, and the air so stiflingly still that the sweat ran
down my whole body clear to my ankles, then I thought how
nice it would be sitting on deck in an easy chair, with the
cool breezes making the bright sun feel just comfortable.
How cosy it would seem, and how I would rest, take the
physical rest I had so well earned, and the mental rest that
would result, with nothing in the blue sky or the smooth
waters to cause the slightest mental action. I would just be
lazy and do nothing but eat, lay around on deck and dream
and sleep. After so many months of constant sight-seeing
and hurried thinking, the prospect of a chance to remain in-

active, mentally and physically, for a while, seemed like paradise to me. It was the prospect of this delightful sail on a smooth ocean, under a perfectly clear sky and bright ·sun, that induced me to buy the excursion ticket at Salt Lake City, and it was in anticipation of this voyage that my spirits kept up climbing into the Sierras. The thought of seasickness never entered my mind, and if it had I should have scoffed at the idea of my being sick if others were. All this and more I anticipated.

What I realized is this and a great deal more. As I said, we went out through the Golden Gate into a bank of fog and a gale of cold, raw wind. The sound of the fog horn at the entrance of the harbor, which I had heard so many days and nights during the past three weeks, was the only thing to indicate that we were not a thousand miles at sea. But that mournful sound soon died away, and when the fog occasionally lifted afterwards, it showed us that we were indeed out of sight of land, upon an ocean I had so innocently supposed was pacific. How much misery I saw there, and how many times I wished I had kept on from the Geysers and ridden up to Portland on the wheel! I could have done it and reached there as soon as by boat, but I did not want to miss the delightful sea voyage. No, I would not then have missed it for all the world. But I would now.

The fog and cold wind made the ladies' cabin the most comfortable place, and for a while the piano and the strong voices of the many veterans on board singing their familiar songs made the time pass pleasantly, but before dark the trouble began. About ten o'clock I went below, thinking I was fortunate to even secure a clean bunk in the bow of a boat where the state-rooms were all taken for two weeks ahead. My bunk-mate, a fine old gentleman from Kansas, had already turned in, but he came crawling out from his bunk, saying, "I can't stand this any longer." I did notice the boat lifted things up higher and let them fall lower than it did during the day, but I felt all right. "O, I stayed here too long, I guess," said my friend, as he started for the round box of sawdust near the bunk. A gentleman in the upper bunk had been leaning out of his bed, intently but quietly looking down in this same box for some time, but this doleful remark of my bunk-mate seemed to suddenly touch his sympathetic nerve, and they mutually, and at the same time, cast away all bitterness in the same small box of sawdust. My friend's head, which was the lower of the two suspended over the box, and which was scantily clothed with gray hair, received a shampoo of a variety of ingredients, but he scarcely minded this in his haste to get away, and I undressed and went to sleep after a while, notwithstanding the place was full of men apparently tearing themselves all to pieces during most of the night.

Yes, I slept some but not as soundly as I have done, for the seventy-five sick men down there occupied my thoughts some. And after a while I got the notion into my head that the boat would not go down into the trough of the sea so far if I held myself up a little, so I did. When the boat went up, up, every nerve in my body tingled, and I felt a prickling sensation clear to the ends of my fingers and toes, and the higher up the boat went the stronger was the nervous action. But I did not feel sick. Then when the boat went down I straightened out stiff and rigid in order, if possible, to hold the boat. Although I saw it did not make much difference with the boat whether I tried to sustain it or not, yet I could not relax my muscles sufficiently to rest easily. But in the morning, before I could get washed, I found out what sea-sickness was, but only to a slight degree, and for an hour or two.

Lying out on one of the benches on the upper deck with the cold, raw wind blowing into his pale face, was a young gentleman of thirty, with blue eyes, but a face so smooth and fair that he looked much younger, another Bartley Hubbard, if I ever pictured one. He had been stripped of the blanket he had brought up from the hole of misery, where it seems he had spent the night near me, the steward saying, as he took the blanket, "he must go below to lay down," but rather than do that he lay shivering in the wind. I had found it impossible to keep warm, even by pacing the decks, and, contrary to rules, had robbed my bunk of its blankets and was walking about covered from head to foot in the warm wool; but it did not take long to tuck that living representative of the leading character in "A Modern Instance" up warm with my blankets, and when the steward came again to take them, Bartley said the captain, or some fellow with a uniform cap, gave them to him. Watching my chances I soon had another pair about me, but Professor Williams, with heavy underclothing and overcoat, was unable to keep from shivering, and so forcing those last ones upon him, I successfully committed a third burglary without being detected, although the steward came to me afterwards and wanted to know "who was carrying off the blankets." I said I had taken my own on deck, but truthfully replied I did not know whether any one else had taken theirs or not.

Bartley was unable to go down to supper, and after I had brought him some tea and crackers we enjoyed the sudden change in the faces of many of the lady passengers, as they sympathizingly patted him on his feverish cheeks, called him "little fellow," and asked if he was thinking of his mother, and then were told he was thinking of his wife and children at home. They didn't pat his cheeks again after that. After we had waited till everybody else had turned in and he had flatly refused to go below, under any consideration, we laid down together on the deck, near the middle of the boat, and slept warm and well all night with the cold wind blowing across our faces.

The first afternoon out the beds were made up on the floor of the ladies' cabin before three o'clock, and the bustling stewardess said to a spinster. among others: "Come, take your bed now if you want to be sure of it." The spinster hesitated, before all the gentlemen then in the cabin, and looked shy, but the stewardess repeated the request with impatience, almost, when the maiden lady replied in a low, complaining voice, as she looked at the gentlemen present: "Why, I don't want to go to bed now." She felt relieved. however, when she found it was only to claim the bed by placing baggage on it.

The same afternoon I was talking with some lady friends, where the deck was rather crowded, when I heard, just behind me, the voice of this same kind, but business-like stewardess, saying, "Come! out of the way, little boy," and turning around to see who the youngster was I saw that whoever he was he had suddenly disappeared, and that I was the only person in her way. The ladies, who had just a moment before expressed admiration for the manly effort that it seemed to them was necessary to make such a trip as I had, now smiled, in fact all did, everyone within hearing, and no one laughed heartier than the "little boy."

And what an appetite I expected to have from sniffing the salt sea air all day, when, in reality, after that short season of personal disgust with the inner man in the morning, I got sufficient nourishment by sniffing the boiled-vegetable air every time I passed the ladies' cabin door. The very sound of the gong was nauseating. and what in the world that young fellow wanted to go around through the different decks whanging away eighteen times a day, and calling on us to go down and eat, when the thought of doing so was more than sufficient! Apparently, from the sound of the gong, it was eat, eat all the time; but I doubt if many did more than go through the form of eating. I did not eat more than one square meal out of the eight on the boat.

Forty-five hours after we lost sight of land the boat stopped and floated around in the fog among a lot of buoys, and soon after got across the bar and steamed up the Columbia River to Astoria, and a short time later to Portland. The whole voyage was a cold, foggy, uninteresting ride; the sun never shone once; but on the boat the experience to me was new, and disagreeable as much of it was, I am not sorry for it. Still, very few of the passengers will take that trip again. We were still further disappointed in finding the atmosphere along the river very smoky, and after stopping over night at Portland, a city finely built, but like San Francisco, with a Chinatown in the very heart of it, we took the train, or most of the boat party did, at 3 P. M., and went slowly up the south bank of the Columbia River.

A bicycle is some bother in traveling on the cars, for where they run such long trains as they do on all these trans-continental lines, and consequently have so much baggage to load, the machine is the last piece to be taken aboard, and as it is always at owner's risk I often have to hand it up as the train is starting, and then jump on myself, rather than leave it to be left, perhaps. The steamship company would neither take it as a part of the one hundred and fifty pounds of baggage allowed every passenger nor allow me to care for it, and I had to ship it by freight, still at owner's risk, at an anticipated expense of three or four dollars, but when I saw it unload on the wharf at Portland, among a lot of horses and truck wagons, I thought the owner was running a great risk of having it smashed by leaving it there any longer, and so I walked away with it, asking questions of no one. Whether the owner took too great a risk by so doing is still unsettled.

The ride up the river by boat, with a clear atmosphere, must certainly equal in grandeur that up the Hudson, but the smoke was too dense to see across the water and we could only catch a glimpse of the shadowy outlines of the high mountains on either side and see for a few seconds the beautiful little waterfalls coming down over the rocks. Then again it was rather aggravating to hear the roar of the river as we stopped in the night at a station somewhere, and to go out and see the ghost of what must have been a magnificent sight by daylight — some great falls in the river.

I have seen and heard just enough of this country to wish to make another trip, but it should be taken four or five months earlier in the year; and other mistakes can be avoided. What there was in the trip to the Geysers to cause it I can't think, for the roads were smooth (no such pounding as there was riding through Illinois), but the result of that trip has been another eruption, not at the Geysers, but upon me. Where there is the Devil's kitchen, the Devil's gristmill, and lots of other articles of furniture belonging to his satanic majesty, it is certainly a devil of a place for a wheelman to visit, but in going there I did not look forward to any such outcome of the trip. And that is just what is the matter with me now. I can't look forward to the unpleasant results. In short I have boiled over again, and as a result of these eruptions I shall carry back with me as a souvenir of the trip, many miniature craters of extinct volcanoes.

CHAPTER XX.

At Shoshone Falls.

HY don't you stop off at Shoshone and go down and see the falls? They are only twenty-five miles from the station," said one of the Union Pacific officials with whom I became acquainted at Denver. This was just at dark the next . night after leaving Portland. I had forgotten what little I knew of those falls, excepting their name, and had no idea of going so near them on this trip, but I left the train at 3.30 the next morning, and about sunrise started out due south. "I suppose there are ranches along the road," said I to the stage-driver at this end of the route. "No, not one; and you can't get any water till you get there," said he. So with a bottle of water, which did not last much more than half the distance, I rode along over the slightly undulating lava beds, which are mostly covered with a few feet of sand and with sage brush, but which occasionally come to the surface in broken masses of dark brown, perforated, metallic sounding rocks.

It certainly was not a very interesting ride of four or five hours, for jack rabbits in great numbers and an occasional gopher were the only living things I saw, and in looking

across the same level, treeless country, far ahead, I had
begun to wonder where the Snake River could possibly be,
when suddenly I heard the roar of the falls, and came to
the edge of a cañon perhaps three hundred feet deep. The
rocks of this cañon, from top to bottom, are composed of
this lava, and it is formed in layers from twenty to thirty
feet thick, looking as if the lava had, at different times,
overflowed the country to that depth, which it really had.
But what was my astonishment when I found, on inquiry,
that these layers in some places number as many as thirty,
and that their depth in many places was several thousand
feet.   For instance, the Columbia River, which I had so
recently seen, has cut its way through lava beds three and
four thousand feet thick.   And this is not all.   These im-
mensely thick beds of lava not only cover the entire surface
of Idaho, but also of nearly the whole of Oregon and
Washington Territory, and parts of California, Nevada, and
Montana.   When it is stated that the entire surface covered
by this lava is not less than two hundred thousand square
miles, forty times as large as Connecticut, one can only
faintly comprehend the statement, and many may not believe it; but the fact remains.   And to me the thought that
I had been allowed to ride over a portion, a very small
portion of this lava that ages ago burst out through some
immense fissure or great vent in the earth's surface, this
thought alone paid me for the hours of thirst endured.
The simple fact that I have seen this lava bed has left on
my mind one of the strongest impressions of the whole trip;
an impression, if not exactly taken on ·dry plate, yet that
was left on a very dry pate.   Still no one need to come out
into this country to see the effect of some ancient eruption.
The hills at Meriden, Conn., and East and West Rock at
New Haven, as well as Mount Tom near Holyoke, Mass.,

hills that I have climbed and ridden over since the bicycle enlarged my means of traveling, these are all lava formations.

There is a fine view of the cañon, looking up the river towards the east for a couple of miles as you go. Then a zigzag road down into the cañon, and half a mile below are the falls. The ferry is just above the falls, and I had to wait some time there, before the ferryman, at the hotel just below the falls, on the opposite side of the river, saw me. The ride across in a leaky row-boat — there is a cable ferry-boat for the stage — with broken oars and oarlocks, only a little way above the cloud of mist, was not the safest one I have ever taken, but with my wheel lying flatwise over the edges of the boat, we crossed all right and I had soon climbed out upon a projecting point in the precipice below the hotel, and obtained a magnificent view of the falls, which are but little inferior to Niagara, far ahead of any other falls I have seen in the West.

Snake River flows down through the cañon with scarcely a ripple, until at the falls it is broken up by half a dozen or more of rocky islands, and after plunging into pretty cascades for a short distance, it leaps over the cliff, which curves in a little, and falls two hundred and ten feet down into the cañon, there not far from six hundred feet deep. Although the perpendicular fall was greater by fifty feet than at Niagara, the volume of water is less, but there is the dark cañon above and below the falls that adds greatly to the impression one receives. Eagles were seen soaring around in the skies in almost every direction, and on a huge boulder just above the falls in the middle of the river, was a nest of young ones being fed by the parent bird.

After spending three or four hours there, I crossed the river again, and climbed up out of the cañon and started back. I took a larger bottle filled with cool spring water

— the location of that spring, as well as many others in this Western country, I shall never forget. I can, in imagination, see them now, almost every one of them. The water, of course, got warm, and before dark I had drained every drop of it. There was no riding after dark, and for miles I pushed the machine along in the sandy rut, thinking of little else than that tank of ice-water in the station I was trying to reach. I might mention, as an instance of how similar situations recall mental impressions, that in crossing the plains from Laramie, the song of "Tit Willow" was continually running through my mind, and for days I could do nothing to rid myself of what came to be very unpleasant, but after reaching California I scarcely hummed the tune once. I was not troubled with the song at all after leaving the sand and sage brush, but with the first return to the sage brush, the tune I had not hummed or thought of for weeks came back, pursuing me with all its unpleasant monotony — the smell of the sage revived it.

About an hour after dark I lost the wheel tracks, and but for the clear sky and north star, should have had some trouble in getting back to the station. As it was I laid the machine down and commenced feeling around in the sand with my hands for the ruts, and wandered about so long I even lost the machine. There are patches of ground, of an acre or more in extent, entirely free from sage brush, and it was in crossing one of these, where there is no bushy border to the sandy road to make its direction discernible in the dark, that I got into trouble. But I found the wheel tracks after a while, and soon after the wheel, and was very careful from that time to keep the wheel from turning out of the rut, for I had to feel the rut with the machine, as I could not see it. It was after ten o'clock when I reached the station, and no lights ever shone brighter in the distance than did those of

Shoshone, and that ice-water, as I poured it down at intervals all night, till the train arrived at 3.30 next morning,
served to quench my thirst in the manner I had anticipated
for so many hours. Thirsty and tired as I was, I felt fully
recompensed by the sight of Shoshone Falls, without visiting
the upper falls, situated about two miles up the river. The
machine has acquired the distinction of being the first one
to visit this place of interest.

At the terminus of the Oregon Railway and Navigation
Company's line at Huntington, I went into the baggage car to
get the machine. "$3 to pay on that," said the baggage-
master. As I had traveled over 1400 miles on the Union and
Central Pacific railroads without being charged a penny for
the machine, this charge for one day seemed to be rather exorbitant, and I said so. "Well," said the baggage-master
very confidently, "I can't help that. It is $1.50 on the other
division, and the same on this." I told him to give me a
receipt, if I must pay it, for I should try to get it back from
headquarters. That he did not like to do, for whatever I
paid him he intended to "knock the company down for it,"
and the receipt would come home to roost, so he compro-
mised by throwing off one-half, which I paid. On the other
side of the depot, the Union Pacific's Oregon Short line came
in, and that was the first and last charge made for carrying
the machine till I reached Baltimore, where the Penn. Railroad Company's price is one-half cent a mile.

After waiting all day at Pocatello, where I put in five or
six hours of good sleep on the platform, on the shady
side of the depot, with the knapsack for a pillow, I reached
Beaver Cañon, on the Utah Northern Railroad, at three A.M.,
and before daylight slept an hour or two more on the floor
of the waiting-room, near a stove that was really comfortable,
for the nights were quite cold up there. I had lost so much

sleep the past week, I could lie down and take a comfortable nap anywhere I could get a chance. The two nights on the boat, it may be remembered, were not accompanied with many hours of sound repose. The first night out of Portland, I talked with friends on the train who were to return home by the Northern Pacific, till. late, and then I wrote till after one o'clock. After that there was not much rest sitting bolt upright, for every seat in the car was taken. The next night it required more force of will to stop off at Shoshone than anything I had done during the trip, for these reasons : I was going towards home, after four months and a half of constant traveling away from it. That thought alone made me very happy,

 and I could not bear to be delayed even for a day ; and besides, I had laid down with four seats all to myself even before dark that night, with the intention of having a good long night's rest. But I did not want to miss any great sight so near as that to my route, and so I took short naps all night till three in the morning, for I did not want to be carried by the station. The next night I took the train at the same hour that I left it the previous night; and thus I had had only one good night's sleep in over a week, when I started out due east early in the morning, Aug. 22d, for the Yellowstone.

Distance on the wheel, 3,251 miles.

PERILS OF CAÑON COASTING. — (*Page 174.*)

CHAPTER XXI.

In the Yellowstone Park.

EXT morning I left Beaver Cañon, taking some luncheon along with me, and it was well I did, for there was no place to get food, and I saw no one all day. But the roads were excellent, level, and running through some beau-tiful meadows, with hills on either side covered thick with pines. There were many streams to ford, though, and taking off my shoes and stockings so often was the cause of much delay. It was the first delay of this kind during the trip. However, I reached the Half-Way Hotel sometime before sundown, after riding fifty-five miles, and was obliged to stop there, for the next ranch was twenty miles farther on.

This hotel is a log hut, with rows of tents on the sides, for sleeping-rooms, and is situated close to Snake River, a splendid trouting stream, the hills in the rear being covered with heavy timber. About dark nearly a dozen passengers arrived in the stages bound for the Yellowstone, and the sleeping apartments were taxed to their utmost; so when the bar-tender offered me a bed with him, on the ground, in his tent, or bar-room rather, I was glad to accept it. Drinks were twenty-five cents there. The next morning

13

one of the horses that had been turned out the night before, was found with a great chunk of flesh torn from his shoulder, and his haunches and other portions of his body badly clawed up. The drivers said it was done by a bear; and that was as near as I came to seeing one on the trip.

The second day I came to Snake River Crossing, which at this point is about two hundred feet wide, and too deep for a forty-six inch wheelman to ford without removing his trousers as well as his shoes and stockings. I had started out ahead of the stages, which had several lady passengers aboard, and supposed I had plenty of time to get across before the stages reached the ford, and so I should have had but for the fact that the water here was too deep for me to carry trousers, shoes and stockings, knapsack and bicycle all at one trip. I had waded once across, through water so cold it made my legs ache, and so deep that it wet a certain short, thin under garment that persisted in dropping down after being tucked up under my blouse out of the way, and had got back into about the middle of the stream when I heard the stage coming down through the woods. Trousers, shoes, stockings, and knapsack had been carried across, the machine still remained to be taken over, and the one to do it was standing waist deep in the water of an icy river, undecided which way to turn. The temperature of the water would not allow of much delay, even were I inclined to wait, and so dashing and splashing through the water as fast as the soft, sandy bottom would admit, I crawled out and laid down on the grass behind a convenient tree, near the machine, curling up and covering myself, though my good intentions were practically unfulfilled by the short garments I then wore. But as good fortune would have it, the lady passengers waited to ride in the second stage, and the men in this one laughed well at what appeared to them uncalled-for modesty on my part in retiring so expeditiously behind so slight a shelter.

Coming to another smaller stream soon after, I hoped to avoid further delay by riding with a spurt down into the water and across, as I had done many times before under similar circumstances, but the pebbly bottom was not so firm as it looked, and the wheel slowly came to a standstill in the middle of the stream, while I quickly dismounted into the water, in so doing ripping both inside seams of my nether garment down to the knees. This necessitated more fine tailoring behind some bushes, and, before I had finished, the coarse grass and sticks beneath me had produced in red a very good etching of that immediate section of country; but the sketch soon faded.

The roads all the forenoon were fully as good as the day before, and it was much pleasanter riding through dense pine forests and along fine, cool streams of clear water. I took my luncheon that noon by a spring that flows into the Pacific, and about half a mile farther on took a drink from one flowing into the Atlantic. I should not have known this but for the stage-driver, on whose heels I followed all the forenoon. There was nothing in the appearance of the surrounding country to indicate that I was crossing the back-bone of the continent. During the afternoon I left the stage far behind, and rode for twelve miles through pine forests, over a road that twisted about and pleasantly found its way through where there were the fewest trees to be cut away.

From Beaver Cañon to Fire Hole, the first stopping place in the park by this route, the distance is one hundred and five miles, and of that, ninety miles is as fine riding as any wheelman could desire. That night, long before dark, I reached Fire Hole, after climbing one long, hard hill, and was ready to start out on short trips to see the wonders, but decided to wait till morning. I took a bath in Fire Hole River in water so warm one would know it came from "Hell's Half Acre," or some other portion of the farm, and the stage-driver offered to share his blankets with me, on the ground of course, in a tent. The next morning the first point of interest visited was the Falls and the Grand Cañon to the northeast. The ride of thirty miles was over the same excellent gravel roads, and through the same beautiful meadows, that abound all over this section of country, but there were six or eight small streams to wade, and a mile of steep hill climbing to offset this, and before I reached the hotel a hard shower wet me through and covered the machine thick with mud. Still the sight of Sulphur Mountain, on the way, was very interesting. It is a hill perhaps one hundred and fifty feet high apparently all sulphur, and at its base is a spring perhaps twelve by twenty feet in diameter that has more business in it than all the California geysers, so called, combined twice over. The water in this spring is constantly boiling, rising sometimes to a height of four or five feet. The Upper and Lower Falls of the Yellowstone River, which are respectively one hundred and sixty and three hundred and fifty feet high, are very imposing, but hardly more so than the Nevada and Vernal Falls in the Yosemite, although the volume of water is a little larger. The river rises in Yellowstone Lake, which is in the southeastern part of the park, flows north, and going over the falls plunges down into the cañon.

But the Grand Cañon! It is useless to try to describe it. There is nothing with which to compare it, for there is nothing like it in the world. A photograph may give the outlines in cold gray, but no artist can paint the colors of the rocks. The cañon is nearly two thousand feet deep, but the sides are far from perpendicular, in some places the angle being about forty-five degrees. But as the soft crumbling rocks slide down to the green river at the bottom the different colors are blended together in a most beautiful manner. Pure white, yellow, brown, fire-red, pink, and all the different shades and tints of these and many other colors are mixed up in striking contrasts. I walked down to Inspiration Point and crawled out on a projecting rock, where a fine view is had of the cañon for five or six miles. It certainly is the most beautiful spot I ever saw. Up the cañon, three miles, the Green River leaps over the falls and comes roaring down through the cañon two thousand feet, almost directly beneath this point, and turns a corner two miles below and disappears, while the bright sun brings out the varied colors of the rocks with a most brilliant effect.

The next day a ride of twelve miles to the Norris Geysers, and eighteen miles back to Fire Hole, was over roads not so good, but the coasting down through the fine woods for miles, with the roads full of stumps, required some lively work and close steering. There were no geysers of any account in action at Norris, but plenty of hot springs. In fact, during a frosty morning one can hardly look in any direction in the Park, which is fifty-five by sixty-five miles in area, without seeing steam arising through the trees from these springs, of which it is estimated there are three thousand in the Park.

In passing a party of campers, for the Park is full of campers, and tourists as well, on the way to Fire Hole, I was kindly invited to spend the night with them, and the tent was pitched near the Fountain Geyser. This experience of camp life was just what I had been longing for all summer, and it fully met my expectations. This party of five young men, two of whom, Mr. John B. Patterson and Mr.

Joseph M. Thomas, were Philadelphia wheelmen, were jolly fellows; and after supper, a meal I relished better than any I had had for months, we all went over in the dark to the fountain. Pretty soon some young ladies from another camping party near by came over, and a bright fire was soon burning within six or eight feet of the geyser, which was then a quiet pool of water twenty feet across. One of the young ladies recited a poem, a love story, in really very fine style, the young men sang "Pinafore," "Mikado," and other selections with very pleasing effect, others waltzed on the coarse gravel, and altogether the party were enjoying themselves, when suddenly the water began to boil, and in less than half a minute it was flying up into the air thirty or forty feet. It was certainly a queer sight, the white spray and steam rising high up into the starry heavens, the bright camp fire making the surroundings all the blacker, and a dozen or fifteen persons looking on with bright eyes and red faces, and their forms standing out so distinctly against the black background.

The machine, that night, was, of course, left outside the tent, and a heavy thunder shower not only wet that, but came near soaking us through. There was no ditch dug to turn the water, and it ran down under us as we lay on the ground. But that was part of the fun of camping out.

The next morning we started for the Upper Geysers, but before I had ridden a mile the left handle-bar broke. The day before, while taking dinner with another party of campers, two young fellows tried to ride the machine while I was very busy eating some delicious ham boiled in one of the hot springs, and I noticed the handle-bar began to get loose during the afternoon, and now it came out of the socket. But by slow riding I reached the Upper Geysers, ten miles distant, and during the afternoon saw Old Faithful send a spray of water up one hundred feet into the air once in sixty-five minutes, as regular as clock-work; but there are indications that the time is gradually becoming longer, the force is subsiding. There is more satisfaction to be had from this Geyser than any other, for there is no waiting. Crowds of people are seen going to this place just before the appointed time, and Old Faithful never disappoints them. It plays for about five minutes, and then subsides as quickly as it commenced spouting. This Geyser is in the form of a small volcano or cone, perhaps ten feet high, composed of white, flakey rock.

We climbed up on the white mound of the Giantess and waited hours for her eruption, for there was every indication of it, one sign being a thumping sound beneath our feet, but she failed to make a display till two hours after I had departed next day. This Geyser is a pool of water fifteen feet in diameter, so clear that one can see down into it thirty or forty feet, and so hot it boiled occasionally while we were lying around on the warm rocks waiting. When it did go off, I was told, it looked like a boiling pyramid, sending jets of water into the air 150 feet. When it subsides, which is not for a day or two, it leaves the crater empty to some depth; when it gradually fills up again, and in a week or two, just as it happens, off it goes again. That night the boys sat around the camp-fire, sung, and told stories, but with my thin clothes on I was glad to crawl just inside the tent, cover myself with blankets, and lie there watching the rest, and thinking of the wonderful experience I was having.

The next morning I started back for Fire Hole, riding with the broken machine as well as I could, and saw the Grotto in eruption. This one is a mound six or eight feet high, filled with large holes through which the water spurts in all directions. And the Growler was muttering, too.

This is not much more than a hole in the earth, but the deep, guttural sound that comes forth every few minutes with a gush of hot steam, leaves the impression that it is well named. I might go on and describe the Castle, the Grand, the Giant, and others, — there are seventy-one of these spouting hot springs in the park — but will mention only one more, and that the greatest of all. It is the Excelsior at Hell's Half Acre, an appropriate name, as you will see. It isn't a half acre alone, but an acre and a quarter of water heated to the verge of boiling. The immense caldron is so obscured by clouds of steam that one only obtains momentary glimpses of its surface, but he who has seen it may well speak of it as an outflow from the infernal regions. There is no sight in the park more impressive. The water, boiling sometimes, is about four feet below the banks that enclose it on one side, on which it is continually making encroachments. These banks jut over it from having been hollowed away beneath, and there is danger in going too near, as it is not easy to tell when they will cave in. The whole surface about is made by a lime deposit, and behind as well as before the visitor are these lakes of heated water, from which arise clouds of steam that are colored green and red by the reflection from the water below. This geyser has been known to go off but once, and that in 1882, when it suddenly burst forth, sending a stream of hot water 300 feet into the air, and boiling over such a quantity that it raised Fire Hole River two feet. It played for nearly a week, then subsided, and has since remained comparatively quiet. I wet my feet in the warm water, then started on toward Fire Hole. The paint pots, springs of boiling mud of red, gray, and different colors, are to be seen in several localities.

The roads in many places are black with small pieces of glass, and I saw chunks of it by the road-side, from the Obsidian Cliffs, mountains of black and different colored glass, two or three hundred feet high; but these, as well as the Mammoth Hot Springs, I missed by not going forty miles out of my route. Still, as it was, I saw enough, much more than I can describe.

Reaching Fire Hole, where the only blacksmith's shop within a hundred miles is situated, I found the blacksmith was off on a drunk, so I had to try and fix the handle bar or walk a hundred miles to Beaver Cañon, for my supply of money was nearly gone. But I found something with which to run a new thread upon the handle bar, and getting out the broken piece I screwed the shortened bar in place, and went on my way rejoicing.

The day before I started back for Beaver Cañon a detachment of United States troops were sent out in that direction from the park, to intercept and drive back a party of Indians who were reported on their way from a reservation to hunt in the park. The first day I saw and heard nothing of them, but the next forenoon, when about ten miles from any ranch, for the ranches are fifteen or twenty miles apart, an Indian came galloping up from across the meadow. According to tradition my scalp should have been the first thing he asked for, but instead he wanted to know, in broken English, if I had seen a party of Indians hunting, and asked where I came from, how many miles a day I could make, and the usual string of questions that almost every white person asks, and then he said, "You know my name?" I replied I had no recollections of ever meeting him before. "My name is Major Jim, *Major*," with considerable emphasis on the last word; and with that we parted, and I reached Beaver Cañon without further incident.

Distance traveled with the wheel, 3,505 miles.

CHAPTER XXII.

Through the Black Canon and the Royal Gorge.

NE day's ride by train from Beaver
Cañon through a section of country composed mostly of sand and
sage brush, overlying that same
sheet of lava, and through Mormon cities of eight and ten thousand inhabitants, where they had made the
desert blossom for miles around, brought
me back to Salt Lake City. Here occurred the first rain
that had caused even an hour's delay in my trip since the
middle of May, three months and a half ago. After leaving
Omaha, sufficient rain had not fallen in the eight or ten
States and Territories through which I had passed to dampen
my shirt sleeves, and when I reached the Yellowstone, it had
been so long since I had even felt a rain drop, that the thorough wetting I received there was really enjoyed. But on
reaching Salt Lake City, I was delayed a week by a cloud
burst on the line of the Denver and Rio Grande Western
Railroad, which swept away seven bridges and a mile or two
of track.

I started out and had gone about 100 miles before coming
to the break, when the train was sent back to Salt Lake
City again. As it was in going West, so now in returning,
I was laid under lasting obligations to another Mormon,

for cash on a personal check. This time it was Mr. D. S. Davis, Captain of the bicycle club. Still the enforced delay was not time wholly wasted. It showed me Mormonism in a different light from that in which I had seen it on my first visit. The Mormons professed to me their thorough loyalty to the United States Government, but their actions belie their words. The act of hoisting the stars and stripes at half mast on the Fourth of July does not strengthen one's belief in their loyalty, and to refer to the returning army of Eastern veterans who are daily passing through the city on their way home as a "parcel of blatherskites," as a Mormon bishop did on a public occasion, these and many other instances are daily occurring to show that the Mormons, instead of loving, are beginning to fairly hate the government.

A book published a year and a half ago entitled, "The Fall of the Great Republic," finds many enthusiastic readers here. It prophesies the breaking up of the government in a very few years, and it is only too plain to be seen that the Mormons would rejoice to see the prediction fulfilled. Whether the strong hand of the government will succeed in suppressing polygamy without any serious outbreak here is, to say the least, uncertain, for at times it would take very little to start a riot.

Sunday afternoon I went to the Tabernacle. It was communion, as it is every Sunday with them, I have since been told, and I suppose all the faithful ones were on hand, occupying the front seats, ready to perform their part of the service. At least, it seemed to be the extent of their mental capabilities, to take a piece of bread and a drink of water when it was offered them. A more ignorant, inferior, almost idiotic set of people I never saw. The women, most of them had sharp noses, peaked chins, and a wild sort of look about the eyes. They looked hard. The men, the gray-haired,

bald-headed ones, looked simple and childish, the middle-
aged ones were dull and heavy featured.   There was not a
noble looking woman, or an intelligent appearing man among
them   This description may not hold good of the whole
congregation, for there were probably five thousand present,
the Tabernacle being about half full, but it is a fair estimate
of those in the front part of the house as I sat facing
them.

   The bread was distributed among the vast audience by
eight or ten men who were continually returning to the front
to have their silver baskets refilled, until the stock of bread
was entirely exhausted.   Two barrels of water, however,
was sufficient to go around, although at one time it seemed
as if even this amount would not supply the thirsty multi-
tude.   As soon as the bread was blessed, in a very brief manner, the speaker commenced his sermon, but was interrupted
after a while by a subordinate, who as briefly blessed the
two barrels of water.   How much impression the sermon
made can well be imagined, when you consider the aisles full
of men passing bread and water, children chasing each other
about and pulling hair, scores of babies squalling — I never
saw a greater proportion of small children in any congregation — and people passing out.

   But in the midst of all this hubbub, the preacher suddenly
stopped.   A young man, perhaps 30 years of age, stepped to
the front and without any apparent embarrassment, asked
the congregation to deal leniently with him, that he would
do better hereafter, but he was guilty of a sin which the
church considered next to that of shedding blood, and so on.
Then his nearest relative made a motion, that as his nephew
had thus publicly confessed his adulterous actions, he, the
nephew, should be turned out of Zion's church, and a sea of
uplifted hands forthwith excommunicated him.

As this young man holds a high office in the church, and is the son of George Q. Cannon, who is still a fugitive from justice, for practicing polygamy, this prompt action of the church may at first seem meritorious, but the licentious reputation of the son has long been known, and it is thought this public confession and prompt excommunication was for effect upon the large number of Eastern people present. But if so, the effect was hardly favorable, even if it was hoped it would be. The whole service was most irreverent and disgusting. Not a head was bowed during prayer, the little children and even babies were allowed to grab for the bread as they would for sweetmeats, nearly all drank the blessed water as if they were really thirsty, and in the midst of this easy free lunch sort of a meeting, with a discordant sound of crying babies, a prominent member of the church unblushingly confesses his guilty actions in a very business sort of a way! It is all a poor burlesque of the religion of civilization.

Not wishing to miss the scenery along the line of the Denver and Rio Grande, a railroad which traverses a section of country through which there are very few wagon roads, and in the most interesting portions none at all, I saw the bicycle handed into the baggage car, and with a pasteboard box as large as a small trunk, filled with pies, cakes, peaches, and grapes, I settled down into a seat in a cozy, narrow-gauge car with the firm belief that another washout on the way would not, at least, reduce me by famine. But accustomed as I have been for months to an appetite of the most ravenous kind, it now surprised even me, to say nothing of the blank astonishment with which the other passengers must have noticed my almost hourly devotion as I bowed over that monstrous pastboard shoe-box. And so, notwithstanding I had laid in rations sufficient for an

ordinary week's trip, when another washout did occur, and
lengthened the ride of thirty-three hours from Salt Lake
to Denver to fifty hours, the stock of eatables fell far
short of the end of the journey.

But what shall I say of the scenery ? Unlike the dreary
hours and days of sand and sage brush along the lines
of the Union and Central Pacific Railroads, here is nothing monotonous. At the outset, the ride for hours is in
a southerly direction, along the base of those grand old
snow-capped mountains, the Wasatch range, until the
snorting little engine turns up a cañon, and, puffing like
mad, pulls the train of twelve cars as far up the grade as
it is possible even for such an ambitious little locomotive
to do. Then two more eight wheelers are attached, and
the three engines take us to the summit in a short time.

The hills along this cañon are covered with shrubbery,
which has already begun to show the approach of winter by
changing its color to the beautiful hues so common in New
England in the fall. If there are long stretches of desert
on this line, we must have passed them that night, for the
next morning, soon after breakfast, an observation car was
attached to the rear of the train, and we all, or as many as
could, took seats in a car that is like an ordinary one with
the top taken off above the window sills. And then commenced the ride through the Black Cañon. The train ran
rather slowly, so that we all had a good opportunity to view
the cañon without that hurried feeling so commonly experienced in sight-seeing from a fast rushing train. The dark
colored rocks rise in jagged and broken masses to a height
of nearly, if not quite, two thousand feet on either side of
the Gunnison River, which comes roaring and tumbling
down through this narrow and very crooked defile in the
heart of the Rocky Mountains, and a most interesting part

of the whole ride was the sight of a long train of cars cross-ing and recrossing the foaming river and winding its dark way along through what seemed to be the very bowels of the earth.

Almost every one of us was soon standing, for who could sit still when there was so much to be seen on all sides, and if one imagined these grand sights lasted only a short time, that was where he was wrong, for the cañon is fifteen or twenty miles long, and we were considerably over one hour in passing through it. Then, soon after, came Marshall Pass. Here the situation was just reversed. Instead of groping along in a deep and narrowly contracted defile, where the only outlook was heavenward, now we glided along up the sides of a deep ravine, rising higher and higher, getting a wider and wider view of the surrounding country, until, after twisting around the sides of the mountains, and passing around more horseshoe curves than we ever dreamed of, we finally reached the top of the range of mountains, eleven thousand six hundred feet above the sea. Here, in an immense snow shed, filled with black smoke, we waited for the second section of the train, for it had been divided in climbing this last grade, and then we started down the other side. A locomotive preceded our train, and the second section followed us. Down we went at a lively rate, coming close on to the heels, sometimes, of that single locomotive, which would then dart on ahead out of the way for a time; and looking back we could see the other train rushing close upon us. Sometimes, in going around and down some of those horseshoe curves, we could look out of the window, high up the sides of the mountains, but only a short distance across, and see the passengers on the other train waving papers and handkerchiefs at us as if to hurry us out of their way.

And so we went, chasing each other down grades that made one think of Mt. Washington Railroad, and at times so close to each other that both trains and the locomotive were all within a mile. It certainly was dangerous, but we enjoyed it just the same, perhaps all the more, and, finally, just before dark, we came to the Royal Gorge, a cañon. not so long as the Black Cañon, but with sides higher, more nearly perpendicular, and closer at the bottom, if that were possible. The sides of this cañon are 2,800 feet high by actual measurement. Down through this cañon the consolidated train rushed as if the very devil was after it, the little low eight-driving-wheel engine being on the point, seemingly, of tearing itself all to pieces or jumping off into the rocky river at every sharp curve, and it was all curves through the cañon. At one point the cañon is so narrow that the track is suspended over the river, it being held up by braces overhead, the ends of which rest against the rocks on either side. This was the last of the marvelous scenery, but it was the best; it was grand beyond anything I can describe. One who crosses the continent without passing over the Denver and Rio Grande, misses the finest mountain scenery there is in the country, I think, outside of the Yosemite. It beats Salt Lake City, with its many-wived Mormons and bottle-sucking babies, "higher than a kite."

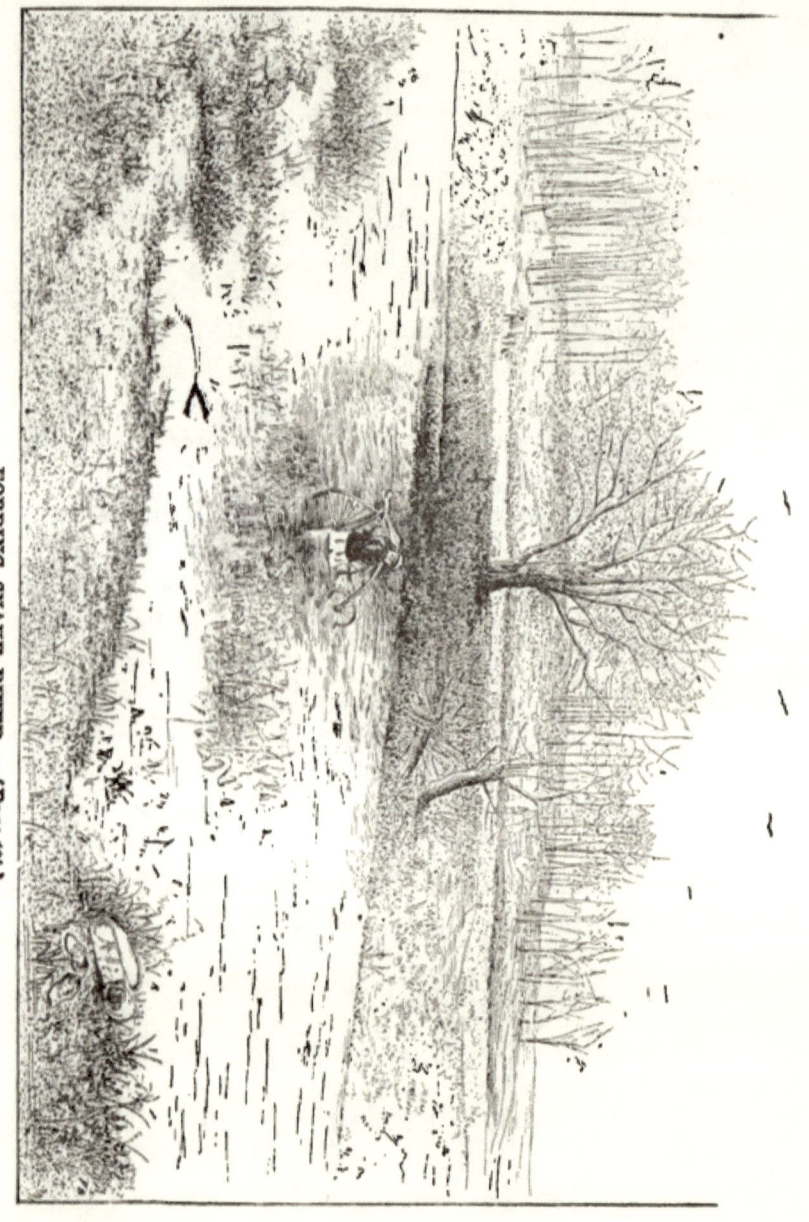

FORDING SNAKE RIVER.—(Page 194.)

CHAPTER XXIII.

A Visit to Prudence Crandall.

REACHED Denver, and went to the bicycle club rooms one evening, meeting Mr. Van Horne, and many other good fellows, but was sorry not to again see Mr. C. C. Hopkins, fancy rider, whose acquaintance I made on my other visit here. The prospect of wheeling across the State of Kansas was not very encouraging, the country being fairly flooded with water, and so I took the train again, and the next afternoon left it at Emporia, a thriving town in Kansas, on the Atchison, Topeka & Santa Fe Railroad, with the purpose of visiting Prudence Crandall Philleo (of almost national renown), at her home at Elk Falls. Here the rainfall had been very slight and the roads were in excellent condition, so that after traveling so many days on the cars and taking no exercise on the wheel, I returned to the saddle with the keenest enjoyment.

But the corduroy knickerbockers, which I then put on again, felt very stiff and clumsy after wearing thinner ones so long, and they will be the last corduroy trousers I shall ever have. The country south of Emporia, for eighty or ninety miles, is a gentle rolling prairie, which looks as fresh

14

and green as in the spring, and the timber and numerous
farm-houses tend to break up what little monotony there is
in the prospect.   But all the enjoyment of the trip was soon
swept away by a drizzling rain which set in on the second
day of the ride, and I was glad to find even a grassy place
on the side of the road to walk on, for in the road the
sticky black clay would clog up under the saddle and entirely stop the wheel.   However, after pushing the machine
along in this manner for eighteen or twenty miles, I was
made glad by the sight of Elk Falls, a town of seven or eight
hundred inhabitants, situated within thirty miles of the
northern border of the Indian "Nation."

The town is surrounded by low hills, and a good patch of
timber is close by, so that the general appearance of the
country is very different from the level, treeless prairie, so
common west of the Missouri River.   Inquiring at the first
house I came to, the man said, pointing to a house west of
us on the brow of a hill, "Mrs. Philleo lives out on that
farm, about a mile and a half from town.   A Mr. Williams
lives with her and takes care of the farm, but she goes
around lecturing some, talking on temperance, spiritualism,
and so on."   I had ridden part way out there, when in
answer to another inquiry, I was told: "Mrs. Philleo, since
she got her pension from New Jersey, has bought a place in
town, and lives next house to the Methodist Church."

So turning about, riding through the place, and going
around to the back door of the house, which was a plain
story and a half, with an ell on the back side, I was pleasantly received by Mr. Williams, a man of 35, with brown
hair and mustache, large blue eyes, and a most sympathetic,
almost affectionate, manner.   "Mrs. Philleo," he explained,
"is at church.   She enjoys excellent health, and it is wonderful how much she, a woman of 84 years, can endure.

Yesterday she wanted to ride over to the farm and see about some things, and before I was ready to come home she started on foot and got clear home before I overtook her, and she didn't seem tired either." Just then Mrs. Philleo came in, and said cordially, "I am glad to see any one from good old Connecticut." As she removed her bonnet, it showed a good growth of sandy gray hair, smoothed back with a common round comb, and cut straight around, the ends curling around in under and in front of her ears; of medium height, but somewhat bent and spare, and with blue eyes, and a face very wrinkled, and rather long; her chin quite prominent, and a solitary tooth on her upper jaw, the only one seen in her mouth.

She smiled with her eyes, and with a pleasant voice, said: "Come, you must be hungry, coming so far" (I had only told her then I came from Connecticut on the bicycle), and she urged the apple pie, ginger snaps, johnny-cakes, potatoes, ham, bread and butter, and tea, upon me promiscuously, and in great profusion. "No; as my grandmother used to say, I never break a cup, you must take another full one. Now do you make yourself at home; I know you must be tired. Why, you have seen enough to write a book. [This, after I had explained more fully the extent of the trip.] When you get home you must write up an account of your journey for some newspaper. [Further explanation seemed unadvisable just then.] Now come into the other room; I want to show you some pictures."

So, talking every minute, we went into the sitting-room, and drawing up rocking-chairs, we sat down cosily together. "I am going to have these photographs of these noble men all put into a frame together. I don't want them in an album, for I have to turn and turn the leaves so much. I want them in a frame, so I can get the inspiration from them at a glance. This is Samuel Coit, who did so much last winter in my behalf, and this is S. A. Hubbard of the *Courant.* This is ———. Why I see you know all of these noble souls. Well, I want to read you a letter he sent me," and she slowly picked out the words of the writer who said, among other generous things, that he would be only too glad to load her down with any number of his books, and would send her a complete file of them. The letter was signed Samuel L. Clemens.

"But," she added, "he has never sent them. Probably so busy he forgot it. I do wish I could see them, for I had a chance once to read part of 'Innocents Abroad,' and I do like his beautiful style of expression. And here is Major Kinney, and George G. Sumner, and Rev. Mr. Twichell. What grand good men they are. And this — you say you have heard him preach! How much I would give to hear that great soul speak," and she handed me Rev. Mr. Kimball's photograph, and several others, every one of which is more precious to her than gold. In this collection also, were photographs of William Lloyd Garrison, Wendell Phillips, and other anti-slavery friends of hers, and I noticed several others of Garrison framed and hung about the house. When I expressed the opinion that the amount of her pension was too small in proportion to the injury inflicted, she said: "O, I am so thankful for that. It is so much better than nothing."

During the evening, the collection was again displayed to a visitor, and it is plain to be seen, the sight of those faces does her a great amount of good. She and I went through them again the next day. After breakfast, I sat down to glance through a book I had seen her reading, "Is Darwin Right," by William Denton of Massachusetts. Soon she came into the sittting-room with a pan of apples, and drawing a low rocking-chair up in front of me said, "Now you must stop reading, for I want to talk," and we talked. In fact, she became as interested in the conversation, and so far forgot herself that, in cutting out the worm-holes from the apples, she once put the worthless portion into her mouth, and munched it thoroughly before she discovered her mistake. The conversation drifted from one subject to another, and on her part it was carried on in a clear, connected, and enlightened manner.

I can only give a few sentences of hers. "My whole life has been one of opposition. I never could find any one near me to agree with me. Even my husband opposed me, more than anyone. He would not let me read the books that he himself read, but I did read them. I read all sides, and searched for the truth whether it was in science, religion, or humanity. I sometimes think I would like to live somewhere else. Here, in Elk Falls, there is nothing for my soul to feed upon. Nothing, unless it comes from abroad in the shape of books, newspapers, and so on. There is no public library, and there are but one or two persons in the place that I can converse with profitably for any length of time. No one visits me, and I begin to think they are afraid of me. I think the ministers are afraid I shall upset their religious beliefs, and advise the members of their congregation not to call on me, but I don't care. I speak on spiritualism sometimes, but more on temperance, and am a self-appointed member of the International Arbitration League. I don't want to die yet. I want to live long enough to see some of these reforms consummated. I never had any children of my own to love, but I love every human being, and I want to do what I can for their good."

After dinner while I was reading — for there is a host of good books in the house — she sat down to copy off a short account of my trip I had written at her request the night before for a local paper, but every few minutes she would stop to talk on some subject that had just entered her mind, and sometimes we would both commence speaking at the same instant. "Go ahead," she would say, or "keep on, I have kept hold of that idea I had," pressing her thumb and forefinger together, and then again she would say, "When you get another idea just let it out." And so two days passed, very pleasantly, for me at least. There was no subject upon which I was conversant, but that she was competent to talk and even lead in the conversation, and she introduced many subjects to which I found I could only listen. At night Mr. Williams's bed and my own were in the same room, and this gave him an opportunity to say of Mrs. Philleo, "I never knew a person of a more even temperament. She is never low spirited, never greatly elated. When things don't go right she never frets." And of him, when he was off at work, she said, "You don't know how much comfort I get from my adopted son. We have lived together nearly four years, and my prayer is that he will grow up a noble man to do all the good he can in this world," and I can add, judging from his conversation, he has a mind so broad and intelligent that he is fully abreast and even a little beyond her in mental growth, and that is saying a good deal. The last thing she said as I left them was, "if the people of Connecticut only knew how happy I am, and how thankful I am to them, it would make them happy too."

Surely she has one of three graces, the greatest of the three, charity for every one. Of strong religious convictions, a thorough spiritualist herself, she respects the beliefs of others, and uttered in my presence not a word ill of any one. The State of Connecticut certainly is to be congratulated that it did not neglect its opportunity last winter. What a shame had this good woman, this great mind, gone to another world without having even that slight justice done it. Very few people in Connecticut realize what a narrow escape they had from a lasting disgrace.

The ride on the return to Emporia was uneventful, excepting that a break in the head of the machine obliged me to take the train sooner than I expected, and after a short stop in Kansas City, to keep on by rail to this place where there are facilities for repairing the break.

At Kansas City I met Mr. C. B. Ellis, dealer in bicycles, and one or two other wheelmen. In meeting, as I have on the trip, many Connecticut people who have settled in the West, it is pleasant to have them all or nearly all express the desire to return East to live, sometime, when they have made money enough. Some place that wished-for event ten years hence, others longer, but all show that the "good old State of Connecticut" occupies a prominent place in their future plans and prospects. It is their ideal of a place to live in. It is mine.

Miles traveled on the wheel, 3,627.

CHAPTER XXIV.

The Triennial Conclave at St. Louis.

EACHING San Francisco in season to witness the encampment of the Grand Army of the Republic, I was quite as fortunate in getting to St. Louis on the eve of the triennial conclave of the Knights Templars. Intending at first to make a stay in the city of but a few days, various causes induced me to lengthen the visit to nearly or quite two weeks, and the chief reason for this was the kind invitation of A. W. Sumner, now proprietor of the St. Louis Stoneware Company, but once an old schoolmate of mine, to remain with him while waiting for my bicycle to be repaired. He and I had not met since we both attended Rev. Mr. Hall's School at Ellington, Conn., nearly twenty years since, and after "Hello, Poggy," and "Hello, Bubby," had come to our lips spontaneously, we talked over and looked back to the time we spent in Ellington with very much the same feelings, I think, that Nicholas Nickleby had when he recalled his experiences under Squeer's at Dotheboy's Hall. Still we bear no ill will against the apple-trees in the rear of the school-house, but think it doubtful if those trees themselves have borne anything since, after furnishing so many switches to be used for our moral welfare and physical up-

lifting. But these reflections were soon forgotten in the
noise and excitement of the week.

The Charity Concert at the fair grounds, the proceeds of
which were for the benefit of the widows and orphans of Masons, was a great success money-wise, but hardly from any
other point of view. The immense band-stand was built on
the inside of the mile track so far out into the field that the
music could scarcely be heard on the grand-stand, which, by
the way, is probably the largest and finest one in the country,
and after the first number had been played the majority of
the eight or ten thousand people who had paid a dollar for a
seat, in addition to the fifty cents admission fee, on the grand-
stand, left it in disgust and gathered out in the field where
something of the music could be heard, besides the cannon
accompaniment, if that part can be called music at all. Seats
were provided for twice the number of musicians that could
finally be persuaded to participate, for many union musicians
refused to play in a concert with non-union musicians, and so
there were many vacant chairs among the performers.

Into one of these seats a press committee's badge made
way for me, and there the noise during the anvil chorus was
fairly deafening. Before the piece was played Gilmore came
over to the anvils on one side of the stand, and rather sternly
placed the men, who wore white shirts instead of the customary red ones, in a different position from the one they had
taken, but as if to soften his orders he said, smiling, "You
are to strike first, you know, but you will do it all right, I
guess." During the performance, as one set of musicians
would play too loud, or to soft, or too slow, or too fast, Gilmore would look sharply at them, and raise his eyebrows
almost to the top of his head, and when the fifty anvils came
in, and the cannons went off, both at first in poor time, it
seemed as if he would fly all to pieces, he had so much to

see to, but after a few beats, and after bending his body sidewise, almost double, and sweeping his arms from above his head down to the floor, he had the thousand performers all playing in very good time. The effect upon the great audience was shown by the way they cheered at the end, and even Gilmore seemed to be well pleased, for he cried "bravo," and bowed to his musicians before he turned about and acknowledged the applause of his audience. When some one of his performers, carried away by the enthusiasm of the moment, proposed "three cheers for Gilmore," he had to fairly yell "hold on, hold on," in order to be heard, and by features and gesture frowned down and nipped in the bud the proposed compliment.

The gate receipts show there were one hundred and twenty-five thousand people in attendance, and of this number I did not see one drunken person. Actually, I have been, many a time, to a county fair in Connecticut where there were not one-hundredth part as many persons present, and have seen decidedly more disturbance and drunkenness. Undoubtedly there were some among this great number who were not sober, but I did not happen to see them and I was around a good deal. It was beer, beer everywhere, and everybody drank it, nicely dressed and otherwise fine appearing women ordering their beer brought to them on the grandstand fully as freely as the men. One hundred and fifty waiters were kept busy all day on the grand-stand alone. Coffee, lemonade, and soda could be had at exorbitant prices, but the price of beer was restricted to five cents a glass by the Brewer's Association.

And in addition to the fact that beer drinking was a question of economy, there was still greater influence brought to bear in favor of beer. It was a very warm day, many were overcome by the heat, but there was no place where one could get a glass of water. I went from one end of the fair-grounds to the other in search of it, and finally was obliged to drink from the end of an iron pipe where they water horses. Water, evidently, is not used here as a beverage. They tell of a Missourian who was knocked off a ferry-boat into the water and was rescued after being in great danger of his life and was asked if he was much hurt, "No," he replied, "thank God, I don't think a drop of water got into my mouth." This is a chestnut out here. Has it got East ?

Some of the members of the Womans' Christian Temperance Union in the Eastern cities, who do such a grand good thing by freely furnishing ice-water to the thirsty crowd at all such out-door public gatherings, might suggest the idea to some of the members of the society in this city with good results. Still, notwithstanding the fact that saloons here keep open day and night, seven days in the week, the number of arrests for drunkenness last year was a little less than forty-two hundred, which is not one per cent. of the present estimated population of the city. It would be interesting to compare this with the percentage of drunkenness in Eastern cities. Here the license fee is $600, and the more I can learn of the practical workings of high license in these Western States, the more I am impressed with the belief that high license must for a long time precede prohibition in large cities, in order to insure any practical, good results.

But even expecting something of the kind, I was surprised at the practical working of the prohibitory law in Kansas. At Elk Falls, where I spent a couple of days so pleasantly with Mrs. Philleo, the same crowd of loungers congregated about the drug stores that are usually seen near the saloons, and upon inquiry, while waiting in the drug store, I was told anyone could get liquor by signing a blank statement.

This statement is filled out by the druggist at his leisure, and gives the name of the disease with which the person is afflicted. The probate judge gets five cents each for recording these statements which are sent to him by the druggists. As I sat there, one poor sufferer passed out from behind the counter where he had probably just disclosed to the druggist the nature of the terrible disease from which he was undergoing inward torment, but which had as yet only shown itself outwardly on the end of his nose. Drug stores have increased three-fold in Elk Falls within a short time, and the increase in other parts of the State is surprising. The probate office has suddenly become a very lucrative position, and judging from the records in this office, Kansas must be the most unhealthy place in the country.

But to return from the subject of temperance to the Templars. For several nights the city was beautifully illuminated in their honor. It is impossible to give a good idea of the beautiful effect of the numerous gas jets used in the illumination. I counted the number of gas-lights upon one of the arches, and found it had 346. Different colored shades were used, and these arches, surmounted with small pyramids of lights, were erected along three or four of the principal streets at the intersection of every cross street. In addition to these large arches were smaller ones extending along on the curbs. The effect, for instance, at the corner of Washington avenue and Fourth street, was like that produced in looking through an immense arbor two or three miles long, completely covered with variegated colored gas lights. Thirty-five thousand gas-jets were used in this manner.

The flambeau battalion paraded the streets on several evenings, burning up a couple of thousand of dollars' worth of fireworks each night, and sending off a dozen or so large rockets at a time, with fine effect, as they marched along, colored lights and a shower of Roman candles adding to the beautiful sight. The trades' display parade was another occasion gotten up for the edification of the visiting Knights, and included a parade of the fire department.

During a break in the procession, I had gone into the exposition building to hear the " Poet and Peasant " rendered by Gilmore's band as I never heard it before, when coming out and crossing over to Franklin avenue, I found the street full of people, all apparently waiting for something. Soon the bell of a fire engine was heard, and in another instant four large gray horses on a keen run came rushing down through the crowd drawing an engine finely decorated with flags and bunting. The crowd opened barely wide enough for the engine to pass, and closed up again, when another engine rushed down the street in the same reckless manner, no one making the slightest effort to keep the street clear. There was something exciting about the affair that is relished by the average American, just as we enjoyed the way those trains chased each other down the side of the mountain from Marshall Pass, but it was dangerous business.

The prize drill of the different commanderies at the fair grounds, and the street parade of the Knights Templar, was a very fine exhibition of what degree of perfection in the different manœuvers can be attained by uniformed men outside of the regular army and State militias. But with me there was something lacking in the procession and the appearance of these bodies of fine looking men. The sight of that procession of veterans in San Francisco was constantly coming up in my mind, and in that there was a something decidedly lacking in this. Here the white plumes, the showy uniforms, the costly banners, the glistening jewels, the elegant regalia, the diamond studded swords and crowns, all this beautiful display of costly equipments to be seen on the streets and in the show-windows, certainly made a finer appearance than anything to be seen at a veteran reunion, but in it there was nothing to stir a man's soul. The sight of a torn battle-flag is worth more to me than all the banners in any Knight Templars procession. The flag cost men's lives, and an empty sleeve has more in it, so to speak, than the finest Knight Templar's uniform in the procession, more of history. of patriotism, and of true religion. "In Hoc Signo Vinces," "Christian Warriors," "Defenders of the Cross," and such mottoes, are here seen on all sides, but "Gettysburg," "Appomattox," "Defenders of our country," are words that are more tangible, and have more meaning in them, to the average patriot certainly.

But this is hardly a subject for a touring bicyclist to get warmed up over. One of the greatest attractions in the city during this month of festivities, is Gilmore's band at Music Hall in the exposition building. The hall is truly what its name indicates. It is built without boxes, and with the stage well out into the auditorium. The auditorium is boarded up on the sides and overhead with narrow beaded strips, which have the musical effect, I am told, of an immense sounding board; and when Gilmore's sixty-five players are all getting red in the face under his energetic leadership, the air is so filled with music that, as has been said, one could cut the music up in chunks and deliver it around the city for little private serenades. Twice every afternoon and twice in the evening, this hall is filled with four or five thousand visitors to the exposition, who during the intermissions wander about the Machinery Hall and other parts of the immense building. For twenty-five cents this exposition is, as it ought to be, the most popular attraction in the West. It is said, however, that, cheap as is the price of admission, over two thousand dead-head tickets have been called for and issued. There is always an army of applicants at headquarters, and the bald-headed secretary seems to have his time thoroughly occupied in writing passes for this omnipresent crowd. But he is an amiable person and performs this unprofitable service with an alacrity and cheerfulness which I have rarely observed in officials who possess the authority to disburse free passes of any kind.

CHAPTER XXV.

The Wheelmen's Illuminated Parade.

THE wheelmen's illuminated parade here, on the evening of October 1st, was a success. It not only surprised and gratified the crowds of people that lined the streets in the most fashionable part of the city, but the effect was beyond what the wheelmen themselves expected. I rode out to the natatorium, about dark, where the wheelmen had already begun to congregate, and it was interesting to witness the transformations in their appearance. One after another came hurriedly in, wearing his ordinary clothes, and disappeared in the numerous dressing-rooms in the building. Very soon out would come an immense green frog nearly six feet high, walking on his hind legs, then came a gorilla, but with an unusual appendage in the shape of a tail long enough for several "missing links"; soon after a great white rooster came strutting about; then appeared the devil in red tights and with wings so broad he had to go sideways through the doors; closely following him was "Cupid" in white tights with nothing to keep him warm (it was a cold frosty evening) but a pair of tiny wings and an eye-glass. "Cupid" is better known to Hartford wheelmen as George W. Baker, who

AN ODORIFEROUS AWAKENING.—(*Page 252.*)

made the wonderful ride from St. Louis to Boston last year in nineteen and one-half days. Many had their faces painted white with L. A. W. across their noses and cheeks in red paint. But I cannot stop now to even attempt to describe the different costumes.

The machines were variously and tastefully trimmed with different colored paper and hung with Chinese lanterns. One machine, or rather three bicycles fastened together and supporting a sort of canopy, was festooned with nearly a hundred lanterns. There were various other designs, and in all there were two hundred riders in line, and probably several thousand lanterns. The ride was over a route nearly four miles in length, and excepting a few blocks, the pavement was entirely of asphalt.

Being at the head of the line, as an aid to the grand marshal, with no duties to perform, and assisted in that work by Mr. H. C. Cake of Clarksville, Mo., and Mr. H. G. Stuart of Kansas City, Mo., I was unable to get a good view of the procession till it reached the exposition building, where the immense crowd reduced it nearly to a single line of walking wheelmen, pushing their machines along as best they could. But the view down Pine street was very fine, where the street for nearly a mile was filled to the curbstones with colored men on the sides carrying torches of red fire, and the middle of the street a mass of moving wheels, burning torches, fantastically dressed wheelmen, and hideous looking animals astride of wheels, and the whole filled in with Chinese lanterns hanging not only from the pedals, handle-bars, and backbones of the machines, but moving along in the shape of trees, crosses, boats, and canopies.

It was such a weird and beautiful sight that it is almost universally acknowledged that of all the fall festivities held here this procession has only been excelled in beauty by that

15

of the Veiled Prophet. And judging only from the newspaper accounts of the night parade of the Boston wheelmen
last fall, this one far surpasses that, which was the first and
only affair of the kind ever gotten up in this country. It
certainly does in one very important particular of a negative
character. There was no molestation of a single rider by
the crowd of hoodlums that followed the parade everywhere.
When it is remembered how, at Boston, bricks were thrown
in the way and sometimes at the heads of the riders, how
sticks were thrust through the wheels, causing innumera-
ble headers, and how finally some of the wheelmen dismounted and engaged in knock-down arguments with the
roughs and drew revolvers on them, it may at least be
placed to the credit of a city that is supposed to be so far
removed in respect to the civilization of the "Hub" as is
St. Louis, that in this particular, as well as in other respects,
the wheelmen have furnished an example that may well be
followed by wheelmen and hoodlums alike in Eastern cities.

Judging from the remarks at the banquet the next evening,
at the Lindell Hotel, given by the St. Louis wheelmen to the
many visiting wheelmen who joined in the parade, the credit
for the great success of the whole affair seemed to rest mainly
upon the shoulders of Grand Marshall E. K. Stettinills and
W. E. Hicks, a "literary fellow" on the *Post-Despatch*, both
of whom, with becoming modesty, tried to shift the respon-
sibility upon the other's shoulders. Hicks has dark hair,
blue eyes, a thin face, small moustache, and is slightly built,
and a little above the medium height. A wiry, active sort
of a fellow, all nerves, just the one to create enthusiasm.
Stettinills, on the contrary, is solidly built, of medium
height, full face, black hair and eyes, small moustache, and
has a sledge hammer way with him that is sure to remove
all obstruction and insure success. One was imaginative,

the other executive, "chiefly executive." One went off like a sky-rocket, the other like a cannon—a good combination, as it proved.

After Chief-Consul Rogers, who presided in a very happy manner, had called upon Mr. Gus Thomas, another literary fellow, to respond to "The Press," and he had done so in a speech that for wit and humor is rarely excelled and which kept the wheelmen in a continual roar of laughter, the presiding officer then said there was in their midst a touring wheelman who had accomplished the "great feat of crossing, etc., etc., etc.," and called upon him to respond. This wheelman had had a Colorado ranchman advance upon him with glaring eyes threatening to put a hole through him, and he did not know enough perhaps to feel afraid; had seen an Indian fully armed and galloping towards him, off on the plains of Idaho near the Yellowstone Park, without having one additional heart-beat, and during his entire trip had carried as his only weapon of defense a dull jack-knife with the point of the blade filed off for a screw-driver, and yet after hearing the account of his trip so greatly exagger- ated, and seeing the eyes of seventy-five or a hundred friendly wheelmen turned suddenly towards him, he trem- bled and turned pale, his breath came and went as if that Indian was after his scalp, he hid behind the back of his chair, he could not think of some things he wanted to say and said some things he did not want to, and altogether presented an appearance that ought to dispel any impression that might be entertained of his supposed courage in going where he has been. He says he had rather wheel another thirty-seven hundred miles than be where he was then.

The Simmons Hardware Company, agents for the Colum- bia bicycles in this city (in whose employ were Messrs. Jordan, Sharps, Dennis, and Smith, and other wheelmen, whose acquaintance I made), had just moved a part of their immense business into a new six-story brick block, which was to all outward appearances substantially built, when one Sunday evening, without the slightest warning, the upper floor dropped and carried with it the five other floors down into the basement, burying and ruining one hundred and twenty-five bicycles and a full stock of bicycle sundries, the walls of the building remaining standing, apparently little injured. This occurred a short time before I arrived in the city, and, consequently, an order for a new head for my machine had to be sent to Hartford; but the delay has given me an opportunity to become better acquainted with the wheelmen, and although at Buffalo, Denver, San Francisco, and especially at Salt Lake City, not to mention other places, the cordial treatment I received made me regret to go on, yet, notwithstanding I have made the longest stay here that I have at any place, I am more loath to leave the St. Louis wheelmen than any I have met, and that is saying a good deal for them.

Distance traveled on the wheel, 3,740 miles.

CHAPTER XXVI.

Through Kentucky.

TOOK the train from St. Louis, after receiving some road routes kindly given by Mr. Harry L. Swartz, to Louisville, Ky. My recollection of the Illinois dirt roads, after a lapse of five months, was too vivid. The result of my encounter with one hundred and twenty-five miles of clay ruts and lumps, had left too many scars behind, and my indignation had not sufficiently subsided from the boiling point, to make me care to wheel across that State a second time; so, after making the acquaintance of a few wheelmen in Louisville, among them Messrs. Thompson, Adams, Allison, and Huber, I started out over the Shelbyville pike.

The pikes in Kentucky are macadamized, the rock used for that purpose being hauled and dumped alongside the road where it is broken up by negroes. It was no uncommon sight to see four or five "niggers," as they are always spoken of there, seated in rows by the roadside in the scorching sun pounding these rocks into small pieces. From twenty to twenty-five cents a perch is the price paid for this rock, and five perch is a very good day's work. The riding, as a general thing was very good, and there was plenty of coasting interspersed, but the many loose stones in the road would not allow very lively work.

Although I did not go through the finest portion of the blue-grass region, it was a very pretty country to ride over, plenty of trees, cool-looking groves, and fine-looking farm-houses set back quite a distance from the road on a knoll, a winding driveway leading to them. Sometimes these farm-houses would have a cluster of tumble-down shanties near them, a reminder of ante-bellum times. All the houses, unless of the recent build, had the chimneys on the outside.

Besides enjoying the ride through this fertile, beautiful-looking country, it was quite refreshing to be able to pass a group of children, quite mature ones, sometimes, without being the object of such facetious remarks as " Get up there, Levi," " Let her go, Gallagher," and so on, words that are always on the tip of the tongue of every white young American all through the West as well as in the East. But no such remarks ever fell from the lips of the colored children. They would open their eyes wide, and grin perhaps, but not a word was said, unless, as it sometimes happened, it was " Good mornin'," or " How de do." Much as I had to regret the ignorance of the colored people — for they hardly ever gave a satisfactory answer to an inquiry about roads and streets — still they never tried to say something smart as I passed by, a compliment that cannot be paid to the white people of Kentucky, or anywhere else.

The first night out I stopped at a farm-house with a widow and a lazy son. The husband had been killed in the rebel army. The next morning at the breakfast table the old lady asked me what kind of bread I had to eat in California. I replied, " Very good, both home-made and baker's." " Well," said she, " my daughter has been visiting in California, and she says they make their bread there in this way : The women take a mouthful of water and squirt it over the flour, and then take another mouthful and do the same, and in this way mix it up. I don't want to eat any of their bread." I explained how the Chinese laundrymen sprinkle their clothes, and suggested that perhaps there was some mistake, but it was no use trying to enlighten a mind that probably, until the war, believed the Yankees had horns and tails.

The bicycle is not in favor in Kentucky. I was obliged to make more dismounts on account of frightened horses than in any section of this country through which I have passed. And not only do the horses and their drivers dislike them, but the women express themselves very forcibly about them. A saddle-horse, left unhitched in front of a house, ran away down the road at my approach, but was easily caught. "I don't wonder he was afraid of the thing. They had not ought to be allowed in the road," said a female voice, with emphasis. The sound came from the inside of the house somewhere, I did not look to see where. Meeting a carriage, in which were two persons, I dismounted, as the horse showed some signs of fright, but it was needless, and as they drove leisurely by the man smiled and bowed to me. "Don't bow to him. I would not be seen bow—", was what I heard issuing in a piping voice from the inside of the dilapidated vehicle. She evidently belonged to the aristocracy — to the same liberal class of females that spat upon Union soldiers during the rebellion.

Toward night I came suddenly upon another saddle-horse around a bend in the road. Saddle-horses are in such customary use, both by men and boys, that it is no uncommon sight to see half a dozen such horses hitched to trees near the school-houses, the scholars riding them to and from school.

This particular horse was hitched in front of a saloon out in the country, and before I could stop he pulled back, broke the bridle, and ran down the road. A man came reeling out of the saloon into the road with a black rawhide whip in his hand, a tall, large-framed man, with full, red cheeks, long face, moustache, and goatee, a typical Kentuckian, drunk, too. "Now you jest take that bridle, and ketch that horse, and bring him back here again, or you'll get a pounden. I am a peaceable man, but I ain't afraid of Christ, damnation, or high water. Now you do as I say," and he walked deliberately back into the saloon, perhaps out of consideration for my humiliated feelings, but probably to take another drink.

Although I was not mentioned in his "little list," from his other remarks I judged he was not afraid of me either, and certainly a Kentuckian who is not afraid of water is a brave man indeed. So quickly mending the bridle with a string, I walked a rod or so, put the bridle on the horse without the least trouble, hitched him, and went on my way. Passing through Frankfort, I went to the north of Lexington, which is situated in the heart of the blue-grass region, and rode on to Georgetown. The term "blue grass" is derived, I was told, from the fact that the grass in that section of the State has a bluish color when it is in seed. The sun, during the middle of the day, was so hot that occasionally I was inclined to lie down on the grass under a shady tree. Once I was stretched out with my head within a foot of a stone wall, and had dozed off almost to sleep, when I suddenly smelt a snake. To one who has handled so many live and dead ones, the scent of a snake is very familiar, and, as may be supposed, I was not long in jumping to my feet. There was no snake in sight, but sure enough out on the road was the track of a snake that had recently crossed, and I felt certain it was

not many inches from my head when I awoke. Judging
from the size of the track left by one I saw crossing the road
a little farther on, this one must have been five or six feet
long.

Reaching Cincinnati on the third day from Louisville, I
had a few moments' pleasant talk with Robert H. Kellogg,
formerly of Manchester, Conn., but now general agent of
Cincinnati for the Connecticut Mutual Life Insurance Company. "Seeing a Yankee from Connecticut will make me
feel good for a week," said he, as I left him.

When I went across Ohio in May, the consul at Cleveland
in directing me to Columbus sent me off into a section of the
State where the roads were miserable, and where I got stuck
two days in the yellow clay. Consequently I never felt like
advising others to follow the misdirections of that consul at
Cleveland. But after traveling so many miles since, and
not being misled by any one to amount to anything, it is curious, upon entering Ohio again, and applying to the consul
for the best roads to Chillicothe, that he, even with the help
of the Ohio State Road Book, should be unable to send me out
of Cincinnati in the right direction. The map that goes with
the road book is a splendid map. It gives every river, all
the railroads, the outlines of every town, the name of every
county, city, and village — everything almost but the roads.
It is large in size, but it is remarkably small in road information, and so of little use to a touring wheelman. At least
the consul and I studied it diligently for nearly half an hour,
and then he decided I must go out to Loveland, twenty or
twenty-five miles, and inquire, just as the consul at Cleveland
sent me to Wellington, and then told me to inquire, just as
any three-year-old boy could direct me.

So the next morning I started for Loveland, but I inquired
before I got there, and found I was going in the wrong direc-

tion, of course. Then I rode across four or five miles of dirt
roads, composed mostly of loose rocks and dust, to another
pike, a splendid one, but at Goshen found I was still going
in the wrong direction; so after six or eight more miles of
dirt roads, I found a pike that leads almost in a straight line
from Cincinnati to Chillicothe. The pikes radiate from the
city as do the spokes of a wheel from the hub, and consequently it is important to start out on the right one, but it
was two o'clock in the afternoon before I found out which
one that was. But it was a good one, especially near Hills-
boro, and the second night I was one hundred and twenty
miles from that useless road book and the friendly but
misleading consul.

Coming, with the help of steam-power for a short distance,
to the Ohio River again, opposite Parkersburg, West Virginia, I rode along up toward Marietta. The roads were
good, running close to the bank of the river which was forty
or fifty feet below, and, with fine farm-houses along both
banks, and trains of cars rushing up and down, the ride was
greatly enjoyed. I kept pace for miles with a stern-wheel
steamer going up the river. The water looked so inviting, I
pushed the machine down behind some bushes next the
river, stripped, and took a good bath. Then I hung the
pocket-mirror against the root of a large stump, left there
by the big flood probably, took the shaving apparatus out
of the knapsack, and had a good shave. This recalled to
my mind where I performed the operation one morning
in the Yellowstone. It was in a pretty meadow between
the Grand Cañon and Morris, and near a pebbly brook.
I had laid the machine up against a pine tree, under which I
was standing, and had just got my face well lathered when
three stages came down the road close by. Several ladies
exclaimed simultaneously, "O, see the bicycle!" but catch-

ing sight of me, with me chin elevated, they murmured something more I could not hear, and went out of sight.

Leaving the machine outside in front of the post-office at Marietta I found I must wait several hours for the next Eastern mail, and so escaping the crowd that in so short a time had blocked the door and filled the sidewalk, I pushed my way out, and rode a mile to the "Mound Cemetery," as it is called, and I believe generally accepted to be the resting place of a part of the nation, the Toltecs of Mexico, who passed from the face of the earth before the Aztecs appeared, who were in turn annihilated by the conquering Spaniards. I had not time to pursue the study of ethnology, but climbed to the top of the big mound, feeling secure there among those quiet folks from the flood of questions that inevitably pour down upon me wherever I stop. But no, a man who heard me inquire the way followed and climbed up the forty-five stone steps only to bore me while I write these words. He could not wait to give the others a chance, those who had waited silently for a couple of thousand years. But the Toltecs have more sense. As I pushed the machine up the steep side of the mound they did not ask me "Why don't you get on and ride?" but I have met hundreds of persons who would not derisively but soberly ask that same question if they saw a wheelman pushing his machine up the side of a house. And doubtless this man would have done the same when I came if he had been where the Toltecs are. (I wish he was.) But he is gone now, and I can almost hear the old Toltec beneath me give a sigh of relief. It may be the wind, though, blowing through the big oak trees that are growing up the sides of the mound.

Distance traveled with the wheel, 4,005 miles.

CHAPTER XXVII.

 BICYCLE excites more attention through Southern Ohio and West Virginia than in any State or Territory across which I have ridden. On one occasion, in Ohio, a district school was dismissed, and the school-master asked me to perform a little for the edification of the scholars. I was climbing a steep hill at the time, in a broiling hot sun, and so declined, but was sorry afterwards that I did so. Crossing the Ohio River at Marietta, and following the north-western pike, east through West Virginia, over a very fair road, notwithstanding the hills, the machine was an object of curiosity to every one. In passing the farm-houses, some one was sure to give the alarm, and in some mysterious way the whole household was instantly aware that the opportunity of a lifetime was at hand, and they were bound to improve it. Out would come "Paw" and "Maw," and four or five children, and generally three or four guests, for the people are great visitors in this section. And after I had passed they would all laugh, not derisively, but because they were pleased. The grown folks really acted childish about the machine.

One morning a little boy on horseback rode on ahead, and aroused the neighbors for miles. On another morning I got started early, and was noiselessly passing the house when the dog, I believe, gave the alarm, and the whole family, nine of them, broke from the breakfast-table and rushed out into the road, the farmer holding a Bible in his hand, with his finger in the place, so that the morning service might be resumed when I was gone. It was a pleasure to answer the questions of all these simple people, but when I passed through the larger towns it was really annoying to be the object of so much interest.

At Grafton, for instance, I stopped on the sidewalk for a minute, and in less time than it takes to write this I was surrounded. Then I moved out upon the curbstone, and instantly the crowd surged into the street and gutter, simply to get in front and look me squarely in the face. Here a reporter, in the form of an elderly gentleman, slightly inebriated, interviewed me, and contrary to my usual feeling when being questioned, I was decidedly pleased this time, and the crowd enjoyed it fully as much. It was only after asking and hearing the answers to his questions over and over again that he was able to put them upon paper, and when I told him the distance I had traveled on the wheel he made a calculation in regard to the circumference of the earth that surprised me, but I said nothing. This is the result of his muddled memory as it appeared in a Grafton paper:

"Mr. Thayer may be regarded as one of the most remarkable men of the age, who has accomplished the feat of traveling more than *half way around the world* on his bicycle. In his modest, unassuming way he informs us he has traveled 4,100 miles on his bicycle since leaving home."

But to counterbalance the annoyance there were many

things about the ride through West Virginia that were pleasing and new.   A very busy branch of the Baltimore &
"Ohar" railroad runs for miles close to the pike, and many
times while I was climbing the long hill the trains would
take a short cut and go through the hill, making the ground
tremble beneath me as they rushed through the tunnel.   The
beauty of the changing foliage was at its prime, the air cool,
and the wind blew the rustling leaves about with a pleasing
noise.   Sometimes I would sit down under a shady tree and
quench my thirst with two or three nice apples (they were
very plenty everywhere) or crack a few black walnuts, much
to the anxiety of the chirping squirrels in the trees, or pull
up a root of sassafras or a bunch of pennyroyal.

I stopped for a few minutes near a pair of bars.   A squirrel came running along on the stone wall to these bars with
something in its mouth, and, jumping down to the ground,
skipped across to the other side, and went on his way along
the wall.   Pretty soon he came back, and in a short time had
another chestnut in his mouth to be stored away with the
first.   As he jumped down to the ground to cross the space
between the walls for the third time, a good-sized rat sprang
out from under a large stone, and chased the squirrel half
way across.   Then the rat went back into his hole and
waited.   I could just see the head peeping out.   Pretty
soon the squirrel came back as big as life, and had got about
half way across when the rat pounced out upon him, and the
squirrel gave one squeak, and was back on the wall again in
an instant.   The rat retired to the hole again with a very
determined look.   I was getting very much interested.   The
squirrel, with more discretion, came slowly down to the
ground with compromising chirps and creeped along, turning
first to one side and then the other, but all the time arguing
the question in his squeaking voice.   The rat came out to

meet him, a few steps at a time, sullen, but settled in his purpose to allow no more crossing on his premises under penalty of his jaw; and the affair to me was getting more than interesting when a small, shaggy dog came running along, in the road, turned, and went under the bars, and the rat went one way and the squirrel the other, without more ceremony.

All this added spice to the trip, especially as I had ridden so many miles through a section of the country where there were neither hills, trees, apples, nuts, sassafras, pennyroyal, nor water — to say nothing about squirrels and rats. Here there was too much water — hundreds of little brooks crossing the road, making unnumbered dismounts advisable. This reminds me of the different remedies wheelmen have of quenching thirst. Some advise taking toothpicks, others pebbles in the mouth, and so on. But somehow I have become accustomed to using water, that is, when I could get it. With the perspiration oozing visibly from every pore in a wheelman's body for hours at a time, it seems only common sense to think that that waste of moisture must be supplied, not by extracting the juice from a wooden toothpick or a stone, but by a liquid in some form or other. When the system is dry it needs water, just as the stomach does food when it is empty. Toothpicks and pebbles may excite saliva in the mouth for a short trip, but as a regular beverage they are of little use.

It is quite common to see three or four kinds of sauce on the table, such as apple, grape, and peach sauce, but it is spoken of as "apple butter," and "grape butter." At one house where I was taking a meal, some one said, "Pass the butter," but that not being quite plain enough, he said, "Pass the cow butter."

The rain drove me into a house one afternoon, and while

waiting there, the brother of the lady of the house came in.
She was a woman of more than ordinary intelligence for
this section, and fairly good looking, and as she sat by the
stove, nursing her baby to sleep, I noticed she spit upon the
floor behind the stove. Humming some tune as she rocked
back and forth, her voice was frequently interrupted as she
expectorated, and for rapidity of fire and accuracy of aim,
she greatly excelled her brother who sat near her. Her lips
were stained and her teeth discolored. Pretty soon her
brother said, "Got any terbacker," and she, without the
slightest concern, pulled out a plug from her pocket and gave
it to him. At two other farm-houses where I stopped the
women chewed, and upon inquiry I find it is a very common habit with the women in this section, as a little boy
said to me, "Yes, some of 'em chew a nickel's worth a day."

One noon I was seated by a table in an old-fashioned kitchen
eating some hot short-cake, that had just been taken from
the open fire-place, when a tall, gray-haired, grizzly-bearded
farmer came in, and yanking a chair away from near where
I sat, he said to his wife, as he sat down, "Where did the
damn Dutchman come from?" Smiling, I answered, I was
a Yankee. "Then you are worse still," said he, and he
muttered something else I could not hear. But after finding
out I had passed through in Illinois the same town in which
their son lived the man became mollified, and after showing
them how the bicycle worked I thought they seemed more
lenient to Yankees than at first.

Hotel-keepers along here show more care for their guests,
in some particulars, than anywhere I have been. One
asked, as he showed me into my room, if I knew how to put
the gas out. This inquiry, although made with the best
intentions, no doubt, rather hurt my vanity, for by this time
I thought I had traveled enough not to look fresh, at least.

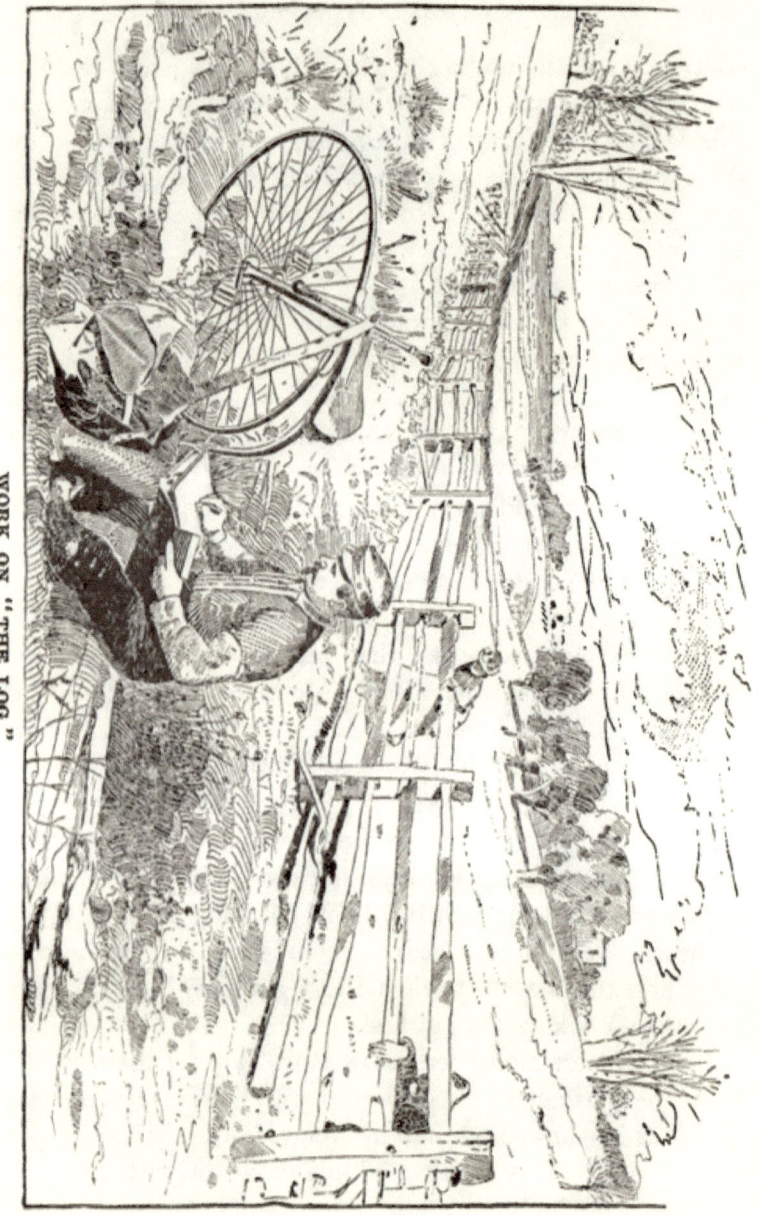

WORK ON "THE LOG."

Another one took me out of my room in the dark to show where the door was that would lead to the fire-escape, which thoughtfulness I certainly appreciated.

Once, at Cumberland, Md., and on the banks of the Chesapeake & Ohio Canal, and the hills, the only impediment to a perfect bicycling trip was gone, and all else remained — the fine mountain scenery, the beautiful foliage, the cool, bracing air, a broad river, a winding canal, and an almost perfect bicycle path for nearly two hundred miles. This charming prospect is in wait for any wheelman who has the good fortune to be at Cumberland in October. I glided along for hours and hours, until I was tired of riding, and yet there was no monotony. The scenes were always shifting.

The Potomac River is very crooked, and the canal follows it closely on the north side most of the way. It is not the tow-path, the path where the mules walk; that is nice riding; that is very poor indeed, but it is the smooth, hard wagon road on the bank of the canal that makes the fine wheeling. Where the wagon road is missing, and this is only for a short distance, there is a smooth foot-path made so by the mule-drivers, and this answers all purposes. Wherever the river does not, the canal hugs close to the sides of the mountain, and so for hours and even days I rode along. On the left the mountains, covered with the various colored leaves, then the canal with the numerous boats moving slowly and silently along, in front a broad, smooth, winding path, on the bank of the canal large shady trees; then the wide, smooth river, on the opposite side the numerous trains of the Baltimore & Ohio Railroad, and then the mountains again. Occasionally the canal would widen into a lake half a mile wide, at other times a perpendicular ledge of rocks on one side and the river on the other would force it into a

16

narrow limit. The ride was most enjoyable, gliding along in the shade and without fatigue for hours.

Occasionally at the locks there was just a little fine coasting, but only a little. The mules on the tow-path made no trouble to speak of, and those in the bows of the boats, with their mouths full of hay, would look out of their little windows and prick up their big ears as they rode by as if they were perfectly contented with their lot: but, when they were taken out to drag the boat and the tired mules along, in their turn, they apparently changed their minds.

At one place I came to a tunnel about half a mile long and started to ride through it, but it soon grew so dark riding was unsafe, so I walked, but before I got through even walking was not very pleasant. I could not even see my hand before me and the nickel on the machine was only faintly visible. The railing that prevented me from walking off into the canal I could only feel, not see, and, altogether, it was the darkest tunnel I was ever in. Had a boat entered the other end of the tunnel before I got there, I should have had to go out the way I went in, but I was soon gliding on as usual.

Leaving the canal at Williamsport, I followed along the road towards Sharpsburgh, just in the rear of Lee's line of battle at Antietam. After spending a little time at the National Cemetery, which is on a hill that commands a fine view of the whole battle-field, and on which, I was told, a part of Lee's artillery was stationed, but out of ammunition, I rode around to Burnside Bridge. Not till I saw that bridge did I fully realize where I was. A picture of it appeared in Harper's Weekly twenty-four years ago, and all those war sketches were so familiar to me, having made a strong impression on my boyish memory, that when I passed a bend in the road, and the three-arched stone bridge came in sight. I felt as if I was walking on sacred ground. More lives were laid down in other parts of the field, I did not know just where, but this spot I recognized instantly, and remembered reading at the time of how much importance it was. and I left it with a greater respect than I ever had for the brave Connecticut men who faced death in that battle.

Getting back upon the tow-path again at one of the fords where Lee's army slipped away across the Potomac into Virginia, I was soon at Harper's Ferry. The brick building still remains in which so many men were imprisoned by John Brown on the night and morning of his raid, and I was shown the spot where he and his men shot down in a most cold-blooded and unprovoked manner several defenseless citizens of the place.

Reaching Baltimore by train I made a stop of a day and a half, but couldn't resist the temptation, after so long an absence from home, to step upon another train that brought me home to Hartford without change.

Perhaps a few dry statistics of the trip may not be uninteresting to wheelmen. During the trip the points of special interest visited were the Hudson River and the Highlands, the Catskill Mountains, Niagara, Pike's Peak, Salt Lake, Tahoe, the Calaveras Big Trees, the Yosemite Valley, the California Geysers, Monterey, Columbia River, Shoshone Falls, the Yellowstone Park, the Black Cañon, the Royal Gorge, and Marshall Pass. The route was through twenty-three States and Territories, and a stop of from one day to three weeks was made in the principal cities in those States and Territories. The distance traveled by wheel, rail, and steamer, was a little over eleven thousand miles; the time nearly seven months.

Distance traveled on the wheel during the trip, 4,239

miles, making a total distance traveled on the same machine, 7,900 miles. The only tire that was ever on the front wheel is still in good condition; that wheel runs almost as true now as it did when it was new. Only one spoke has ever got loose or broken in it. The rim of the little wheel, although repaired once or twice, is still in good shape, the middle looks well, and the whole machine is in good serviceable condition In fact, it carries me nearly every day now, over rough pavements and sometimes out into the country eight or ten miles over frozen ground and dangerous ruts. I often got reduced rates on railroads, being a newspaper correspondent, but this help was counter-balanced by paying local rates which are always higher than through rates, but the total cost of the long trip, including repairs, clothes, and every expense whatsoever. was $284.70.

www.ingramcontent.com/pod-product-compliance
Lightning Source LLC
Chambersburg PA
CBHW020338030726
47496CB00007B/1937